The Wild Witches of West Bygod

Paul Lubaczewski

Madness Heart Press
2006 Idlewilde Run Dr.
Austin, Texas 78744

Cover by John Baltisberger
Interior Layout by Lori Michelle
    www.TheAuthorsAlley.com

For more information, address:
    john@madnessheart.press

                www.madnessheart.press

Acknowledgments

First and foremost, I wish to thank my beta readers: Steve Knol, Dorothy Frank, Edward Mignot, Jessica Charles, Tricia Resnick, and, of course, my wife Leslie. Having other eyes on a book saves you ever so much hassle down the road and also gives you innocent victims to blame your own mistakes on later if anyone notices one. Really, y'all have my undying gratitude. I'd also like to thank my fellow writers, a weirder fraternity I could not hope to be part of, especially Sab Grey, Andrew Snook, Jeff Strand, and Douglas Alexander for giving me blurbs and thinking I was funny. Speaking of which, I would like to thank all the zines, bookstores, and podcasts that have helped me promote my work in the past. The list is lengthy, just know I could kiss you all dead on the mouth if I could afford another restraining order. Finally, thank you West Virginia for being so rugged and untamable and full of so many nice, kind, down to earth people and finally giving me a place to live where I could honestly picture staying forever.

Author's Note

In Appalachia, the word MeeMaw is the common word for Grandmother. I've noted that in western West Virginia and Eastern Kentucky, there's a variant, Maw Maw. Since I had two grandmothers to work with, and one of them was from the western part of the state . . . well, it seemed to be a good way to differentiate between them.

Chapter 1

"Everybody has talent, it's just a matter of moving
around until you've discovered what it is."
—George Lucas,
speeding ticket magnet, also George Lucas Jr.
Yes, a Junior, bet you didn't know that, did ya?
Wait, Star Wars geeks, of course you did.

———◆———

TWO MEN SAT on an old stone farm wall overlooking a field
that was obviously deep in the country. The night seemed
endless and unknowable stretching out in front of them,
barring the twinkling of lights off to their right. Those were
completely knowable, which is why we barred them from this
metaphor. The metaphor of the unknowable night doesn't
work so well if you toss in "Except for those buildings over
there." In many ways, the men seemed like polar opposites.
One was clean-shaven, his hair conservatively trimmed, while
the other's bright red beard sprouted out at interesting and
unique angles, possibly hiding birds within its depths or lost
tribes of gnomes and goblins. Yet, they sat together with the
ease of two who knew each other well.

"Sae, dae ye hink thes is gonnae be th' a body?" the one
said with an accent so thick you could have successfully
used it to thicken stew.

The other man appeared to mentally translate what he
just heard before replying, "Well, if it's not him, I'm
damned well screwed to know who else it would be."

"Ye cannae be sure, yer loon coods hae mebbe . . . had puckle rolls in th' hay at skale ye dornt ken abit."

"Pardon?"

"Thaur micht be a dobber, ye rockit!"

"Still not getting it."

A third man approached the wall, serious-faced as well as being dressed dourly, he looked like he had just been attending a funeral. He leaned his face into their conversation. "He's saying there might be a bastard child out there somewhere."

"Oh," said the first man.

"Cannae ye kin plain sassenach, Ah jist said 'at? A dobber bairn. Learn tae listen, ye fools!" The man's bushy eyebrows seemed to merge with each other as he squinted in irritation.

"Well, we'd best hope there isn't one. I've got me a feelin' we'll be needing him to be the one soon enough," said the first man as they all went back to staring out into space.

☽○☾

Sometimes, you know—even with enough hindsight to have come to the realization that it was a bad decision—that given a chance, you would do the same dumb thing all over again. Like it was just your destiny, something you couldn't avoid even if you wanted to. Like "the guy choice." Some days you had to admit there was the guy choice or the not guy choice, and while you might not be a bro, you definitely were a guy. The day your parents' DNA mixed and decided what sex you were, you were pre-ordained to do many dumb things in life for no other reason than "Guy." Any actions, once the guy aspect took over, should be forgiven; they never actually were, but in a just, fair world, they would be. Toxic masculinity has a side that is totally harmless to everyone but the guy, more humorous and unpleasant masculinity than it is toxic. Football teams are often involved in a lot of those choices, unfortunately, not all of them.

The inevitability of guyness, the unbearable stupidity of great big bolshie balls thinking, it was what had led Matt Hawley here. Here being trying to get to sleep in a cheap motel near Front Royal, Virginia, a place he had never expected to drive himself to. Day one of his two-day drive to a fresh start. Well, that's what it had been billed as to him when he was informed that's what he was doing. A lot of times, after the penalty phase of our stupid decisions, someone, often our mom, offers us a "fresh start"; if we're not so lucky, it might be the Justice System doing it. It felt more like keeping him from being a bother than a great opportunity to Matt. Perspective was important in life, and Matt was pretty sure not everybody was sharing the same one here.

When Ashley had looked at him with her startling green eyes and informed him, "It just isn't working out," Matt had choices. First off, he could have looked further into what she meant by *it wasn't working out*, but he was too broken up to even think about that one. Matt might not have been so willing to achieve such an even split of their things if he had known it involved her being on her back screaming the name of the DJ at the club she bartended at. Again, perspective is important; Matt's perspective had been, "It's all my fault it's not working out," instead of the more accurate, "What's not working is who gets to sleep in this bed with Ashley." Matt wasn't so stupid that he hadn't suspected right then and there that he was getting hosed here and that there was more to this than just a personality conflict, but low self-esteem stepped in to help him out and said, "You really do suck, it's clearly all your fault, so give her what she wants, then go find a place to crawl off to and die."

When it came to who got the big things, the apartment

and the Xterra, both of their names were on the lease and on the purchase receipt for the SUV. Who got what? Since everybody was being so reasonable—and in Matt's case, completely clueless—a split would need to happen. This was where the inevitability of guyness had struck, assaulting him with a lack of common sense. He chose the SUV. Obviously. He couldn't help it, it was the guy choice, and the split had not succeeded in totally emasculating him. Worse, he was so brokenhearted about the whole thing, he wanted to get out as soon as possible, hopefully leaving in an angry dramatic huff, which is hard to do if you take the apartment—they are notoriously immobile. Maybe it wasn't the worst choice long term; short term, it dawned on him a very short time later that it definitely was. The long view was that if he had taken the apartment, she would still be looking for a place and living there in the meantime, most likely rent-free since she would point out "It wasn't her apartment." In theory, that split would mean *she* would be the one leaving, but unless the DJ he didn't know about yet took her in, he knew damned well that he was weak-willed enough that Ashley would have just stayed as a "roommate" until she could "get on her feet." She absolutely had enough self-control that she wouldn't have stormed out and driven off into the night.

Like Matt had.

Leaving him without a place to stay while he looked for another apartment in the crowded city, and without a security deposit because it was currently staying with Ashley in his former apartment.

This was when guyness struck again, this time with a solution to his situation. A really basic solution, but we're dealing with primitive thinking here.

The wrong solution again, because it turns out it's very hard to get to sleep and get to work on time if you are currently living in an SUV. That and the smell that comes with an urban camping adventure is not welcome in an office environment. No matter how hard you try, the smell of someone living in a vehicle is only one half-step from homeless, and it's a pretty short half step. The perma-stench and the unexcused being late led to him being unemployed in no time flat. Bereft and homeless, Matt turned to the one place a man in his twenties does in this situation, the one place he could always turn to when the chips were down: the people who loved him most.

His mom soon said, like really soon, like as in an unseemly short amount of time, "You know, you haven't seen your cousins in West Virginia for years now. Maybe a fresh start will do you some good. If nothing else, it will make the break up easier, you know. Not seeing her at all the same places, not having to talk to mutual friends. Give you a clean break so when you're ready to get a new place or a new girlfriend, you won't have so much baggage. They'll be thrilled to have you for a bit."

That's what she said. Matt was positive that wasn't what she meant. What that had really meant was: "Your father has remodeled the basement into a man cave, and he'll be damned if he's going to have you sleeping on his Nirvana pillows and getting in the way when he wants to watch the Giants."

He looked at himself in the motel mirror, always a depressing action, which is why motels make sure that there's a large one in every room. It can't be proven, but they probably clean up on the suicide demographic and know their clientele. Matt stood around six feet even. He had auburn hair trending towards the lighter side, and his steel-gray eyes looked remarkable and out of place contrasting with his darker hair. His features tended towards sharp, angular cheekbones and a sharp nose. Those features were offset by his more rounded looking chin, giving him an open and honest appearance to the casual observer. Matt was not in rock-solid shape, no six-pack abs, more three-pack and some open rings, but nor was he overweight in any way, something he worried about with his jawline. He figured if he ever let himself get overweight, what was now a pleasing jawline would turn into double chin city. He had been an average student in high school and college, maintaining Bs but never aspiring further. Matt's favorite movie as a child was *Home Alone;* he had also enjoyed *Edward Scissorhands*, overall, but at the time, the old scientist dude had frightened him. Matt's blood type is O positive, which may not seem very important now, but you never know, he may need a blood transfusion later. His first pet was a cat named Homer, after *The Simpsons*—which is not the security answer he gives for passwords, that is Arnold, go hack him now. Matt also once ate an entire pizza in one sitting as a dare in high school. He has a mole on his elbow, which he is not self-conscious of; he often forgets it's even there. Matt wears Old Spice brand deodorant because Axe is too douchey. Sometimes, Matt hums show tunes without knowing what they're from. He votes, but isn't political per se, and no, he won't say who he voted for. His childhood nickname from his mom was Mattie. We just felt we should get all of that out of the way now (I see someone's been taking those online writing classes I recommended for this book-editor).

Before checking into his flea nest, he had seen a cave today, which had never been on his agenda before today, not until he saw all the signs for CAVES on the highway. Matt had done this because he wanted to feel like this was a trip for fun, not for some obscure punishment for not being able to manage his personal life. It was amazingly expensive—well, it amazed him, at any rate, as to how much they charged to see a cave. He thought it was pretty cool, not as cool as what they charged for it cool, but cool nonetheless. It turned out there was more than one cave that you could pay money for a tour of in the area, and he knew deep down that for the rest of his life, he would hear that he REALLY needed to see the other one from everyone he told about seeing this one today. Matt had doubts about if he should even put the pictures up on Instagram for just that reason.

Matt had gotten beer and food from a local supermarket and was now engaged in the time-honored tradition of men in motel rooms the world over: feeling miserable and bored because they were stuck in a motel room in a strange town where they knew nothing and nobody. If a man in a motel room was actually enjoying himself, odds were pretty high he'd be willing to deny it later in a court of law to try to avoid some *serious* trouble. Matt considered missing Ashley for a little while but dismissed it out of hand. He had found out about the DJ by this time and didn't want his train of thought to go any further down that weed-strewn path than it needed to. He had found out too many times and too painfully already in the last few weeks that he possessed a very vivid imagination.

Sighing, he killed the lights and tried to sleep to the ungentle, unpeaceful, and not at all lulling noise of the nearby highway. This lasted for five minutes, until he realized that the entire motel room shook every time a particularly big tractor-trailer went by. So instead, he went to a nearby convenience store, bought two more six-packs of beer, and passed out later with the TV turned on to *Adult Swim* at a loud enough volume that he couldn't hear the trucks anymore—or the people in the next room doing the kind of thing that may be held against you in divorce court.

He dreamed of aliens and action figures. Thankfully, he couldn't remember what they were doing, not even that thing with the ladder and the goat.

The next morning involved a momentary panic at waking up, more specifically, waking up with a gummy mouth in a strange motel room with an entire fleet of tractor-trailers shaking the bed. Matt's first thoughts when his eyes cracked open had been *Zombie Apocalypse* followed quickly by *The Rapture*. The fact that the Rapture came in second said a lot about his lapsed religious beliefs and which possible event Matt took more seriously. Putting on his clothes and shoes, he stumbled out the door with one pseudo-coherent thought in his brain: coffee, followed by the incoherent thought of banning all tractor-trailers forever and for always. The beer had come from a place a short walk from the motel; the solution could come from there as well.

His brain was slightly more in gear by the time he wandered in the door of the roadside convenience store. Matt managed a nod to a painfully perky looking clerk before he headed right for those large tubs of black re-humanization that he needed oh so badly. He bought a couple; it was a Two-Fisted Tales of Coffee sort of morning. As a total afterthought, he also grabbed an energy drink for the road and some kind of pastry concoction that promised cheese filling. He knew it contained more of a cheese gummy part in the middle, but he was being optimistic.

When he went up to pay, the clerk decided to make conversation against Matt's wishes. "So," he asked happily, "where y'all headed?"

"Raleigh County, West Virginia," Matt mumbled, struggling to tap his card on the payment pad before realizing he had to insert the chip in this one. He could sense the silence that followed that pronouncement and glanced up at the clerk, who looked a little stunned. "Why do you ask?"

The vacuous look of morning happiness came right back in an instant. "Oh, no reason; y'all just don't sound like yer from around here is all. Wouldn't of figured you for goin' to Beckley is all."

"Visiting relatives not far from there," Matt grunted, relieved to finally get the transaction to go through so he could work his way through the two cups of life that steamed on the counter in front of him—and, more importantly, away from anyone who wanted to talk about anything.

The clerk handed him his receipt, and as Matt turned to leave, the clerk added, "Y'all have a blessed day."

"Ummm, you too," Matt replied, heading for the door. That was weird, he wouldn't have figured for Wiccans down here. Go figure (FREE TRAVEL TRIP! It's just a thing Appalachian people say. There are no mobs of Wiccans littering the mountains, only your normal amount).

☽◯☾

Today he was planning on taking his time driving. Not so he could see much in the way of sights, although there were plenty of signs for various roadside attractions, Matt was just ambling. He had figured that on the day he got in, he'd be more or less stuck at the farm for the night, and he really wanted to keep that amount of time to a minimum. It wasn't that Matt disliked his cousins, in reality, he hadn't seen them in years, but therein lay the problem. He had no idea what they would have to talk about . . . except maybe what a loser he was for getting politely yet firmly shipped off to stay with them a while. He assumed his dad had already talked to them at length about things, and Matt wasn't looking forward to all the leg work he'd have to do to change their opinion of him.

Matt wasn't even really mad at his parents about this. He'd made such a big deal about moving out when he went to college, and he'd made a *huge* deal of only staying back at home briefly when he graduated before moving right back out again. He was an independent man, and he could take care of himself! They certainly weren't expecting him back, asking to use the washer and have his old sheets taken back out of storage for him to sleep on, at twenty-five. Matt could make the defense that he had *tried* to keep it together on his own, but it was a pretty feeble defense when you're knocking on your parents' door with your clothes in a trash bag. They probably would have let him stay, no, scratch that, they would have, but his mom had gone this route for a face-saving move on everyone's part.

Matt promised himself that he was going to make the best of it, heck, he might even like it for a little while. He'd certainly liked visiting when he was a kid, so he had to consider it a possibility. All right, that might be being overly optimistic, he had also liked Rugrats when he was a kid, and watching the show recently out of nostalgia had made him wonder if he'd been slightly "special" as a kid. There might be some issues, there were new adults to contend with, like, parental level adults, for instance. He'd have to get used to his aunt and uncle and MeeMaw, who he really didn't know now; who knew how they'd be running their house? On a plus, they had boys around his age, and he remembered playing with them fondly. Somehow, Matt doubted they'd want to while away the hours throwing rocks anymore, but he might be able to find some common ground. Adding to that awkwardness, to fill in the gaps in his memory, he'd done some research on the area and strongly suspected this was going to be the total sticks. So, if he could avoid being stuck out there for an extra hour or two, all the better, positive attitude be damned.

With that in mind, he decided to make some stops. Internet research is a magical, wonderful thing; it enables you to know that you can buy Indian food in Roanoke for lunch, for instance, so he did just that. It also lets you know of a large chain brick and mortar bookstore in the Blacksburg/Christiansburg area, so he stopped there and bought a Seanan McGuire book. Something more important in the same area were places where you could buy some very, very high-end beer. Matt really didn't drink that much normally, but booze cures boredom, and he suspected boredom was going to be an issue. He also found something called a "pepperoni roll" at a local convenience store when he stopped for gas.

The pepperoni roll would, in turn, cause another stop just through the tunnel into WV, specifically to buy more pepperoni rolls from a supermarket. He had no idea what was in them other than pepperoni and cheese, but they were better than crack cocaine, as far as road food. Less messy than chips, cheaper than fast food, perfection covered in dough. There! That hadn't been that hard! He'd barely crossed into the state and, already, he'd found something he liked about it; this was looking up! His more negative self pointed out that sure, they might have some food that he liked that he wouldn't be able to get back home, but then again, Indian food was probably better in India and he wouldn't want to live there either.

He was also willing to concede the place was pretty to look at, but only in a grudging what-I-can-see-from-the-highway sort of way. No state looks its absolute best from an interstate. Interstates go through areas where people generally don't live, and they generally don't live there for reasons. Not to mention the barriers and the blasting just to create the highway brings the look of things down. But Matt would be willing to concede that the massive mountain range he went under via tunnel to enter the state was pretty cool looking. At least what he could see of it when he wasn't dodging tractor-trailers and looking for Virginia state police leading up to the mountain, both of which were everywhere and anywhere. Thankfully, he had been warned about their proliferation by his cousins while arranging the trip through email.

It really didn't strike him until he finally pulled off the

turnpike and found himself sitting at a crossroads about to turn in the direction of the farm. He was really all the way out here, not in the city anymore, not in the suburbs, not anywhere. He was miles from everyone he was used to, no buddies to call to play X-box with, go clubbing with, or go eat with. Just him in an SUV full of his junk in the middle of nowhere, West Virginia about to live here for who knew how long with people he hadn't seen in years. Seeing it in this light, Matt almost wanted to turn the car around and run for home, at least until he reminded himself that he had nowhere to live back there. Not to mention that years of letting Ashley make most of the decisions on where and when they went out meant all of "his friends" were actually "her friends" and he had no one to go back to. If he had, they'd have taken him in, and he wouldn't have been sleeping in his SUV.

The anger at the memory of her perfidy was enough to make him put down his panic attack, turn the SUV onto the country highway, and head for his cousins. Matt wasn't quite ready to curl up in a ball and cry just yet, maybe later, though; it was always an option that was open to him.

))((

Bill Baldwin dragged his corpulent form up the hill. In theory, there was a road here; in practice, he had just gotten the Suburban detailed and there was no way in hell he was leaving half the transmission behind him just to avoid walking. About halfway up the steep incline, he did find himself looking longingly back at the enormous black SUV and wondering if it might be worth it to pick up an old beater pickup for when he had to come up here and visit the crazy old bat. Maybe get some old Ford truck he could pick up for three hundred off an employee or something, drive it until he snapped the shocks, spend fifty bucks to fix it again, and sell it to some hillbilly for a thousand.

The Wild Witches of West Bygod

Bill was a man of the real world, a world of suits and ties and, goddammit, air conditioning. He shouldn't be out here in these god-awful hills dealing with someone like her, kin or no kin. He had worked damned hard to get into the halls of power just so he wouldn't have to spend so much time near these yokels! On the completely realistic other hand, he couldn't say she didn't get results, and results were what mattered to the shareholders, not how he got them. He only hoped and prayed they never found out exactly how it was he was getting those results. Nobody liked a shareholder revolt; instead of bricks, those people threw expensive lawyers at you, which could be a lot deadlier in the long run.

The shack had come into view, and he shuddered involuntarily at the sight of it. Bill thought of it as a shack; for many people out here, it was a house, but he wasn't really from here anymore. He had hated this place even as a child, but Mama had insisted they come up here to visit his Maw Maw. Little Bill would pout or cry the whole way or try to find a way to be nowhere near their own house when it was time to leave. Of course, if Mama had to postpone a trip to visit Maw Maw because she couldn't find young Bill, he'd get a hiding to remember. But if it took long enough to find him, it would postpone a trip for a day, one more day to hope for a miracle, like his Maw Maw dying overnight by getting eaten by a bear, something that would get him out of having to visit her.

The woman didn't even have an indoor toilet, for the love of god! It wasn't like he hadn't offered to pay to have one put in enough times. Hell, he'd offered to tear the whole terrifying place down and build a brand-new house for her on the same spot. The cackling baggage had laughed at him and told him he didn't understand nothing about nothing. Bill understood plenty, like how the modern world operated, for one thing. Heck, she was so outdated that he didn't even know if that old wreck of a pickup truck that used to belong to Paw Paw she kept tucked in a rickety shack even still worked, which, in Bill's mind, showed how exactly much she didn't understand anything. What if something happened up here? Who was she going to call? How was she going to even leave if she needed to? It was silly, her clinging to old mountain ways when there was a whole world outside she was missing.

The only thing Bill was willing to concede was that her magic worked all right. He went up to Maw Maw's, he asked, and it happened. A lot of people in these parts only wished they had that kind of pull with the ancient old crone. Bill Baldwin did, which is why Bill Baldwin had gone from growing up in a shack not much better than the one he was approaching to owning two different mansions. Bill knew where he needed to get in life, what positions he needed to occupy, and when, and Maw Maw made damned sure he got there with the barest of efforts on his part.

A lot of people gave a lot of things to Maw Maw to get her to work any magic for them. All Bill Baldwin had to do was ask.

☽○☾

Matt stopped the SUV again when he pulled into the drive. It was a long driveway leading to the house from here, even though he could see the gigantic ancient structure clearly in the orange light of dusk. He wanted a moment to compose his thoughts and, most importantly, rehearse to himself what "best behavior" counted as. He had been dating someone for years, and in that situation, "best behavior" starts to slip. You get used to each other's inappropriate jokes, cursing, belching, political opinions, etc., etc., and you begin to forget how to act like you are still in the workplace when you're on your own time. He reminded himself yet again, "No jokes about the Pope farting, even the really funny one involving the incense and the candles behind the rectory." Reminded of his manners,

Matt took a deep breath and put the Xterra back into drive.

He slowly crawled up the stone lane, thinking to himself that it looked just like the really lame artwork you saw for sale cheap in thrift stores back at home; he was almost surprised someone hadn't set an easel up in one of the fields. He knew there were cows somewhere around here, an animal Matt had always had an indifferent relationship with since he was a kid. Matt wasn't surprised that along with the cows came the fragrance of cows; he might have the windows up, but it wasn't sufficient to keep the soft sickly-sweet fermented grass smell from filling up his nostrils. He had to hope he would get used to it; he kind of remembered getting used to it as a kid and hoped he maintained some of that childish malleability. Now that Matt thought about it, he remembered bouncing up better as a kid when he fell from heights that would leave him on the ground moaning now; so, considered like that, maybe his malleability wasn't what it used to be.

The house was an ancient thing. It had been in the family for generations. He had never been told why it hadn't been his dad's family living here instead of his cousins. In theory, Dad was the older brother, so that would make more sense. Dad never really seemed to want to talk about it much. But now that Matt was out here, he figured Dad didn't owe an explanation, and he thought maybe he could kind of see where the guy was coming from. People who lived in cities spent their whole lives trying to afford a place way out in the country, and people who lived in the country tried to figure out how to make it in the big city. It was just a fact of life that people thought it would all be better somewhere other than where they were. No matter where you were in life, you just naturally assumed it sucked when compared to something else you couldn't have. Maybe Dad had done the impossible and found a place he could be perfectly content with. If he had, he didn't need to explain that to Matt.

Edwin and Tyler, his cousins, were already on the front porch, having seen him coming down the long lane. The two could not have looked much more diametrically opposed if they had tried. Like, "he's a little bit country, and he's a little bit rock n roll" different. Edwin was wearing a t-shirt and a dirty ball cap, looking for all the world like he had just escaped a Kenny Chesney video—but only by promising he was off to do something rural and rustic and very salt of the earth-ish, giving him no time for music videos today. Tyler, on the other hand, also had an appearance of having just escaped a video, but in his case, more of a Social Distortion rockabilly one. As Matt was grabbing his things to get out of the SUV, he could see the tattoos peeking out from Tyler's cuffed black dress shirt. It occurred to Matt that his cousins might have changed a lot more than he had over the years and there might be more of a feeling-out process with them than, say, his aunt and uncle.

As he was getting out of the car, the screen door banged open and out came Uncle Donnie. The larger man pushed past the brothers and came off the porch with a large smile on his face. Before Matt even had time to fully react or expect it, he found himself being slapped on the back and butted in the gut by his uncle's spare tire in the depths of a massive hug.

"Welcome to West Bygod, boy!" the man bellowed in his ear.

"Hi, Uncle Donnie, good to be here," Matt lied. It could be good to be here, but he wasn't sure yet that it *was* good to be here. The one thing Matt was sure of was the circumstances of him being here, which were pretty far from good. That and his back was probably going to be sore tomorrow from the slaps; the man was strong. Still, it pays to be nice.

"Well, you remember yer cousins, right?" Donnie asked, turning towards his sons, who were waiting patiently on the porch. "I'll let the three of you say your hellos while I go inside and see what's taking Debbie so damned long in the kitchen."

With that, his uncle turned and went back in the house, leaving the three twenty-something males standing there awkwardly. (This is a base state for young men thrust into a social situation together. No one wants to start a conversation in case it is viewed as a sign of weakness by the other males. If anyone speaks first, they all suspect deep down that this may lead to feelings that might be discussed, and the next stop after that is picking out doilies. This is known instinctively by your younger male of the species. Being friendly and outgoing when not being forced is considered un-macho and therefore to be frowned upon. Never saying "Hi! How are you?" sincerely until you're 35 at the earliest is a popular male model of behavior. Nobody knows why. Maybe in the wild, the other males would beat you up and take your woman if you made polite conversation around the cave campfire, and men still worry instinctively about it.)

"So how y'all been, Matt?" Edwin broke down and began the butt-sniffing process of the younger male.

"Well, it was a good drive down and . . . " Matt faltered.

He was surprised when Tyler grinned widely. "Yeah, I know. We heard. I'm livin' with the folks after my divorce, so it ain't like I got any room to talk. Don't let it get y'all down none. After dinner, me and Eddie will help you get moved into your room, get yer tech shit set up. That is, unless Adrianna goes and drags him off to the house to make more babies after dinner."

Edwin punched his brother in the shoulder. "Shut up, Tyler; just because Melanie got wise and ran for the hills ain't no reason to give me shit."

"Yeah, hill of pills more like, you dick," Tyler shot back.

"So . . . " Matt chuckled at the exchange. "I see you two really haven't changed all that much."

CHAPTER 2

"If you don't believe in ghosts, you've never been
to a family reunion."
—Ashleigh Brilliant

———— ◆ ————

IT HAD BEEN years since Matt had been here, not since
before he was a teenager at least, but walking in the
wooden screen door brought it all back to him. Frankly, not
much had changed; there were slight changes in the
decoration, but they were only slight. This was keeping in line
with the fact that his grandmother still lived on the property
and would probably skin his uncle alive if he so much as
touched her house in any manner she didn't approve of. She
had moved out into a smaller outbuilding that his dad and
uncle had fixed up for her years ago, but make no mistakes
about it, in all but name, this was still "her house."

Matt's uncle came out into the living room with his
Aunt Debbie and someone who Matt could only guess was
Edwin's wife. Before Matt could say anything, his aunt
swept him into a large hug, which Matt tried to reciprocate
while at the same time trying to keep vital air going to his
lungs. Aunt Debbie may have looked like she had gotten a
bit doughy, but her arm strength could bend steel easily,
and she was a hugger.

"So happy y'all came down to stay with us," she said,
releasing him as he tried to remember not to noticeably
gasp for breath. The woman she turned him towards was

dressed in a blouse and jeans, with long blond hair flipped to the side. "This here is Adrianna, Eddie's wife. Ade, this is our city boy nephew Matt, he's come down to carpetbag for a while."

Adrianna gave Matt a quick hug, saying, "She's just messing with you about the carpetbagging thing, I'm pretty sure. Mostly sure."

A flash of hair flew by at knee height, and Aunt Debbie called out, "Hunter, don't you want to meet your cousin?"

A small voice called back, "Can't now, busy!"

Edwin blushed a bit. "That's my son, Hunter. Be thankful the kids will have their own table. What he can do to food . . . " Edwin shuddered. "I didn't even know you could get a pea that far up your own nose. The baby isn't as bad, but the mush they eat is gross."

His aunt bustled off to get things ready, and dinner was served shortly thereafter, which (thankfully) kept awkward standing-around-waiting-for-dinner conversation to a minimum. Matt was pretty sure that the whole family dinner thing was being done for his benefit. He could tell just by looking around and spotting the dust in a few key spots that the dining room didn't get a lot of use. Which made sense. The last time he had checked the dining room at his folks' place, it was being used for storage; his parents ate in front of the TV.

He wanted to ask if MeeMaw was going to join them but at the same time was trying to forestall that family reunion. There were a lot of thank you cards for ten dollar checks he had neglected to send over the years, and he wasn't looking forward to the reckoning over it. He was being forced into a confrontation with the secret guilt that haunts many full-blown adults, knowing deep down that they should have sent the thank you cards, the ones that they completely blew off. (It's a mystery why that isn't the first thing a therapist asks when someone goes in for treatment for unexplained anxiety issues. Just open right up with, "You forgot to send the card for that five dollars for your birthday in the sixth grade, didn't you?" It would speed things along by a lot.)

Matt's dining room theory was confirmed as they all shuffled in and Tyler said, "Man, it's weird eating in here when it isn't Thanksgiving or Easter." That earned him a quick scowl from Aunt Debbie for busting the Walton's family dinner myth so quickly.

Food was a pretty simple affair, roast beef and mashed potatoes, but after all the driving he'd done that day, it was more or less the best thing that Matt could have possibly hoped for. It was good and filling, and there was plenty of it. Just the thing to make him feel better.

Matt figured this is why roadside truck stops do so well: they sell big wads of all you can eat comfort food, which is exactly what you want after hours of cursing the parents of every driver within a mile of yourself. (What you say about the police hiding behind every berm is between you and the lord, unless your kids are in the car and repeat it verbatim to your wife later. They invariably will, and even faster if your mother-in-law is present.)

They all were at the table, except for the children, and it lent a sense of family to everything, something that Matt really hadn't felt in years—his family all loved each other, sure, but hanging out together was a rarity. The children were being supervised at their own table in the kitchen by Edwin and Adrianna, who both traded off making mad dashes to keep Hunter from smearing the baby with something disgusting that may have been food at one point.

Any hopes he had of getting through dinner without it getting uncomfortable ended when Aunt Debbie said, "So, Matt, since you're new here, you can certainly come by and see our church. At least until you find something more to your liking."

Matt almost choked. He'd been expecting it and was prepared for it, just not at dinner. Especially not at the very *first* dinner together like that. After drinking a sip of a local micro-brew Tyler had brought out, hoping to cover his shock, he replied, "Ummm, well, the thing is, I'm a Buddhist, Aunt Debbie."

The room went silent. Every piece of cutlery hung in midair, every piece of food that was being masticated remained unchewed in the moment, and even Edwin's children being fed by Adrianna in the next room seemed to sense the moment and fell into radio silence.

Aunt Debbie's smile took on a brittle character for a minute, then she said, "Oh, well isn't that nice. Very . . . very peaceful, I've heard."

Life was allowed to restart on the Hawley farm.

Matt couldn't be sure, but he swore he heard a faint cackle come from the outbuilding where his grandmother was eating alone. He'd been told he'd have to go visit her tomorrow at the latest, since she didn't like to walk all the way up to the main house. The timing of her laugh was almost like she had been in the room with them. Clearly, the silence after his announcement had been too much for his brittle psyche and he was hearing things. He hadn't been sure if saying that was going to work, but it was the only way to get out of going to church. He wasn't really religious at all, yet he found that claiming to be a Buddhist got you out of those situations. It was something nobody knew much about, certainly not enough to prove you weren't being an observant one, but it was considered unobjectionable by the general populace.

Uncle Donnie snorted. "Sounds like Mom's watching *Beverly Hillbillies* re-runs again. She always laughs too loud at them; I keep saying it's insulting and a mean-spirited stereotype, but she tells me not to be such a stick in the mud."

With Matt's sanity proven intact by his Uncle's confirmation of the laughter and the moment broken, everyone returned to eating.

Aunt Debbie finished her own plate and got up, saying, "I don't mind cooking for everyone, but dessert is up to y'all. There's ice cream in the freezer, and I got a chocolate pie from Kroger. My duties have ceased. Y'all live here or near here, so I'll see you soon enough, but this lady is going to go watch TV. Rinse your dishes before y'all put them in the washer. If there are clumps on there tomorrow, remember what I said, I know where y'all live."

With that, she got up and left, which seemed to be the cue for Edwin as well. "I better help Adrianna with the kids. We gotta get 'em put down soon or there'll be hell to pay when they're cranky tomorrow. I'll see y'all in the morning," he said.

The three of them left in the room took it as their cue and cleaned up the dishes and got dessert. Once they were sitting back down finishing up, Uncle Donnie asked, "Not that we're not thrilled to have you for a while, but why aren't you staying with your folks?"

"Do you want the real reason, or why my mom said it would be a good idea?" Matt replied.

"Don't tell me. He's my brother, so I'm betting I can guess. He redid your room, and the cheap-ass doesn't want to lose his man-cave," his uncle said with a chuckled.

"That would be my guess as to the honest answer, yeah," Matt replied, happy it was his uncle who had actually said it and not him.

"Know how I know that? I'm a year older. When I went to college at Marshall, I came back to find all of my stuff in the attic, and he had an 'entertainment room.' Well, you're welcome to stay here, that's for sure; it's the family home and all. Only thing I ask is that after you have some time to settle in a bit, you work. Y'all can either work here on the farm, we can always use the help, or go find yerself something in town. With that pronouncement of doom delivered, I'm gonna go watch some TV. I leave yer Aunt too long, I'll never get the remote back." With that, the big man got up and went out to the kitchen.

As soon as he was gone, Tyler said, "Don't let him fool you, he's gonna fuck around on Facebook until *South Park* comes on."

For whatever reason, Matt thought that was funny. "Really?"

"Yeah, don't let his 'man of the soil' routine snooker you. He partied when he went to Marshall. I've seen pictures from his college days. He put them up on said Book of the Face when he was reminiscing with buddies," Tyler said, grinning.

"My dad can be like that, but it's hard to take the adult routine seriously when he played grunge at me all through childhood." Matt shrugged back.

"Yeah, *eat your peas and do your homework because all my heroes are dead* sort of thing, it just sounds weird," Tyler replied before changing the subject. "So, I gotta ask, why on earth West Bygod? I mean, don't get me wrong, it's pretty and all, but I can't really think of it as the land of opportunity. So, why come down here at all, even with your folks giving you the boot?"

"Well, to be honest, I didn't have any better ideas when my mom suggested it," Matt replied. "And Dad did make some sense, when he wasn't bitching about me drooling on his throw pillows where they were letting me sleep. I mean, who in the hell buys throw pillows with band names on them? But he wasn't *all* wrong."

"About what? I mean, other than the drool thing, I can only assume there."

"I was acting pitiful and making things bad for myself because I was moping. I mean, I could have rented a hotel room for a night or two after I lost my place and maybe not lost my job, for instance. I didn't even really look for a job when I was at my folks' place. They figured a change might do me good. I don't know, maybe they were right about that. Coming down here. I just went along to get along, I guess."

"So, any drunk two a.m. texts?"

"Whaddya mean? Texts to who?"

"Oh come on. You never came home lit, or, I don't know, woke up in your SUV lit, and thought, maybe she'll take me back if I say something great, like RIGHT NOW? Shit, I wake up the next day after every time I go to a show or something and I'm afraid to even look at my phone. Heaven fucking help me if Melanie actually said yes one of these times. I'd have to leave the country or some shit," Tyler replied.

"Oh that, no, I haven't," Matt replied, looking down at his beer, which had some local monster legend on the side of the can. He couldn't help but think the monster was giving him a stink eye. Of course, that was just the way the eyes looked, but since Matt was feeling self-conscious, he decided it was personal. He continued. "Not that I'm any better, I just haven't because I'm afraid her new boyfriend would answer and I'm depressed enough by that point, thank you!"

"Well, enough of this morose ass shit, let's get y'all's stuff out of the SUV, and I'll help you hook up your electronics. Don't ask Dad, he has no idea how any of that shit works." Tyler winked, his interest in the previous discussion already gone.

"Only because y'all keep changing the damned passwords, ya' tattooed pain in the ass!" Uncle Donnie's voice boomed from the living room.

"Once, I did that ONCE, and he's never forgiven me." Tyler shrugged.

$$\text{☽◯☾}$$

Numerous figures were at the family graveyard out across the field that night. Many families had family plots on their property that went back generations in West Virginia; the Hawley one went back to the early 1800s. No light lit the scene, none was needed, despite the fact that it was one of those eldritch scenes that are supposed to be lit by a full moon in a book like this. Unfortunately, the moon on this night had not heard of this literary conceit and was only a little more than a crescent—not even a real crescent moon, more of a croissant really—and the entire Gothic horror effect was completely ruined. You couldn't even see the ancient and, in some cases, crudely made stones, some with high grasses in front of the names and dates—which trust us, on a full moon looks entirely creepy, especially if a light breeze comes by and brushes them against the stone. Bad scheduling really, and nothing could be done about it then.

One of the figures spoke, a man dressed in a kilt and a flowing white shirt—who looked suspiciously like the one man from the beginning of the book. "Weel, mah fowk, has anyain hud a swatch at th' cheil?"

Most of the other figures looked completely blank at that, but three who were wearing older clothing of homespun huddled among themselves before one of them finally turned to the others and said, "He asked if any of us have had a chance to look at the young man."

The original figure growled, "A' fowk knows whit Ah said, ye dornt hae tae translate!"

The translator turned to the first figure. "I'm sure they do, Grandfather, but for the younger generation, it speeds things up a bit."

The first figure stood up, made sure his back was straight so everyone could see him standing there in his kilt and linen shirt. "Weel has onie ay ye?"

Another of the figures, dressed in a dark suit and tie, raised his hand, looking suspiciously like the other man from the beginning. "I was planning on seeing him tonight. I was his grandfather, after all, so if he wakes up by accident, at least it will be a familiar face," he said

" Weel, make sure 'at ye dae; we cannae afford tae lose anither member ay th' fowk efter his faither."

The man in the suit and tie turned to look questioningly at the ones who had been doing the translating.

The one who had translated aloud last time shrugged and said, "Don't fuck it up."

)O(

Tyler and Matt were in Matt's new room finishing hooking up the important things—i.e. Matt's connections to the outside world. It had taken a while to get everything in and set up, but life was now functioning. Well, the bits that made life feel normal, at any rate: his phone, his desktop, and the TV. All of which took passwords to get it hooked in, which Tyler actually had written down for him in case of a power outage. It was also nice because it gave him at least one person to one-on-one with and get used to. The room itself was . . . well, it was a room. Rooms are basically boxes to hold people and their stuff. It had a nice bureau for his clothes, it had a nice wooden framed bed, and now, it had Matt and his stuff.

"I don't know why Dad doesn't just ask me where I have the passwords or to write them down for him," Tyler grumbled as he was hooking up the TV.

"Don't you just have a cable splitter?" Matt asked.

"Naw, we have a cable run out to the house for the internet, which cost a fortune, but for TV, we still rely on the West Virginia state flower," Tyler responded, finishing up.

"State flower? What?"

"Satellite dish. Everything runs off the Hopper," Tyler replied. "All right, we're all hooked up, and look at all the beer you bought. What? You thought us hillbillies didn't have decent beer?"

Matt turned on the X-box and flopped down on the bed with one of the controllers. "Maybe a bit, you never know, be a good little boy scout and be prepared. You wanna play?"

"Yeah, sure; don't worry, I got a mini-fridge in my room with local micro-brews in them. Dad drinks nothing but Sam's and doesn't want me crowding the fridge up with my 'Damned hipster crap,'" Tyler said, handing Matt a beer he'd brought with him and grabbing the other controller.

"My dad is the same way, except with Yuengling. Whatever they drank in college, I guess. Yuengling at PSU with my dad. I guess Sam's was big at Marshall," Matt replied.

"God, I hope I never get like that."

"Like what?"

"You know, stuck in a rut, never bothering to try new things."

"Odds are in its favor, I'm afraid."

"But we can see it now and fight back. Hey, don't sweat the whole work thing too bad, by the way. Buddy of mine owns a record store nearby. Dad just wants to make sure everybody's working on something, he hates to see people slumming. It makes him feel like he's failing as a parent, I guess. So, it's that or help out on the farm, and the record store will get you started until you can find something better; at least it doesn't smell of cow shit. Well, most of the time anyway; things happen, after all. Dad'll probably bitch less about that than my job," Tyler said as he dug through Matt's box of games.

"Well, you have a job, at least, and put in *Zombi Four*, that game is awesome."

"Horror games, huh? Yeah, that's cool. Anyway, Pa says I get paid to scribble on people at the tattoo shop, which is such bullshit. The man has two different tribal pieces himself," Tyler said, putting the disc in. "Anyway, don't worry about it for now. Figure tomorrow all you have to do is finish unpacking and go out to the other house to visit with MeeMaw for a while."

"Anything I should worry about with that?"

"I wouldn't even know to tell you, her mood depends on the day."

☽◯☾

Beatrice Baldwin looked out her window at the fire in the fire pit out front. Yes, the water should just be about ready now. She gathered up the things she needed and got up slowly. Seemed to her that she did everything slowly these days. It frustrated her to no end; she had things to get along with, but this rotted old husk never seemed to want to move the way it used to.

Beatrice hobbled her way to the porch and down to where her huge old pot hung over the coals. The water bubbled vigorously as she set her sack down on the bench. She knew the boys that lived in this area had snuck onto her property to see what she was about; they did whenever they saw the fire burning out front. Let 'em. Part of being what Beatrice was, was letting people know what you was.

She opened jars and threw in pinches of this and dollops of that and, finally, the body of a large copperhead Bill had caught under her porch last week. She held the thing high, making sure there was no doubt as to what it was before throwing it in. Beatrice could almost imagine the cringes of fear from her unseen audience down the hill.

Next, the old woman began to chant as the steam rose all around her. The words had no meaning whatsoever, it was all for show. Finally, she dipped in a ladle and brought it to her lips. She didn't actually put any in her mouth, the stuff tasted awful no matter how much basil she tossed into it, but she found that it made for a better show that way. It was all a show, letting the local folks dream of dark secret potions. What she really used the goop for was keeping away rats. They couldn't stand the smell of it; Beatrice couldn't say she blamed them. But why just put out traps when you could get inside the heads and the dreams of everybody living in these hills?

$$\supset \bigcirc \subset$$

Matt had the strangest dream that night. He was positive it was a dream; the topic matter certainly felt like a dream. He was curled up in his bed at the farm after finally seeing Tyler off to his own room around one a.m. They had almost ended up staying up even later, until Tyler's phone beeped at him to remind him he had an appointment to work on someone the next day. He'd begged off and gone off to his own room, saying that having a hangover handshake was not going to do at all so it was time to pack it in. That worked for Matt really, gave him some time to settle into his new surroundings.

Matt had played the X-box a bit more after his cousin left. He wasn't even going to bother setting up his channel preferences on the dish tonight, and he hadn't been that interested in watching TV yet anyway. Better to do something a bit brainless that emptied out his thoughts a bit for sleep, like sip on beers with excessive alcohol content while making computer-animated zombies splat on the screen. It was just about all he was up for at the moment, and it brought a bit of normal back into the situation. Life just didn't feel like it could be that bizarre or unsettling if he had just taken a chainsaw to a festering animated rotting corpse.

(Zombie slaughter: what normal feels like! That should be some kind of a corporate logo! Maybe for Quaker Oats or something. Wilford Brimley would have to wear zombie makeup for the ads, but it'd be great! "Zombie Killing, a good thing to do, and doing it with a warm bowl of a Quaker Oatmeal is a good way to do it!")

After a bit, he had decided he was finally calmed down and settled in enough to crawl into bed and kill the lights.

He hadn't set up his bedside clock yet, it was still in one of his boxes or bags, and frankly, for tonight at least, it could damned well stay where it was. He didn't need to get up tomorrow, so knowing the exact time it happened wasn't a real priority. Matt had laid there for a bit, wondering how many days grace he had before his uncle brought up getting a job again. Not that he minded all that much, deep in his heart, Matt really did want to treat this like it was a fresh start. He couldn't foresee this being the rest of his life. Never moving back home was ridiculous, but for now, he kinda felt like Mom might have been on to something. Not that he was going to admit that to her any time soon; he was still a bit sore that his mom hadn't let her baby bird back into the nest to tend his broken wing. It didn't matter, really; for the moment, he kind of felt like he had a clean slate, like all the mistakes he had made living in the city were wiped clean. Nobody here knew what a screw up he could be, and as long as he never, ever acted like his real self, they never would. At least he had achieved an understanding with himself as to what an idiot he could be like and could take steps to prevent it going forward. He gave himself four months before he messed it up, but by then, maybe he'd be better prepared for going back home. Resolved that he had set a date before he burned any bridges by his own stupidity, he had drifted gently off to sleep.

Sometime in the early morning hours, the dream started.

"Boy, y'all gotta get up for a minute," a voice said loudly.

Matt's eyes cracked open. It was dark in his room, but yet he could see . . .

He sat bolt upright. "Who are you? What are you doing in here?"

"Son, I've known you since you were a baby; y'all should look closer."

In the pitch-black room, he could see someone in front of him, a luminescent man in a dark suit, someone he hadn't seen for many years. "Pa Pa?"

"Yep, just come to look at you now you're home, is all. Lots of folk here on the farm want to get a good look at you," the figure standing by his bed replied with a soft smile.

Matt felt something nagging at him as he stared at his grandfather. Whatever it was, was ignored so he could say, "Couldn't you get a look at me in the middle of the afternoon?"

"Well, I was hoping to do that too. This is along the lines of an invite to come visit over at the family plot. Lots of folks want to meet you there," his grandfather replied.

Bingo! That was what was nagging at Matt. "Umm, Pa Pa, you're dead!"

"Well, don't hold it against me; don't make me a bad person, after all. After you visit your MeeMaw tomorrow, come by to pay your respects to what come before you. And mind your MeeMaw, you're a lot closer to her than you think."

There, that was what this dream was all about. Nagging guilt because he had forgotten to send a thank you note to MeeMaw the last time she sent him a check for five dollars, when he graduated High School. This was all a dream about his guilt. Good enough, that made sense. Dreams were when you were supposed to work these things out, after all. Now that he got that out of the way, he could wrap this dream up and move on to something involving Swedish Stewardesses and baby oil. Matt had no idea why those types of dreams had to involve Flight Attendants and why they had to be Swedish, but who was he to mess with the conventions of the Great American Dirty Dream?

"Well, Pa Pa, thanks for the invite and all, but if you don't mind, I'm gonna cut this dream off and try to get back to the one involving someone who, no offense, is a lot cuter than you. Maybe a woke girl who wants a voyeur when she shaves for the first time," Matt said as he put his head down, congratulating himself on updating his perversions to something more topical and timely on the fly.

"Well g'night, boy, see you tomorrow. You might explain what in the hell you just said there, but somehow I don't know if I want to know."

☽○☾

Matt's eyes cracked open around ten the next morning. He wasn't bright-eyed or bushy-tailed, but he was surprised to find he wasn't nearly as worn out as he expected. Two days of driving and moving all of his stuff would have been plenty in its own right, but on top of that, he'd been playing X-box with Tyler well into the night. It was just as well that he had; he'd had all kinds of weird dreams even with everything to tucker him out. Who knows what it would have been like if he hadn't given himself some time to unwind by ridding a little video world of hideous Zombie mutants and drinking beer with his cousin. It was possible that his grandfather would have swung through the room like that "Wrecking Ball" video, and that most likely would have left a serious mental scar, not to mention it was a severely dated reference. Priorities, and for his first night in West Virginia, he thought he'd had his spot on.

Now that he was up, there was coffee to be attended to. Possibly food, but definitely coffee. He could shower up and visit his MeeMaw later, but for now, he needed to hit the bathroom to pee and then toddle down to the kitchen to ensure future trips to the bathroom. Maybe it was the mountain air, but between knowing just what he needed last night for his own mental health and his day falling into place, he felt clearer than he had every day since the final time his former apartment door had closed behind him.

When he got to the kitchen, he found Tyler sitting at

the table playing with his phone. His cousin looked up when he came in and said, "Sup? Coffee is on, and it is fresh. That is one nice thing about this house, especially if you like to sleep in, coffee is *always* on. Food, you'll have to root around a bit to see what we have, but coffee, coffee you never have to worry about. If there is ever a coffee embargo, all of West Virginia is gonna call off sick with a nasty headache."

After Matt had gotten a cup of coffee and tossed a French Bread Pizza in the oven for the breakfast/lunch of the late riser, he sat back down at the table.

Tyler looked up again from his phone and asked, "So, big plans for your first big day out here in the wilds of Appalachia?"

Matt took a sip of coffee and shrugged. "Well, I have to go out and visit MeeMaw or she'll kill me, or worse, make me feel incredibly guilty in some passive-aggressive manner. Other than that, I don't know, check out the property a bit, maybe drive into town, see if there's any excitement there, try not to create bad excitement on my first day in the area if there isn't. Pretty boring really, more or less just trying to land on my feet a bit."

Tyler flashed Matt a smile as he got up. "As long as you aren't looking to strike it rich while you're down here, you'll do fine. People are a lot nicer than out-of-state people give us credit for." Tyler paused at the door. "But one thing: y'all had definitely best go out and see MeeMaw. I ain't had anyone to fuck around on the X-box with at the house since Edwin moved to his place and got hisself children, I'd hate to see y'all get yerself killed by a pissed off retiree on day one."

Later that afternoon, showered and as human as he thought he was going to get, Matt steeled himself to walk down the path that led from the main house to his grandmother's little house. It wasn't that he was afraid of the woman, it was just, well, it was his MeeMaw. He rarely saw her because of the distance between home and here, and she could be weird. Once he got old enough to think about it, Matt had always assumed MeeMaw started being weird back when she had just been Louise May Turner and had maybe enjoyed the sixties a little bit too much. Time had just added habit to it over the years.

This was a favorite topic for him privately, watching his elders and betters try to act and talk adult when he knew deep down inside they had been far less adult than he somehow managed to appear when they were his age. Like his dad demanding to know when Matt was going to grow up, for instance, while listening to band after band who were renowned for their heroin use. Way to set a good example, Pops! Teenage rebellion had gone on for a long time before Matt had even been born. It humored him to see how many people tried to pretend that they'd totally missed it after the fact. If you asked, they'd say they were in church the entire time, making care packages for orphans.

Including his MeeMaw, the one whose personal little house looked like it had escaped out of a 1956 copy of *Better Homes and Gardens*, who knitted, who drank herbal tea. Matt knew there was the other version of MeeMaw his uncle and dad must have grown up with, the perpetual flower child, vanishing with her husband to his family farm in the mountains of Appalachia after seeing enough of the world to satisfy her. Matt tried to remind himself of this as he stood at the door. Once upon a time, the woman who was about to be judging him as only a grandmother could had once wanted to go to San Francisco with flowers in her hair.

He rang the doorbell, which seemed only polite. Her door swung open immediately, which wasn't a huge shock, she was expecting him and had probably been watching for him.

"Matt!" she exclaimed as she opened the screen door. "Come in, dear!"

Matt noted that she hadn't changed much at all—that timeless nature of people once they get old. She was dressed in a dress shirt and a long skirt. She may be dressed that way, but somehow, he expected there were mountains of tie-dye stashed away somewhere in this pristine house for when she didn't expect anyone coming by. Her hair was kept long and flowing, but still, she reminded him of Meryl Streep in that she was very precise in her expression and movement. She presented a dichotomy, a person who presented herself as someone who very much wanted to "go with the flow" but was hiding an exacting, strict mind, both fighting for dominance over her.

She hugged him deeply and exclaimed, "My! I'm glad all of y'all have stopped growing, just so I can get used to how you look now. Seems every time I see you, you've grown a foot!"

"I think I'm done now, MeeMaw. This seems to be it," he said, smiling back wanly.

"Well, there's growth and then there's growth. We keep doing it all our lives, we just stay the same shape as we do it. Well, until you get my age, that is, then you start shrinking a bit. Come to the living room, dear, and sit down. I've got some milk and cookies, your favorite, if I remember correctly," she replied, beckoning him inside.

Matt translated the part about growth in his head, thinking she must mean personal growth, like emotional or something. He kind of doubted she meant getting fat. He wasn't positive, but he doubted it.

The living room was immaculate. She either didn't get a lot of guests or she cleaned early and often. The place looked like an ad for Lemon Pledge, smelled like it too.

She pointed at the sofa. "Take a seat, dear, I'll go get the milk and cookies. Be right back!"

Still looking around to take in the room, he took a seat where MeeMaw had indicated. Matt was surprised to see that there was a picture of his part of the family on the mantle. Nobody had ever said anything, but somehow Matt had always gotten the impression that MeeMaw and the family had not been happy with Dad's decision to go to Penn State over WVU or Marshall, and even less happy about him choosing to stay up north with Matt's mom, whom he'd met at college.

(Sometimes when you're a little kid, you pick up on a vibe when you come to visit relatives. Kids pick up way more than adults ever give them credit for.)

His dad may be the black sheep, but Matt could only hope that black wool didn't pass on by association. Matt had to figure it didn't; she had been a doting grandmother as far as he could recall. He'd never felt anything but love from her. She could seem a bit spacey at times, but, well, couldn't all grandmas? Wasn't it a genetic imperative to forget to keep track of what the real spending power of five dollars was the second your grandchild was born? Matt was positive, judging from his friends as well, that the instant a grandchild was born, new technology could be safely ignored for the rest of time; they sent you a waiver with your AARP membership: "Holder of this card does not need to know what your damned gizmo does, and if you bother them any more about it, the cardholder will start reminiscing about the good old days at length, so back off, Sonny Boy!" He was pretty sure it was right there in the membership packet along with tips on how to draw out making a purchase at the checkout aisle for an entire geological age (remember, do not even take out your checkbook until the coupons, even the expired ones, have been rung up, never bring a pen, ask for one . . .).

MeeMaw came in carrying a plate with some sugar cookies on it and a glass of milk. Sitting there now, it all came back to him. MeeMaw always made sugar cookies when he was coming down to visit, and since he had cousins close to his age, she'd always made a point of hiding some away where Tyler and Edwin couldn't find them so Matt would have a chance of getting some too. It was a cherished little thing she had done just for him, something he hadn't even thought about in years. There was a lump in his throat as he took the plate and glass from her.

She daintily sat herself across from him in a recliner before saying, "My stars, I am so glad to have all my grandsons in spitting distance again. For the life of me, I didn't think I'd ever see you again."

"Well, I'm here now; but, MeeMaw, I'm sure you could have come to visit at some point. Dad misses you, I'm sure. He just gets busy with work, so it's hard to get away," Matt replied with what he hoped was with care and tact.

She sniffed a little at that. "No, your father and I . . . well, the house up there is a bit cramped. It would have been a bother." She shook her head for a moment. Her eyes looked sad just for an instant before she turned the smile back on and asked, "So, I'm to understand you'll be staying with us for a little while then?"

"My mom thought it might be best at the moment. I had a bad break up and all, and she thought if I just stayed around home, well, I might just mope. I guess she figured fresh air in the mountains might help me," Matt replied. He didn't think it would do any good to lie to his grandmother about why he was here, it would come out eventually if she didn't already know. Of course, that didn't mean he had to tell her *why* he'd had the breakup or that he'd been living in his SUV until his parents had given him temporary shelter. She probably didn't want to hear it anyway, no point in depressing the woman about the state of her genetic tree.

"Oh my, yes. You shouldn't mope, I suppose. Do you think you'll be able to find work? I mean, what is your trade, Matt?"

"I work in web design," Matt replied dutifully.

"Oh, is that something involving the internet?" she asked suspiciously.

BINGO! Full onset Elderly Computer Oblivion! He quickly recovered from his mental exaltation about being right about her relationship with technology and said, "Well it is, MeeMaw, but I don't know if I'll be down here that long to worry about working in my trade. In the meantime, Tyler said a friend of his might give me a job."

"Oh my, I do hope it isn't in that awful tattooing thing he does for a living." She tsked.

"No, no, just minding a store for a friend of his. Not really using my degree, but it'll give me something to do."

"Well, that's nice then. And quite nice of him too; I'll mention it to him that I appreciate it."

Matt looked at his grandmother, who reminded him of nothing as much as Betty White or some other perfectly straight grandmother type. He couldn't resist. "So, this is totally out of the blue, but I'd been wondering about it. How did you pick my dad's name again?"

"Oh, I can't remember, dear, it was so long ago."

Matt knew for a fact that his dad was named Robert after Bob Weir of the Grateful Dead.

Chapter 3

"I always wanted to be a farmer. There is a
tradition of that in my family."
—Björk Guðmundsdóttir,
who it should be noted works as a famous quirky
musician, an occupation not known for its
proximity to cow butts. Pig butts, sure, but
producers usually wear pants in public

———————◆———————

AFTER TALKING TO MeeMaw for a while about almost
entirely grandmotherly small talk (how was his dad,
how had college been, etc.), Matt was at loose ends.
Serious loose ends, like, he didn't know much about town,
he barely remembered the layout of the farm itself. Tyler
was at work and would get home when he did and no
sooner, that was just the nature of tattooing. Matt fidgeted.
He had this big long trip to get here so he felt like he should
be *doing* something now that he *was* here. He wasn't so
desperate that he was going to check in the barn to see if
his uncle and Edwin needed help, no point in going crazy
about things, especially if it involved cow poop. He still felt
like he should be doing *something*, just nothing bovine
related in any way whatsoever.

Matt remembered someone mentioning there being a
family graveyard on the property. The more he considered
it, the more he thought maybe he had just remembered it
from when he used to come here as a kid. Matt used to be

fascinated with graveyards when he was a child, when the concept of death was the most completely alien thing on earth and therefore needed to be studied and considered from an outsider's point of view. Matt still found them to be interesting, the ancient stories represented by the stones just sitting there to be puzzled over. He had yet to hit that age when graveyards stopped seeming fascinating as much as they started feeling inevitable.

He made his way to a long dirt road that cut along the property and towards the hills in the distance that held the family plot. Matt decided that since he had nothing if not free time today, he'd walk it instead of driving. It was only about a half a mile or so from the house, and it seemed silly to be all the way out here in the country and the wilds yet still drive just to go that far. He owned an SUV, and somehow driving seemed in defiance of the whole getting-out-to-the-wilds SUV spirit, didn't mean other people wouldn't do it anyway, just that he wasn't at that point in his life yet. You were supposed to use the SUV to get yourself somewhere where you could have some life experiences, not as a tool to avoid life experiences, even if they were only moderately pleasant walks. The weather was warm and sunny. There was a light breeze blowing away from the barn itself and therefore wafting the smell in that magical direction known as "somewhere else." It seemed to be a perfect day for a walk. Assuming there wasn't a shift in the breeze, of course, but even then, it would still be pleasant, if just a little bit more fragrant.

He needed to get his thoughts in some kind of order if coming down here to West Virginia was going to do any good, and a walk seemed like the best way to do that. He could be inside, screwing around on the internet, trying to discover what his new home area had to offer, but he was willing to concede that at a time of stress when one really needed to contemplate what they were doing with their life, the last place on heaven and earth to get good ideas on the subject was the internet. To distract yourself, sure, there was an endless array of ways to humor yourself, a happy chuckle, or you could get mad about something that didn't really affect you. It was all available at a click. One of the internet's favorite pastimes was allowing yourself to go right to towering offense by something stupid a celebrity just said or "news" articles from sites like NauturalLawPatriotNewz. There were, of course, always cat videos, if you were a happier person by nature, and memes were, of course, plentiful. All of that was in full and thriving supply on the internet. Five seconds of Twitter and Facebook and you could get full cat meme bliss with a side dose of righteous indignation in just moments of your time, often from the same person you were following. But that meant it was not really the right place to go if you were trying to put your life in order in your head. You should probably give that at least a couple of minutes of peace and quiet. Not too much, mind you; you spend too long on your own without funny YouTube videos, you start thinking weird thoughts. Next thing you know, you're forming a death cult on a remote mountain that worships space spatulas or something. And even though your cult will eschew all material possessions, you will still have a kicking website and, as a matter of course, YouTube videos. (This is a truism; obsessive people ALWAYS have the best websites.)

What were we talking about again? Oh yeah, Matt needing some quiet time. Let's continue from where we were and see if he gets some, shall we?

Matt was trying to achieve that state of quiet useful contemplation as he walked, he really was, but it wasn't taking. Instead, he had just begun to wonder, *Would the suicide cult leave members behind to maintain the cult's twitter feed? "No Spaceship for you Chad, you boned transcendental screaming, you have to stay behind and get into arguments on the twitter feed. Remember to use lots of hashtags! #notacult #weprefertheorangekoolaide and #nosillierthanscientology."* He was considering how lonely an existence that would be when the grass beside the road parted in a rush!

What erupted from the grass and crossed the road directly in front of him had to be the largest snake Matt had ever seen in his life outside of a zoo! Long and black and fast, it slipped across the road in an instant and vanished into the grass on the other side! Matt picked himself up off the gravel road, where he had landed when he jumped backward in terror from the snake, and reminded himself, *Oh yeah, the country, they have non-domesticated animals out here.* There was even a possibility the monstrosity that had just vipped across the road was harmless, but Matt couldn't bring himself to believe it. He was more likely to believe that the snake had a secret lair and was plotting to take over the world. It had been a pretty big snake; an animal doesn't get that big without devouring small children and livestock.

He stood there for a moment and dusted himself off, considering whether he could truly trust that the snake was gone so he could continue. It was a snake; untrustworthy was in their job description, it was right there in the bible. They don't call people a bunny in the grass when they think they're lying. If it was a little rabbit, he could trust that. (Maybe you should try calling people "bunnies in the grass." Try it with total strangers, let us know how it goes. We're honestly curious.) At least now he wasn't worried about any *other* snakes, that one would have surely killed them all by now in its quest for world domination.

Matt stood for a moment before he conceded to himself that he would have noticed the grass moving if the thing had decided to swing around for the kill. That didn't mean he wasn't still at the ready to flee as he moved past where the snake had vanished when he moved on.

As Matt started down a hill, he could see the graveyard off to the side of the road at the top of the next hill. He was surprised to admit to himself that it looked incredibly photogenic there in the distance. This was a series of hayfields, and the cut stone walls and the large tree that overshadowed the whole family plot created a spot of shaded tranquility in the sea of recently sprouted grass. Matt could kind of see why so many relatives had chosen to be buried there. It wasn't his goal in life, he hoped to be cremated and loaded on to the Mars lander one day—because aim high and all. Still, if you had to be socked into the ground, it looked like an amazingly tranquil place to do it.

As he got closer to it, he could see the graveyard better and considered it a place out of time. Not like it had run out of actual time, like it was going to be torn down or something, just from another time. It reminded him of the historic graveyards you could visit on incredibly lame tours back home that nobody had been buried in the last hundred years. The kind where the guide is just doing this to nab enough money to make rent while going to school and sounds *exactly* like somebody who is only doing it for some quick extra cash. If you ever *had* any questions of your tour guide, which nobody ever really did on any of the tours he'd gone on, there was no possible way this person would be able to answer them. "I'll look into it and see if I can give you an answer when we're done," they'd say. Meanwhile, the twenty or so elementary school kids taking the tour on a field trip from school had already looked it up on their phone, one of which would start tugging on your sleeve to tell you. Not that Matt was willing to admit to this ever happening specifically to him. This graveyard had that kind of historic look to it, only without the bored guide and the pack of smart-ass kids.

Except it wasn't history, people from his family were still being buried here. His Pa Pa was in there, one day his MeeMaw would be too. Matt wasn't sure about his mom and dad's plans, but he was pretty sure Uncle Donnie was already planning to make this spot his final resting place as well. It felt kind of neat to be connected to some kind of family history in a way he really wasn't back home. His other grandparents viewed their family history in terms of "Remember when we went to the Grand Canyon and we had that ice cream?" Important stuff to them but not exactly historical, unless they had done something like spilled the ice cream on a visiting senator and had been wrestled to the ground by the security detail for it or something. If they had, they never mentioned it. Probably embarrassed by it.

Now that he was standing here, he was surprised it meant so much to him to be staring at generations of Hawleys. The graves went all the way back in time to a point where the stones were so worn now as to be barely visible, even with the grass cut routinely. Little rough stone nubs stuck out of the ground, whatever they had said worn away by the ages. He knew because he had learned it on a visit to the farm from his Pa Pa when he was still alive. The graves went all the way back to the first member of the family to come here from Scotland, Mungo Hawley. Matt couldn't remember why his Pa Pa said the man had left Scotland, but with a first name like Mungo, Matt had always suspected it couldn't have been good. He had found out later that Mungo was actually a pretty traditional first name, but first impressions and all . . .

Matt figured he should at least stop by and pay his respects to Pa Pa. Matt had always liked the man when he'd been alive and hadn't been that happy about his family not coming down for the funeral. It had seemed like his grandfather was always tired from working the farm, but even so, he always made time on their visits down here to dote over his grandchildren. It would be weird to walk all the way out here to the family plot and not stand there for a moment in silence. Matt felt he owed him that much.

Finding the grave wasn't that hard, it was the newest

grave there and the only one with any loose dirt on it. Matt stood in front of it, feeling like it would be stupid to talk. The man was dead. It wasn't like he could hear Matt, no matter what you believed. Instead, Matt stood there quietly with his hands folded in front of him and listened to the wind blowing through the fields outside of the stone walls, which was unnerving in and of itself since it had been a calm day before. It almost sounded like whispering to him.

Matt was willing to write the thought off as being silly, but it still made him want to go back to the farmhouse, maybe even stop by the barn to see what Edwin and his uncle were up to just to see another human being. He chided himself for being a geek as he closed the gate to the family plot behind him. Matt couldn't help but note that whatever wind had been blowing a moment ago ceased as soon as he got back out. He shrugged it off as just a trick caused by the way the air broke around the walls and started trudging for the house.

As soon as he was gone, a voice could be heard if you had the trick of listening. "Sae wa in the heel didn't we say anything to him?"

There was silence for a moment before another voice replied, "Well, he is new, we don't want to scare him."

"Bairns the-day! Afraid ay their ain shadows. Och, we dornt want tae scaur heem! In mah day, we went lookin' fur ghosts an' goblins sae we coods barnie them. Noo 'at we ur ghosts an' goblins, we cannae say a wuid in case we frighten fowk! Bah!" the first voice grumbled.

Another voice sighed and said, "Times change, we have to learn to be not alive in the now and not keep living in the past."

"Whit in th' heel diz 'at pure techt anyway?"

"It means we stick with the plan."

Matt had his doubts about his idea of saying hi as soon as he got closer to the barn. He could see that his uncle and cousin were bringing the small herd of cows in for the nightly milking, which meant they were busy. The great mooing mass was making their way into the building like some bovine version of an old film showing a shift change at a factory. You could almost wonder, as you watched it, if the mooing was idle chatter asking each other how the day had gone, if they had seen an interesting cloud or a really pretty flower while they'd been out grazing or something.

He was just about to turn and go back to the house when he heard Uncle Donnie call out, "Hey, Matt! Why don't y'all come over, if you're not doin' nuthin' at the moment!"

Matt groaned inside. He knew that phrase from childhood. Whenever anybody in any circumstance said the words "If you're not doing anything at the moment," they were about to present you with something to do that you'd rather not be doing at any moment. And not just for a moment either, this was going to chew up a good chunk of your time; and it was never, ever anything you had been hoping for a chance to do. Nobody says, "Hey if you're not doing anything at the moment, why don't you come over here and take this Formula 1 car around the track a couple of times while eating chocolate off of this swimsuit model?"

Unfortunately for Matt, he couldn't think of anything to beg off with in time to stop his mouth from saying, "Be right over!"

His mind raced through the possibilities as to what he was wanted for. His favorite to hope for was "Could you tell your aunt that . . . " This would mean going to the house, which definitely had less cow poop in it. Also, there was always the possibility of a snack of some kind at the house, and maybe a pre-dinner beer.

His uncle had a big smile on his face when Matt

approached the gate leading into the milking area, the smile of a man who was about to dash Matt's hopes for a snack.

"Why don't y'all come on in, I can show you how it's done, and then y'all can give us a hand with the milking. That way, if that thing with Tyler don't work out, y'all can drop right into helping here," the man said with a broad, happy, honest country smile that Matt didn't believe for a moment was sincere.

He suspected deeply that this was "Mess with the city boy time!"

Well, he knew how to deal with this! Nobody was making a fool out of Matt today! "Sure, I guess, if you don't think I'd get in the way," he said, his mouth overriding his brain again. Clearly, nobody was making a fool out of him, he could do it all on his own without any help, thank you! One of these days, he'd have to have a serious talk with his parents about raising him to be this polite and all the long-term damage they had done by it.

"Well, follow me. I'll show you how, and then you can do a few yourself!" Uncle Donnie said happily before turning and heading into the barn.

Matt sighed gustily. He was trapped, and there was no denying it. He remembered he thought it had been neat as a little kid, so maybe it wouldn't be so bad, he lied to himself. That was the way of it! Make this a positive experience. He had never really milked a cow by himself as an adult, and when he got back home, it would be a life experience that none of his other friends had. Assuming, of course, he made new friends that weren't his old friends, who were also HER friends . . . Wait! Negative thinking! He needed to stop that train of thought right at the station!

He went into the barn through the door where the giant pasteurizing tank was, rather than climb over the fence and go in that way. Yes, he could have done it; yes, he was wearing hiking boots; but Matt still had hopes and dreams of keeping them as manure free as possible. Somewhere in the back of Matt's mind was the strong foreboding about this. The reality was that most dreams don't come true. He would be scrubbing off his boots at some point, and no way was that thing with the stewardesses likely to happen.

He saw Edwin working through one side and his uncle working through the other, locking the cows into their stalls. This further drove home the factory analogy; the cows invariably went to where they were supposed to go to await milking. They knew the routine at the old mill: up to their work station and let's get it over with. And just like those at the factory, food and shelter were the impetus, the barn being shelter for the night and the grain that his uncle and Edwin were pouring into the trough in front of the cows, the food.

Matt was trying to stay as inconspicuous as possible on the outside chance that Uncle Donnie and Edwin would become so absorbed in their normal routine of milking the cows that Donnie would forget about him entirely, thus allowing him to slip out without molesting cow boobies in any way. This was not to be. As soon as the bovines were fed, his uncle called him over with a wave of his hand. His uncle was rolling out something that looked like a small bundle of machinery but connected to a Cthulhu worth of tentacles. A CyberCthulhu.

"C'mon over and let's get this show on the road," Donnie said in a tone of voice that sounded entirely too cheerful, considering his proximity to an electronic Old One.

Trapped by his own politeness, Matt wandered over to where his uncle had stopped the trolley behind a cow.

"It's real simple," Uncle Donnie said, grabbing two large buckets and sliding in next to a cow.

Matt followed, but not too close because of the proximity to the back end of the cow and anything that might be there.

His uncle quickly got into position on a stool next to the cow and, with a practiced series of motions, dipped out a rag from the soapy water in the bucket and quickly wiped down the cow's underside.

"First you gotta disinfect them. Then y'all gotta check for mastitis," he said. With that, he grabbed a small metal cup that looked a little bit like a stainless-steel coffee mug and gave a couple of yanks on a teat. Holding the cup up for Matt to see, he said, "This lets you get a quick look at the milk. If y'all see any lumps or any discoloration, she needs to be milked by hand."

Matt winced at that a bit, both because it sounded gross and the solution sounded incredibly carpal tunnelly.

Finally, his uncle grabbed the stainless-steel Elder God looking thing off the cart, first hooking one end to an overhead pipe creating a gigantic suction noise and then taking the four dangling tentacles over to the cow's udder. Each one made a noise like the doors on the old Star Trek show as they connected to a teat, sucking it into the contraption.

Uncle Donnie smiled up at him. "Now we wait. Y'all gotta hand milk out the last little bits into the other bucket to make sure they don't get mastitis, but other than that, easy, right?"

"Ummm, I guess so," Matt replied doubtfully.

"Well, we'll wait for her to finish up, and then y'all can do the next one."

"Oh, good," Matt replied flatly, but the heavy dose of sarcasm he said it with seemed completely lost on his Uncle. "Umm, one thing."

"Yeah?"

"What's mastitis?" Matt asked quietly so Edwin didn't hear from across the aisle where he was working.

"Bad."

"Oh."

As soon as the cow was done, his uncle wheeled the

cart the equipment was on down one cow and said, "Here you go, you can give ole four-thirty-six a whirl."

There was an expectant pause before it dawned on Matt that he was expected to do this by himself. He grabbed the bucket and the cup off the cart with one hand and the stool with the other and maneuvered himself into position. Trying to get this done as quickly as possible, as he was sitting down on the stool, he got the rag out and wiped down the cow's udders. The moment the warm rag touched the animal's teats, Matt heard the spatter of urine being unleashed, said widdle splattering onto not only him but also onto the animal's freshly cleaned udder.

"Yeah, they'll do that; just have to wipe 'em down again," Matt heard his uncle say levelly from the aisle.

Matt grumbled as he did it, just not loud enough that his uncle could hear him. He didn't want to look like a wuss about this. Next, he grabbed a teat and the cup and pulled. At least this part he remembered from when he was a kid, so that would be easy enough. He looked back at his uncle, who had stepped back, probably to see how Edwin was doing, and gave a yank. A moment later, Matt's vision was blocked by the sudden swish of the cow's tail as it caught him directly in the face!

Its urine-soaked tail.

"Oh, gross!" Matt spat.

"Aww geez, sorry there, son. I forgot she can be like that when you're starting her off!" his Uncle exclaimed, darting forward. "Let me tie her tail up for you!"

"Thanks," Matt said darkly.

Finally, it was time to put the milking machine on. Which the cow took as her cue to wee again. After wiping down the teats again, he hooked the machine up to the pipe and got back down on the stool to put it on the cow's individual teats. As soon as the cow felt the thing start to pull a teat in, Matt was almost knocked from his stool as the cow's rear leg came up to kick at him! He shoved the foot back down, but the process repeated itself three more times. Star Trek noise, kick, swat shove, Star Trek noise, kick, swat shove, curse loudly, Star Trek noise, quickly stand up to avoid the hoof.

Matt looked over to see his uncle smiling slightly. "Well you seem to have this in hand, as it were, why don't y'all do a few more to get a real feel for it. I'll go get another rig and start working further down the line. Make sure you hand milk her out to finish her.".

As he watched his uncle walk off, Matt realized that this had been the most elaborate "Get a fucking job" speech he had ever been a party to. Get a job or get cow piss in the face. The choice is yours, young man!

$$\mathcal{DOC}$$

On many of the roads of Appalachia, the speed limit is something along the lines of a dare, as if the state's road department had said, "No, we're honestly curious to see if you can pull it off." In theory, you could possibly do 45 on some of these roads, but we're betting you go hurtling off a mountain if you try it. Drunk driving on a mountain road takes a very, very brave man; unfortunately, alcohol creates very brave, very dumb men often enough. Both of those things go a long way to explaining why almost every road in the area has at least one guard rail that's completely mashed in, just waiting for a replacement so that the overly confident or inebriated can crumple the next one.

This gravel road did not even rank guard rails. If you messed up here, you were in the hands of the angels, and you would be meeting them shortly so you could complain about the screwup. It didn't stop the worn pickup from throwing rocks as it went flying by at breakneck speeds, even for a paved road, one without the potholes this one was littered with. Someone was clearly more worried about their present than their near future.

There was a couple inside the cab of the truck, though you'd be hard-pressed to see them through the fogged-up windows. It was odd that they would fog up, it was a warm day, the vehicle didn't have air conditioning to make a temperature difference, and it hadn't rained all day. The man, who was driving, tried to scan the road through the misted window but refused to take his white-knuckled hands off the steering wheel to wipe the window clean. The woman was just slumped against the door whimpering softly, her orange-red hair plastered to her sweat covered face.

"Don't you worry none, Amber, we get into town, it'll all be all right," the man said, almost as if it was a mantra he'd been repeating since they'd gotten into the vehicle. "Ain't nobody gonna be able to touch us, we get ourselves into town!"

The skies darkened, and still, the man refused or was unable to pull his hands from the steering wheel to turn on the truck's lights. He was counting on knowing the way up this mountain, and he figured he was damned close to the top now! It would be all downhill after that, smooth sailing right into the valley!

So strange to completely forget a corner on a mountain road you'd driven all your life.

The crashes the truck made as it plummeted from the road boomed up and down the valley. Soon, the echoes died down, and the only noises left were the pinking of cooling metal and a rear tire still spinning fruitlessly. On the bumper, which had gotten thrown from the crash, you could just make out the bumper sticker that said, "Baldwin For Senate."

$$\mathcal{DCC}$$

Finally, after doing five cows of his own, Matt saw that his uncle and cousin were already more or less finished with the rest of them. Matt made a mental note that there had to be some work in West Virginia, and no matter what he did, he was going to make sure he found it. He had enough bovine secretions in his short time helping with the evening milking to last a lifetime. It made him wonder if he'd ever be able to look a glass of milk in the face again. Record store or something else, it didn't matter, his barn days were over as of now!

Taking advantage of there being no more cows in need of milking, Matt took it as his cue to book for the house before his uncle found something more disgusting to do to prove his point, like manual bull semen collection. He wasn't really sure that was how they collected it, but if there was any possibility, Matt knew in his heart of hearts that if he hung around here, he'd find out one way or the other. And frankly, he didn't want or need to know how they got it. Maybe it involved getting the bulls drunk, making them watch old Carnation commercials with Barry White playing in the background; the mind boggled at the concept.

He took his boots off when he got to the back steps and wondered what new boots went for around here. It seemed to him like it might be easier buying new ones than washing the ones he'd been wearing. One thing he definitely knew was he wasn't wearing them inside. Aunt Debbie seemed pretty easy going, but he suspected that attitude might end when it came to cow poop being tracked inside and onto the carpets.

After getting a shower, he went to see about food. Matt was pretty sure that the big meal last night was a welcome for him coming to the farm and not a nightly deal, so he'd need to forage for himself today. Certainly there were no smells of any large feast being made wafting up the stairs to him as he got dressed. Thankfully, he could just about feed himself if the need arose, but he also began to understand the need for Tyler having a fridge in his own room. Assuming Tyler didn't just have his filled with beer.

Their age was a beer intensive time period in a young man's life, and bottles take up a lot of space. If there was food, he could understand the need to have your own snacks tucked away.

He was just coming downstairs when Aunt Debbie called out from the kitchen over the sound of the microwave to confirm his suspicions.

"I'm going to assume y'all know how to cook your own dinner. You're welcome to whatever you can find, but I didn't raise two boys to be full-grown men to do any cooking except on special occasions."

Matt entered the kitchen to find his aunt tapping her heel, waiting for the microwave to go off. "That's fine," he said. "Mom was the same way after I turned sixteen, and I have yet to starve to death."

She turned to him, smiling. "And how much of that is due to fast food? I know Tyler eats total crap since the divorce if he don't eat at home."

"I can cook, I swear!" Matt insisted. "I promise your kitchen is safe with me."

"Well, all right. If that no-account son of mine gets back from work any time soon, tell him to eat something that don't come in a twelve-ounce bottle or in a paper bag, please." With that, the microwave beeped, and she took out what looked to be one of those cheap entree things from the frozen food aisle—the stuff you know only remotely ever had any meat or meat by-products in its creation despite the description but has the exact right mix of salt and grease for you to forgive it. In a smooth movement, she took out a tray of fries from the oven and quickly put two plates together, one for her and the other, he assumed, for his Uncle Donnie.

"We'll be in the TV room if you want to be social. But I have to warn y'all, it's NASCAR tonight, and I know that isn't that popular up North," she said as she carried off the two steaming plates of food-like product.

"Thanks for the warning, Aunt Debbie," Matt said sincerely as she left.

He had just started rooting around in the freezer and was considering the chest freezer out on the back porch when he heard someone coming down the drive. Going to the front, he saw what looked to be an elderly Ford barreling down the road, sending up a cloud of dust. Instinct told him that it had to be Tyler. The fact that his aunt didn't seem particularly interested in the new arrival more or less confirmed it for him. Since Matt had no idea what he wanted to eat yet, they could probably have dinner together.

Tyler bounced in the door, carrying a bag that looked suspiciously like it held a six-pack. He took one look at Matt and said, "Pa suckered you into doing farm work today, huh?"

"How in the hell did you know?" Matt demanded.

"Your hair's wet, which means you showered, and the only reason I could figure for doing that this early is cow shit." Tyler grinned before asking, "You eat yet?"

"I was just digging around."

"I'll whip us up something, and then we can hang out upstairs. I figure after today, you might want to hear about that music store job, huh?"

"Yeah, somehow I don't think milking cows has a bright future for me, more of an 'obscured by a piss-soaked tail' future, and I can allow myself to pass on that."

Chapter 4

"Whenever you are asked if you can do a job, tell 'em, Certainly, I can! Then get busy and find out how to do it."
—Theodore Roosevelt, stuffed animal model.

———◆———

ONCE THEY WERE upstairs and sharing a boxed lasagna from the oven, Tyler broached the subject of the music store again, but obscurely.

"So what kind of tunes do you Yankees listen to, anyway? I mean, I figure it has to be kind of different, right?" he asked.

"A lot of people up there listen to mostly pop crap, same as anywhere, really. That's how it becomes pop crap, a bunch of people listening to it, I suppose."

"And you yourself?"

"Well, I mean, I hear some of it, the crap is hard to avoid, obviously. But I also listen to some other stuff, a few different types of metal, some club goth, some neue deutsch harte stuff, y'know Rammstein, Hamatom, Megaherz, Eisbrecher . . . stuff like that," Matt said and shrugged.

"Guess what one of the most popular styles of music is down here as far as the record store goes?" Tyler asked with a look of someone waiting to spring a surprise.

"I'm sure it would be, I don't know, racist or classist or something, but I'd still guess, what? Country and western? Gospel?"

"How much do you know about psychobilly?" Tyler asked with a wicked grin.

"You must be shitting me. Really? I mean not like I know anything about it but . . . "

"And that is why you should count your lucky stars you have your cousin Tyler. Let me hook my iPod up to the Bluetooth on your computer, and why don't we see about giving you a crash course. The main ones you need to know are the Meteors and the Cramps. They more or less came up with it back in the seventies, and you'll be a heathen if you don't know them. The who as to why this area is so into it is Blitzkid, they're from down in Mercer County and are probably the biggest band to come out of the area ever. Oh yeah, we'll do some foreign stuff too. You like German stuff, you speak German?" Tyler enthused.

"No, I took French in school. It's just that really heavy techno metal sounds better when it's being barked at you in German. Just seems more natural. They could be saying anything, like that meme: tell someone you love them today because life is short, but shout it at them in German because life is also terrifying and confusing." Matt shrugged again.

"French, you say? I have just the thing, Banane Metalik! Give me just a sec!"

A little later, they were both sitting there sipping beers and listening to .mp3s through the computer's speakers when Matt said, "They sound like the band in the street from *Nightmare Before Christmas* playing French punk rock."

There was a pause as they both considered the statement before Tyler said, "Not one single thing in that previous sentence was not totally awesome, you know that, right?"

"True."

☾☉☽

Matt would be doomed to losing part of his night sleep again. Just as before, he would be woken by his grandfather, and just as before, he thought he must be dreaming. This time, as he looked around the room in a daze, he realized that he also wasn't alone with his Pa Pa. Two other figures had joined him, both dressed like they had escaped some horrible romance novel and were looking to expand their horizons to horror flicks! Matt's eyes bugged open at the sight of them.

"Boy, y'all need to sit up," his Pa Pa said kindly, shaking him awake.

Matt came bolt upright and stared wildly at the newcomers. "Pa Pa, who . . . ?"

"It's all right, they're family too, but—"

His grandfather was interrupted by a man (in a kilt of all things) who growled at his Pa Pa, "Ah can spick fur myself, if ye dornt mind ." Then he turned to Matt. "Ye ken thes is nae a dream, reit? Ye can see us clear as day, an' yoo're waukin', yoo're seein' th' ghosts ay yer fowk come tae spick wi' ye!"

Matt stared at the three of them blankly.

The other man with them, who was dressed in more traditional early American clothes, sighed and then said, "He said you aren't dreaming, you're awake, and you can see the ghosts of your ancestors, i.e. us."

"Who are you people? I mean, other than ghosts?" Matt gasped, drawing his knees up to his chest in fright. He put them right back down when he realized it was something silly that he hadn't done since watching horror movies as a child. (But it should give you an idea of the fear level we're dealing with here. "Revert to childhood frightened" should be a thing.)

"Wa diz thes git keep repeatin' me?" The man in the

kilt smacked the other man in the arm. He turned to Matt and said, "Aam th' foonder ay th' fowk, yer stoatin, stoatin . . . weel thaur ur quite puckle ay them. But aam th' first in thes coontry, Grandfaither, Mungo Hawley."

Matt looked blank again, and the man in homespun sighed again. "I keep telling you, Seanair, nobody kin understand your accent here." The man turned to Matt and said, "I'm your great, great . . . well again, there are a lot of them, Pa Pa Ezekiel Hawley. The man you can't seem to understand is my grandfather, Mungo Hawley. He was the first of our family to come to these mountains from Scotland around the time of our nation's birth."

Matt looked stunned for a moment, then said, "Oh. Okay." He thought about it for a moment before something bothered him about all of that. "Did you say Mungo? MeeMaw mentioned you, is that even a real name?"

"Och aye, it's a traditional Scottish nam, an' ye hud best shaw yer elders some respect an' nae poke fin ay it, loon!"

Matt looked at Ezekiel, who just shrugged and said, "Be nice, he founded the family, after all. But yes, it's traditional. You should just be thankful nobody found it in the family bible and decided to be just as traditional in later namings, you or your cousins could have it."

Another thought occurred to Matt. "Excuse me for saying, you don't sound very West Virginian, or Scottish for that matter, Ezekiel."

"Well, it was a time of good fortune for the family, so I was educated up North."

Matt turned to his own Grandfather. "Pa Pa, what in the hell is this all about? I'm dreaming, right?"

His grandfather patted his leg as he sat next to him. "Ask yourself something, son, do you feel like you're dreaming?"

"No, but y'know, lucid dreams and all?"

"Whit in th' guid god damned heel is he talkin' abit? Whit oan earth is a lucid dream?" Mungo muttered to Ezekiel.

"Let me ask you something, son. Has anyone in your dreams been that hard to understand?" His Pa Pa smiled knowingly, walking him down the path to realization.

"I can usually understand them, especially if they're technically speaking English. Except for that one dream after watching too much hentai," Matt admitted.

"I will cherish my ignorance as to what you meant about that last part," Pa Pa said as his smile went a bit brittle.

"Ah spick sassenach braw, it's nae mah faut nobody can listen worth a jobby!"

Ignoring his muttering elder, Matt's grandfather continued. "Son, y'all have a special gift. Not even everybody in the family has ever had it. You being able to see and hear us is part of it. Part of us being here now is to let y'all know about your birthright. Also, to be honest, they wanted a look-see at you." Pa Pa smiled.

Still positive he was dreaming, he was willing to brush off disbelief, but a thought occurred to Matt. "Why haven't I ever been able to talk to ghosts before?"

"Son, in the big city, y'all can barely even hear yourself think, let alone hear something as, well, ghostly as we are. Not to mention so damned many souls just a clamoring for notice, it all just becomes white noise, really," his grandfather said.

"This has got to be a dream, this just can't be happening," Matt said and shook his head.

Ezekiel stepped away from his own grandfather, quickly and sprightly at that. He had known the old man for a very, very long time and knew instinctively when the man was going to blow.

And blow he did, bellowing at Matt, "Whit in th' heel ur ye talkin' abit? Yoo've bin a given a stoatin an' wonderful gift tae gab tae th' deid, hink ay aw th' things we ken ye dornt! An' ye sit thaur greetin' loch a bairn wi' fricht an' nae believin' th' evidence ay yer ain een?" The big ghost took another deep breath (which was probably not necessary, considering that he was a ghost) before continuing. "Aw we ask is ye swatch efter yer fowk an' yer lands loch a cheil! Yit ye still sit thaur whimperin' loch a scared lassie tellin' yerself it is nae happenin'!"

Seeing Matt's lost and terrified face, his Pa Pa patted him on the leg again and said, "What your Pa Pa Mungo meant there, y'all have responsibilities, that's true, to your family, to yourself, but y'all should still consider yourself lucky anyway. Y'all got generations of family to learn from. Anywhere on this farm, and quite some distance away in these mountains that gave life to all of us, all you have to do is ask and we'll be right there to help."

Matt leaned forward and whispered to his own Pa Pa, "Does it have to be Pa Pa Mungo? He scares the shit out of me!"

His grandfather nodded and whispered back, "Me too, son, me too."

Ɗ☾

A week went by. There were almost nightly talks with his grandfather. Pa Pa explained that he thought that maybe in cities, magic and mystery had gotten eaten up by science and logic, but not everywhere. Not here specifically. Here in these mountains, people still had belief and room to spread out and feel the earth beneath them. Here in Appalachia, magic still existed, and it mainly existed in the venerable families who had brought it to this land from the old country. Families like the Hawleys, for instance. Not every member had the power to actually use it, though; usually, there was only one in a generation. His Pa Pa had it, and he had made it even stronger by marrying a girl from another old family. That wasn't why he had married Matt's MeeMaw, but when he started to say exactly what he had seen in Matt's grandmother, Matt had been forced to cry out for mercy and beg for him to never bring it up again. Her eyes were the best part of the description; when he went on to say something about her hips and other parts, Matt's mind had shut down in self-defense.

It was a lot to take in. And not just the part about MeeMaw's butt back in the 70s.

But being haunted wasn't all Matt was doing with his time. He and Tyler had become fast friends and hung out often. They'd even gone into the big town in the area a couple of times together. What that town consisted of were the remains of an old industrial town. You saw them a lot everywhere manufacturing and production had once thrived, so that wasn't particularly unique. There were plenty of places that had once had a major boom and then whatever industry had provided for everyone one day just left almost overnight. It wasn't totally destitute, though; there was a massive piece of it on the east side of town that was really only a gigantic strip mall, which provided jobs and commerce for the area. Matt could rest assured he would never want for fast food or generic steak again!

He also sent out a lot of resumes online. None of which he had heard back from yet, despite his constantly refreshing his email with hope that he might get a job he actually wanted. He had suspicions about whether or not he would. Matt was willing to admit he was trying to stay in his field from college, and he only assumed that the competition was hot in administration. Or maybe it was his out of state credentials. That could be it as well. Or, it could be that they called his previous boss and got the story of him smelling like ass for multiple days because of him living in an SUV. He couldn't rule that out. Whatever the reason, he decided it was finally time to make the necessary cow-poop-avoiding move. If he couldn't work in his field, he decided a record store was as good as anything. It beat working in strip mall hell at least, or worse, the Mall mall. If he was going to make minimum wage, he damn well didn't want to have to wear a tie to do it while trying to be polite to the kind of people named Karen who shopped at chain stores. With the threat of farm labor still over his head, he told Tyler he'd do it.

Uncle Donnie had started making comments along the lines of, "Y'know, if y'all are bored, me and Edwin, we could use your help down at the barn!"

Cow pats versus selling vinyl platters. It wasn't a hard choice.

It was time to get on with it. A week off goofing around with Tyler around the farm had been fun, but it was time to—shudder—get a job. So today, they were driving to a town slightly further away, because, "They have a quaint little downtown, and quaint equals hip record shop, which beats working at the mall," according to Tyler. Matt had to admit, once they got off the turnpike as he trailed behind Tyler, that it was quaint. The place reeked of "tourist money removal machine." If they didn't have a vape store and at least one art collective somewhere on this strip, the lease to open one had already been signed. Matt couldn't help but be surprised by one thing that was out of place for this type of town: the parking was easy. It didn't seem possible, but the city planners had put in exactly enough parking spots for the amount of traffic the main street received. The people at the *Weekly World News* should be called and told, but odds were they wouldn't believe it. Those editors lived in New York and knew that was far past the amount of BS even their readers would tolerate. You had to keep things at least a little plausible.

Since Tyler knew the guy who owned the place, Matt let him take the lead and just trailed along behind him, taking in the architecture, which was all late 1800s and very pretty. The store itself was a short walk—well, calling it a store was an educated guess, really. What it was, was layers of posters for various bands and show flyers (some dating to the 1800s, if Matt was to guess) with a door letting into it. But the sign above did say Compacted Discs, which had to be the name of a record store, or a chiropractor. At least up north, chiropractors didn't go in for quite that much poster art, preferring to steal their decorations from various Orlando Dentist offices while at Disney World on vacation.

Inside, the dim light illuminated that it did indeed hold racks of CDs, vinyl records, and various other bits of record store paraphernalia like t-shirts, posters, and DVDs, and not chiropractor equipment. Talking heatedly on a cell phone behind the counter was a man that *looked* around Uncle Donnie's age, but judging from the GHOST t-shirt and the bleached spiky hair, he wasn't nearly as willing to admit to that fact.

"I swear to Christ, Tommy, if I have to close the shop . . . if I get out there and you're as fucked up as you sound to me over the phone, I won't fire you, I will push you the fuck off the roof myself!" the man snarled, hitting end on the call.

Obviously too involved with the call to notice the door buzzing when they came in, the man gave a start when he saw them standing in front of them. "Oh shit! Sorry about that, didn't hear y'all come in. Hey, Tyler, how the fuck you doin'?" he said. Turning to see Matt, he said, "Oh yeah, okay, that your cousin? He don't look like a pill head, so that's good. What's your name, kid?"

"Ummm, Matt," he replied tentatively.

"Look, Umm Matt, I'm gonna make this quick. Nine bucks an hour to start, ten after a month. I need a new manager for the store. Every chance it could be you, that'd be fifteen, and that's damned good money for around here. If you cover the rest of today for me, that would go a long way towards just that. I also do construction and got trouble on a job site. I got five Mexicans and five hillbillies standing around with their thumbs up their ass and a foreman who's a god damned drunk who can't figure out what to tell 'em to do. Tyler worked here back in the day, he vouched for y'all. He can show you what to do. So, whaddya say, kid? Y'all want a job? It starts right now."

"Umm, okay?"

The man didn't even answer but grabbed his jacket. His car keys were in his hand in an instant. He was heading for the door and called over his shoulder, "Tyler, have him fill out an application for tax purposes, show him where shit is! I'll call you later to let y'all know what the fuck this was all about!"

"Talk to y'all later, Ashley," Tyler said and grinned as the man fled out the door.

"Spare keys are on the hook! Lock up when y'all close!" the man replied, and then he was gone.

Matt stood there, stunned and dumbfounded by what had just occurred, until Tyler punched him lightly on the arm.

"Looks like y'all just avoided shoveling cow shit for fun and profit!" Tyler said. "C'mon, I'll show you around!"

☽◯☾

The battered and rusted 70s Ford pickup was parked at the top of the hill right outside the shack. The dusty red door creaked open loudly, and Bill slung his weight down in stages to the ground. If this thing died coming up here, well, he'd only paid four hundred bucks for it, so it wasn't the end of the world, but he damned well wasn't hiking up the hill again. Bill suspected he might be coming up here quite a bit soon, and each individual trip was worth the money he'd paid for the truck just for saving him that trek up the damned hill.

After getting himself extricated from the elderly pickup and brushing himself off, the coal boss reached back in across the seat and retrieved a box that was clearly chocolates along with a bouquet of flowers. He was no fool.

65

Maw Maw would want a thank you. Being as he was kin, it didn't have to be much, but the old woman wanted to know that she and her help were appreciated. As desperately as he had needed her help over the years, he certainly wasn't fool enough to risk her ire. What had happened to the people she'd helped him with over the years bore a close resemblance to what would happen if you got her ire, and Billy didn't build up his little empire to end up like that!

People in his line of work held out sometimes, you couldn't get them to sell off their land even if you offered the idiots above market price for what they had. Some of the damned fools wouldn't even give you mineral rights, which were damned nigh useless to them anyhow. Bunch of damned ridiculous claptrap about heritage and history and birthrights and some such nonsense. When money didn't work, when even having a couple of the boys maybe beat someone up or kill the family dog didn't work, well, Billy had one last ace in the hole the other companies didn't have. He had Maw Maw. She didn't convince people to leave by talking to them, but people left, either of their own accord running for their life or in a casket, but they left all right.

He was going to need Maw Maw more than ever soon enough. This last thing had worked out great, and the company would be turning a tidy profit from it, it was true enough; but you always had to think ahead in this business. You had to chase every seam and get there faster than the other guy, find better ways around the regulations. Keeping things profitable was a constant chase. The selling prices weren't always what they used to be, even he knew coal was on its last legs. So, if you wanted to make big money while you had the chance, you had to get while the taking was still good. Some overseas natural disasters had the price of coal up at the moment, so now was the time to strike!

And there was a good seam just to the east of here that,

all through the years, coal baron after coal baron had just not been able to touch. A series of farms that almost seemed to cluster together for protection. Everything and everywhere outside of where they sat, at the very least mineral rights had been sold, but not these. No matter what the offering price, no matter what the type of mining it was, neither land nor mineral rights to the coal sitting there underground had been sold by the families that lived on those hills.

Well, Bill's pet geologists said there were some fine seams there, just ripe for exploitation. The kind of stuff he needed, fast in, fast profits. Billy intended that, one way or the other, he was going to succeed where everybody else had failed! He wasn't a fool, though; he was pretty sure this was going to take Maw Maw and her special brand of persuasion for him to pull it off. There had been plenty of goons back in the old days, and it obviously hadn't worked, but his way never failed to get the result he needed!

"Well y'all gonna stand around sweatin' yer fat ass off or is ye comin' in?" a querulous, elderly female voice called from inside the shack.

Bill sighed gustily. She was in one of those moods. If you didn't know her, you'd think that she was always in a mood, but there were moods and then there were moods. She'd pointed out his weight, that made it a MOOD, which deserved capital letters. Thank all that was holy he'd brought chocolate, that ought to shut her up. The wood of the porch creaked loudly under his weight as he stepped to the door. Bill used to be afraid of the noise it made when he was a kid, but being as it made the same noise all his life, the fear had started to lose its grip on him. Steeling himself up, he pulled open the rickety green screen door and went in.

She sat there in her rocking chair in what she called her "parlor"; parlor was a good name for it really, it certainly didn't look like a living room, and it reminded him of a spider's web. It was filled with ancient furniture and decorations, all of it most likely passed on down to her from some previous earlier spinster that had sat right there. For all that matter, SHE looked like something passed down from a previous time, like ancient Egypt, for instance. She grinned at him, a collection of wrinkles wrapped in an ancient black dress, a shawl over her shoulders despite the warm day. The woman *looked* like the witch she was. Hell, the woman looked like she was posing for the cover of *Ye Olde Time Witches Monthly*, with helpful articles like "How to Not Give the Evil Eye by Accident" and "Our Cruelty-Free Newt Substitutes!"

"Howdy, Maw Maw," Bill said with forced cheerfulness, holding the flowers and chocolates he'd brought in front of himself like a shield.

"I see ya brung me a present. Musta worked out all right for ye," she said, eyeing the box of chocolate.

Bill smiled a bit at that, despite his nervousness. "Yep, worked swell," he said. "Found their pickup truck down in a holler. Family from up north what inherited . . . well, they were a bit happier to listen to an offer."

"Well, put that stuff down fer now and sit yerself a spell." She pointed at the large, old stuffed chair that sat directly across from her rocker. Bill dutifully sat. "So," she grinned knowingly, "is that all y'all be needin' at the moment, ta thank me? Or is there summun' else y'all think have more land than they ought to be havin'?"

Bill gulped; it was like the old hag knew! How did she always know? Nothing for it now. "Well, maybe down the road soon. Maybe y'all know it. There's a group of farmers out near Raleigh County, they're sittin' on a good ole seam or two, and after all these years, can you believe it? They still got the mineral rights!"

For the first time ever, he saw a look of concern go over the old woman's face, which usually only had anger or contemptuous amusement to show for it.

"I warn ye, grandson of mine, y'all better be ready for a fight if'n y'all want that piece of land," she said.

Bill harrumphed, protesting, "I didn't get where I am today by being afraid to bust someone in the jaw!"

The look of contempt found its way back on to her wrinkled visage. "As long as y'all know what yer fixin' to bite off then. Now, when am I gonna be seein' my great-grandbabies again?"

CHAPTER 5

"When the great history of trouble is written, my
family will stand extremely high in the table of
contents."

—Allan Sherman C,
a student who was expelled from college, which
should tell you about the kind of person who tells
jokes for a living . . . No, wait! Ignore that last
part.

———————◆———————

THANK GOD IT turned out that the record store was
usually slow. Like, not going out of business soon slow,
but also not "get in, get out" big-box-retail fast either.
It was a place where people expected to take their time to
browse. That gave Matt what he needed most out of life, a
chance to settle into the gig, easing him into having
another part of his life secured down here. Tyler had stayed
with him the first day, but if Matt was being honest, Tyler
spent a lot of that time sucking up the free wi-fi on the
phone while he watched YouTube videos, occasionally
calling out, "Hey! Check this out!" Somewhere in there, he
did explain most of what went into running the place, but
it clearly wasn't a top priority. Other than the cash register,
it mainly involved keeping track of stock and ordering
stuff. Matt could do this. If anything, most of his day was
spent on his *own* phone, sucking up free wi-fi and watching
movies, but occasionally, people came in to break up the

monotony. An additional bonus to this place over a fast food joint or a mall store, he could vape inside as long as he went into the back room, and there was indeed a vape store a half a block away. In reality, it wasn't far off from hanging out in his own room at the farm, with visitors stopping in every once in a while to give him money for things. Oh yeah, and he could play whatever weird music he wanted; people expected, nay, *demanded* weird music when they went to a record store. (Nobody has ever walked into a record store and heard Pat Boone playing and even once, in the history of man and thought, "Boy this place is COOOL!" Maybe they said, "What in the *fuck* is this?" because nobody has played a Pat Boone record this century in any manner but sarcastically, but even then, they never said it was cool. Kids, go look up Pat Boone on wiki; trust us, you will find all of what was typed there *incredibly* accurate. The man made an ironic heavy metal album and somehow it lost its irony and just became dorky.)

Matt was screwing around on Facebook with Hamatom blasting on the overhead speakers when the insipid little doorbell thing went off, informing him that he was no longer alone. Looking at what walked through the door, it took him a moment to remember to close his mouth. What that was exactly that came sauntering through the vestibule was not a cute southern girl like what you would see on a "Farmers Only" commercial. No, not in the least little bitty bit. This girl had tattoos, she had magenta hair done up in a 50s style pin-up hairdo, and she had a dress on that made it very clear that there was an hourglass keeping time as she walked in. (There are more noir fiction clichés we could probably wedge in there, but you get the point.) It was all Matt could do to get his head pointed back to his phone, but now he had no earthly clue whatsoever what he had been about to type on Twitter or any clue that he actually had Facebook open instead of Twitter, so he ended up hashtagging a meme like a spazz.

All he wanted to type was "hubba hubba," assuming that meant what he thought it did—it was old-timey talk, so it was hard to say.

Matt found himself staring blankly at his screen, trying to consider what he should do here. In theory, he should be minding the store and making sure nothing walked out with her that she hadn't paid for, though God alone knew where she could possibly hide it. In practice, watching her every move would totally make him look like a complete lech, which was also to be avoided like the plague. Guys who leched on hot looking girls were guys who never got to send that girl a friend request on Facebook!

It was in the midst of Matt's existential crisis that the girl walked directly up to the counter and demanded, "So where the hell is Ashley?"

Matt started from his mental conundrum. "What? Oh, he hired me so he could do the construction thing."

Her heavily made-up, perfect china doll face sunk into a pout. "Well there goes my fun for the day!"

"Oh?" Matt's eyebrow went up.

She giggled a little. "Ashley likes to think he's still hip. So, every time I come in, I make up band names and ask if he has them in or can get them. Fucking with a Gen X hipster is cruel, but hey, there's only so much to do in this town."

Matt's face went flat for a moment, then he nodded. "Okay, I can see that."

"So if I asked y'all if you had the, say, Bass Slap Undead Frogs, you wouldn't take out the big book of ordering or turn on the store computer ordering program to look, would you?" she asked, leaning her elbows on the counter and propping her chin on her hands.

"Nope, Google," he said, showing her his phone.

"Damn, if y'all work out here, I sure am gonna miss him," she sighed. And just like that, she was completely over it. She turned and pointed to a speaker. "So, you into this?"

"Yeah, I like a lot of German stuff; friend hooked me on to Rammstein years ago, and . . . well, there are other bands in Germany and all."

"Y'all aren't, like, a Nazi or anything, right?"

"Well, I'm mainly Scottish, and as far as I can tell, we fought them, so no. It just seems to me that German is the exact right language for this type of music. It just sounds so grumpy; it seems to fit. They could be singing about anything, for all I know really, don't speak a lick of it. Suppose it could be Nazi stuff, but these bands seem pretty popular, and Germany has laws." Matt shrugged, giving her the same pat answer he gave everyone.

"So, whaddya feel about psychobilly?" she asked, eyeing him suspiciously.

"My cousin told me I should like it or I would be a forlorn and lonely social outcast here," he said flatly.

"Smart man, but that isn't a yes, so you're still up for debate. Okay, so who's your cousin?"

"This seems like a lengthy interrogation to purchase music, if you don't mind me saying."

"Y'all ain't local, and frankly, I'm nosy. My mamma said it would be the death of me one day. But since it ain't gonna be today," she pressed him, "who's y'all's cousin?"

"Tyler Hawley; he works in a tattoo shop in town," Matt relented in the face of that insurmountable logic.

"Bogus! I've known Tyler for years, and he has never once mentioned a cute cousin who likes German goth metal!" She snorted. "It takes a long time to do these tattoos, he should have said!"

"Maybe he was busy doing a job; if he did those, they look good," Matt protested. "Look, if you don't believe me, ask him yourself, but I'm living with him and my Uncle Donnie and Aunt Debbie up at the farm!"

"I might just have to do that." She grinned, hopping back up. "Welp, I mainly came in to screw with Ash, but if y'all see Tyler, tell him I said hi! But trust me, you'll see me again. I come in here to do more than just mess with the help!"

With that, she turned and walked to the door. Matt couldn't help but watch her hips swish as she walked. As she pushed open the door, she paused and turned back. "Oh yeah, I didn't get your name."

"Oh, I'm Matt."

"I'm Madison. See y'all around, Yankee." She winked as she left.

𝇈

It was his day off, and he had promised to go spend some time with MeeMaw. Actually, that wasn't entirely true, she had imperiously told his aunt, "Tell my grandson it wouldn't kill him to come visit me, I've missed him! Even if all damned Yankees sound like Dan Rather!"

It wasn't that he disliked his grandmother, he loved his family. It was just that Matt just felt amazingly uncomfortable around the old woman. They had, like, nothing in common whatsoever. When she was his age, they still had rotary phones and filmed things in black and white for reasons other than being artistic and moody. He could just feel the sucking silence between them, made worse by uncomfortable attempts at small talk, until Matt would get claustrophobic and count the moments until he could leave without being rude. But Matt also knew that he would be a complete idiot to ignore a hint that a visit was wanted, especially when it had been delivered so gently and with such sledgehammer delicacy like that.

She already had a glass of milk and some cookies set out for him when she ushered him into her living room. MeeMaw must be bored out of her mind; she had probably been looking out the window for him to trudge out here. Matt made a mental note, uncomfortable or not, that he should probably make a point of visiting more often. He got bored sometimes living here, and he could just drive off at will. She never went out much at all. He guessed that at her age, a lot of her friends were dead or moved away years ago, and without Pa Pa around, it had to get stunningly dull. Mind, she did seem to get visitors often enough, so maybe she just missed Matt and had just been expecting him after her failed attempt at subtlety.

MeeMaw smiled sweetly at Matt as he sat down, her best older hippy grandmother warmth generating expression settling in place, and asked, "So, how y'all settling in, sweetie? How's the job?"

"Oh, oh yeah, it seems to be all right. Doesn't seem to be a lot to do to it, but I've got a good chance to make manager. What, with Uncle Donnie and Aunt Debbie not really asking for much in the way of rent, it'll give me a chance to build my savings back up. They kind of took a hit with the whole thing back home," he replied, thankful that he had more or less good news to report to her. Grandmothers like to hear that kind of thing. They tend to think serious problems are your parents' fault and, therefore, your parents' problem, while praise and spoiling were exclusively their bailiwick.

"That's nice," she replied, sitting down demurely, looking ever so proper with her long gray hair pulled back tightly and her plain skirt sitting well past her knees. "So," she asked, "how are y'all getting on with the family?"

"Well, I don't really see Eddie much. Between the farm and his own family, he's always busy. Uncle Donnie and Aunt Debbie have been great, especially now that I have a job. Me and Tyler hang out a lot," he told her, hoping that would make her happy.

"That Tyler can be a wild one, y'all make sure he don't get you into any trouble," MeeMaw replied, almost as a warning.

"We mainly play video games, MeeMaw." Matt swam to Tyler's defense.

She sniffed at that for a second, then leaned forward a little. Her expression wasn't quite so grandmotherly as before, it was more of the piercing and probing variety. "So, how y'all getting on with the *rest* of the family?"

"I . . . I don't know . . . What rest of the family?" Matt looked confused.

"Don't sass me, boy. I know they been visiting you in the house," she snapped. She sniffed again and added, "Your Pa Pa told me his ownself."

Matt could only sit there, stunned. Part of him had just assumed, even now, that he had been dreaming or going mildly insane, which he hadn't ruled out. Even the part where he had felt completely awake, and even when Pa Pa had specifically said, "You're not dreaming." Matt had really been trying to hold on to his sanity here; dead people don't come to visit! If they did, you had just found yourself in some kind of horror movie that they only run on TCM at Halloween. It was the only way he could make sense of something like that. They aren't real, and if you think they are, then you need to get your medication tweaked! These nightly visits had become his secret shame and biggest worry at this point, and here was his grandmother saying . . .

"Ummmm . . . " was all he managed.

She seemed to take pity on him and gave him a warm smile. "It's all right, sweetheart, it runs in the family pretty deeply. Your Pa Pa could do it, and even though I married into the Hawleys, so can I. Usually, one in every generation of Hawley can. I just couldn't think of a nicer way to tell y'all than that. So, how are you getting on with them?"

Thrown off balance by the frontal assault, Matt could only answer honestly. "Pa Pa is all right. I guess. For something I thought was a figment of my imagination. But the other one, what's his name, ummm . . . Mungo, he kind of scares the hell out of me!"

MeeMaw chuckled at that. "Well, he means well, but I must admit he takes some getting used to. I'm still not sure if I'm all the way used to him yet myself. But, for all of his bluster, and as hard as it is to understand him, he is the founder of the family here in America. He brought the name and whatever special thing that the bloodline carries with him, so y'all have to try and respect that."

Matt was not seeing it. The him bringing the family here part, that was pretty easy to believe. He'd seen his father eat steak while watching the Giants play, he could easily believe his family was descended from someone as savage as Mungo. No, the part Matt wasn't seeing at all was "Getting used to him."

His grandmother was silent for a moment; she stared out into the middle distance as if she was in thought. Finally, she turned to him and smiled again. "Maybe, maybe it would help y'all if'n you knew where you come from. Maybe it would help some if you know Mungo's story of how he come to wash up on these shores."

"Do you really think . . . ?"

"Yes, yes I do. Now y'all can just set yourself right there and I'll spin you a yarn . . . "

$$☽◯☾$$

She cleared her throat and began. "Mungo Hawley. Well, he didn't come to America quite willingly. Not everyone come here as the land of opportunity, unless you considered it an 'opportunity' not to end life dancing at the end of a short length of rope. Or in Mungo's case, burning at tha stake.

"See, the powers that the family have, they go back all the way to before man can remember. Once upon a time, the people of the family bloodline, they would have been shamans. They would have been holy men and women, the clerics of the old religions, respected and powerful people. But that all changed at some point. In this case, it wasn't the normal source of all things bad in Scotland, the British, but more the Irish. They brought with them the god of the Romans, Jesus, into the land of the Pict kings, which brought a few bad lines in the Old Testament to contend with. Now at first, it could have all co-existed, this new religion and the powerful magicians of the old one. But, slowly but surely, the word *witch* got more and more popular to bandy about. It stemmed right from the old religion witfa and wiffe, or male or female witch, depending. But now the words had gotten a new connotation of someone who communed with Satan, which pardon me for interrupting the story here, but Satan is not someone I've ever had the occasion to meet, let alone worship.

"Well, those older Hawleys, they saw the way the wind was a-blowin' and they started to find ways to hide what they were. They called it medicine and good luck now, just not too much good luck, mind you. A Hawley sheep almost never died or got lost, and a Hawley was almost impossible to pull the wool over in a business deal, ha ha."

(Matt couldn't help but note there that his MeeMaw had actually *said* ha ha, which he thought was weird.)

"But they were smart, they never took advantage, they made it a point to keep the family's good fortune to perpetually comfortable instead of attention grabbing rich. They made sure to never lord their good fortune over their neighbors as well, because ain't nobody who likes a smart-ass. The gift and their willingness to share it around made sure that they were well-liked and respected as well. People may be willing to denounce a neighbor who got the better of them in a trade, sure enough, but if your neighbor was the only reason, say, your son still walked the earth after he got whooping cough . . . maybe you just learn to pay better attention in your trading.

"So that left young Mungo Hawley as the heir to the land and the gift, well not that young, he was already thirty. Due to a freak accident involving a stampede of sheep, a cliff, a broken wagon wheel, and a bit of very fine scotch, he was sole inheritor to the Hawley name and fortune, such as it was. Even before their unfortunate and unlikely passing, his parents had lamented about his unmarried state. But Mungo had always put them off, saying he'd marry for love or not at all. Fine sentiments, but it should be noted here that the generation locally had not exactly produced the best looking crop of young women in the societal circles the Hawleys moved in. So, while the other men of his generation locally took to drinking their future spouses attractive, Mungo held firm.

"That was until the local minor noble Lord Catach's daughter, Sorcha, became ill. Now, from what he's described to me, it sounds like what we would call typhus, or what they called Aryotitus fever. She had reached the point where the rash had begun, following an alarming fever. The doctors of the manor said they doubted they could do much for it, but one said there was somebody who might succeed where they failed, Mungo Hawley. The doctor warned that Mungo's ways might not seem like the methods of modern medicine, but his results were often better.

"Lord Catach dispatched the doctor to fetch Mungo with enough coin to entice him to come and the promise for more after. Normally, the summons of the local Lord would bring most men running, but not Mungo, Mungo wanted it to be worth his own while or not at all. The Lord's first instinct was to just summon the man, but luckily, the doctor in question knew Mungo and his feelings towards people who had titles, which he quickly explained to the Lord in the politest manner possible. Lord Catach was finally persuaded to give the coin if he wanted to see the miracle worker perform miracles and not to have the doctor see a door slammed in his face with a growl of, 'A body mair deid title is a body less oppressur ay th' common cheil!' which is what they would have most likely gotten if the Lord had just commanded Mungo's presence. To translate, 'I don't care what his title is.'

"So, properly remunerated for his time, Mungo rode to the Lord's manor, begrudgingly, which is how he did most things. Once he met with the girl, he knew what it was that ailed her immediately. Typhus was not uncommon. He ordered some things done which are just common doctoring, like burning the girl's bedding and much of her clothing, despite her feeble protests. He knew how typhus moves, and he assumed it was a flea or the ilk that had caused the illness in the first place, so best to be rid of them before he did anything else, lest his labors still end with the girl just getting sick again. But the one thing that he also did, he swore to Lord Catach he could save his daughter.

"Unfortunately, this galled a local member of the clergy, but then again, what doesn't? That particular gentleman swore up and down that nothing short of divine intervention could save the young lady. He had further suggested that for a suitable, large contribution, he, in his role as a man of God, might be willing to have a word with the big fellah upstairs about maybe intervening in this particular instance. This is one of the problems with men of God, if'n y'all ask my own particular opinion, they got too much free time on their hands, and Lord knows, idle hands and all that.

So anyway, the Lord has Mungo living in the manor now, caring for his daughter, and the reverend is a-settin' there fuming at his chapel. Wouldn't y'all know it, the young woman does get better, slowly but surely. Slowly because Mungo t'weren't a damned fool, he had heard the whispers the blasted priest had been telling anyone who might listen that if the girl got well, it could only be witchcraft. People were supposed to be beyond all that silliness, but if that priest had his way, they'd be sure to remember where they'd left the dunking stools and all that kindling in storage in case it came up again.

"A funny thing happened along the way to her getting well. Not surprising, mind you, not surprising at all, when you consider a young woman who, for reasons of her illness, was forced to spend all of her time with an eligible, slightly older, bachelor of some means, who was also her savior. Actually, it might have been more funny if nothing along those lines had happened, her falling deeply in love with our Mungo and him feeling similar. It would seem like the world wasn't working right.

"But now the happy couple had some new problems, not the least of which was a member of the aristocracy wanting to marry a commoner. More importantly, a commoner who wished to stay that way, thank y'all kindly. Her father, thankfully, was grateful as all get out, and that made him understanding of the situation. When Mungo asked his permission, the Lord gave it, joking, 'Oh, so that was why you were so willing to save her, was it now?'

"If that was all of their problems, we wouldn't be having this conversation here. But that priest was a viper who talked wherever he went and who most likely had some designs of his own on the young lady his own self. So, he'd been thwarted twice, once in bleeding the Lord's back accounts of all its contents and, on top of that, a chance to get his feet under the table somewhere a damned sight more comfortable than the local parsonage. Worse, the insinuating little weasel had friends high enough up the ladder who were open to the suggestion that maybe a witch burning might be forgiven as a bit of country high spirits, and who maybe might even secretly approve of it as a way to keep the butts in the pews.

"Luckily for Mungo, Lord Catach was wont to give in to his daughter's whims. Or, maybe he was just getting rid of her because he was sick of giving in to her whims. Y'all never can tell with history, and Mungo always spoke highly of the man, so I never wanted to point it out. Anyway, he decided after catching wind of what the priest had achieved that it would be best for the young soon-to-be couple if they left for a country where they were slightly less likely to find out exactly how flammable they were, namely, America. More specifically, this new land of Virginia that had produced such a free thinker as Thomas Jefferson, and maybe not Massachusetts, which had its own history with uppity clergy who were good at fire starting.

"Mungo wasn't too keen on leaving home. It was all he knew, y'all understand, but he also knew that he'd never do better than Sorcha, who I've met, as will you, I'm sure. Trust you me, she was so out of his league, it would be like the Yankees playing a t-ball squad, and I'm saying this as someone who loves Mungo dearly as family. If your bloodline has a certain charm and grace to it, it came from her. Lord Catach saw to the purchase of some lands along the frontier of the state—quite a bit of land, really, it was hard to get people to live here then—and would arrange for the sale of Mungo's own lands later, promising to bring the coin the sale provided to the new world in time for their wedding.

"The couple came first to London and then to America by boat, something Mungo doesn't enjoy talking about in the least. The most I could ever get out of him was, 'Th' most crabbit experience ay mah entire bludy life. Moontains shoods be gart ay lain nae water. Ah didne e'en ken a cheil coods flin' up 'at much! Ah hud tae jist burn th' clase when we finally cam ashair, Ah cooldnae wear them encrusted in boak as they waur.'

I've never been able to translate that one hundred percent, but basically, he didn't like it none, and I think his stomach didn't either. As it may, though, the still unmarried couple were still purchasing the things they needed to take with them to their new farmstead when Lord Catach arrived some months later. This changed things considerably, for before they could leave to go to their new life, they'd need to also prepare for a wedding.

Young Sorcha didn't seem to be putting on any localized weight yet, if y'all get my drift, but Lord Catach wasn't fool enough to push his luck on the matter. So, he insisted they be wed before he'd go back to Scotland.

"Mungo and his new bride were wed in Alexandria, finished getting more than ample supplies, hired what folk they'd need, and headed for their new home. So there y'all have it, well, most of it. He built this house, well, the original house what's been built on to, same as the main house, which he also built. Over time, well, it was too large a piece of property for any one family to farm, and there were people coming over from Europe all the time. He and his children and his children's children would sell off separate good working farms over time. With a caveat, of course, that the Hawleys always had first rights to the land. If anybody wants to sell, well, nobody can force a family to stay where they don't want to, but if they want to move on, they sell back to us at market value, and we pick the next family.

"It ain't happened often, but it has, and then we pick a new family that comes in. In fact, one of the families on the overall patch now, they was Amish when they came here. Think they're Mennonite now, or some such, nice enough folk, but a touch dull. That idea, it's created a community, there ain't no town that holds it together, no mayor's office needed, but a community it is. And the thing it does, it protects the Hawley's secret. Course the people living round here get something out of it, long prosperous lives, better than many have had over the years round har, so it's a fair trade all around.

"Which leads to this; since the gift has come to sit on your shoulders, my boy, while you're here, I know your uncle expects you to hold a job, but I expect you to hold another one. Won't have to do much really, just learn and lend a hand when you're able. But you're a Hawley on Hawley land and with the Hawley gift, so I expect you to do your duty to your family name. And for one other reason."

"What's that?" Matt asked, surprised to get a word in edgewise and still trying to take it all in.

"Because a good boy like y'all loves his MeeMaw and wants to see her smiling," she replied sweetly.

☽☯☾

Beatrice Baldwin sat in her rocking chair, alone in her cottage. She liked to sit there when she was thinking, or gloating, for that matter. Tonight was a bit of both. Her grandson might be as sharp as a sack of rubber razors, but he had his uses. His short-sighted greed was the key to everything and anything the old woman wanted. Not material things, money and big houses, those were for short-sighted fools like young Bill to be impressed with; no, not any of that. She wanted a stronger power than that, something rooted in these hills. What she wanted continued and went far past just upthrusts of land. In his own clueless, greedy, and grasping way, Little Billy was invaluable to her getting it. He provided her the cover she needed from this world to accumulate the power she wanted from outside of it.

There was deep and old power in these mountains; you had yourself the right kind of mind, you could tap into it. Power that went from these lands to ones just a hair's breadth away, where things lived that had been banished from our world altogether. You tap into that, then you'd find out what having power was all about. You start using those things, no end to the things one could do. With enough power, for instance, she could trade this tired, wrinkled old body in for a new one, a hot new one with a fine caboose and big cans, for starters. Oh, there were a lot of other things she had in mind, but she was sick and damned tired of being an old crone, and if she was going to have powers, she was gonna have herself a fine smokin' body to go with the harem of fellas she intended to keep to help her enjoy it with.

But that was the problem, power and having enough power to break through that wall to get to the real power behind it all. Now that kind of energy was hard to come by, it came from the ground underneath your feet. That kind of magic, well, it was like water in a cistern, you get too many people using the same one and the water was always left shallow no matter how much it rained. But, if there was a way to maybe move some of the people who the good lord had supplied with jugs away from the water . . .

Times like that, it came in mighty handy to have a young fool of a grandson who was always looking for property to steal with good coal underneath it. It would get even easier if the idiot didn't make any mistakes with his campaign and maybe learned to lie to people a bit better. A Senator, he got himself a lot of power towards making laws, laws changing things like seizure and eminent domain, for instance. His greed was the kind the world accepted as perfectly normal; he picked the people to move and she moved them. He got his coal, and she got the power lingering in the mountains, power that let her access the world right next door. No one was the wiser; coal companies had been strong-arming people off their lands for generations, and that was all everyone assumed was happening now. Bill provided her the cover she needed to drive people off without anyone questioning why.

It was a fine arrangement, just so long as the big dummy didn't manage to spoil it. Such a shame about his cousin; now that boy had some power of his own, she could have made something real and useful with him. But before she could even start to explain it all to him, poor soul had discovered them pills that were all too common here. He was gone from an overdose so fast, most people hadn't even known he was taking them. She surely didn't.

But, you mold the clay you got and use the pitcher you end up with, not wish for the clay you ain't got. Billy'd have to do; she was going to *make* him do.

Chapter 6

"I'm good at fitting in, and I think I'm fairly
perceptive about moods and psychic
environments."

—Timothy B. Schmit,
backup bassist for Randy Meisner, and probably
a true statement if you think about it. Look, not
every joke can be topical, you know!

——————◆——————

EVEN WITH THE recent revelations by MeeMaw, Matt still
had a job to go to. Despite the fact that it was *way* less
interesting than having mysterious powers over illness
and as yet undefined other stuff (which he desperately
wanted defined better before he blew something up or
worse), the job did something that his strange powers
didn't. It paid American. So, it was another glorious day of
telling people, "I can order it if you want!" only to have
them order it themselves on the internet and never return
to the store.

He had discovered that early on, despite sales being
decent because the store was happy to carry oddball stuff
and used stuff cheap, it was never as much as it should be.
Matt estimated that a quarter of the people that came in
were looking for things that may not even possibly exist on
this planet. Every once in a while, though, they would exist
in the magical land of the catalogs, but rarely in the store
itself. So at least a few times a day, he would go over all of

them, looking for whatever obscure piece of music the person said they were looking for, only occasionally even finding it. Even more rarely, the person would actually order the thing. Still, for all the annoyance, it kept cow shit off of him, which remained of vital importance to him. So, Matt tried to be happy for the gig.

Another perk would be walking in at any moment. Madison. Matt had no idea why she came in every day, but he was happy she did. She usually had something funny to say, and she was certainly better looking than a large percentage of the clientele, by which he meant all of them. Since she came in almost daily to paw through the racks, he had begun to feel like they were friends. Well, if not friends, then work friends at the very least. The ten or fifteen minutes she was in the store was usually the highlight of his day since he could talk to her and actually joke back with her.

Matt heard the door beep and looked up from his phone. She was right on schedule and headed over to a rack that she had probably pawed over a million times before now.

"Howdy, Madison, how's things?" Matt asked.

She glanced up at him. "Nuther day, nuther fifty cents after taxes." Instead of her normal routine of paging through the records, she diverted at the last moment, coming right up to the counter, and put her elbows on the counter and asked, "So, what are you up to Friday?"

Matt began to answer. "Well I—"

Madison cut him off immediately. "Jenny comes in at five on Fridays, so instead of drinking with your good for nuthin' cousin, instead, y'all are taking me to see a band."

"I am?"

"Yes, you are. A friend's band is playing near Beckley, and I know y'all live closer than I do, which means if you had been getting out enough and getting to know what nightlife there was, you would have already asked me if I'm

88

going. I refuse to see a music fan wither on the vine, so you're going with me!" she informed him happily. "I will be here around closing, and expect a friend request from me so we can make sure everything is on. We good?"

"Ummm . . . sure, I guess," Matt said, stun faced.

"I do so love an agreeable man. I'll see you Friday." She smiled and whirled around and left.

☽◯☾

Hours later and Matt was on to Job number 2. Well, a job was what it felt like anyway. Get home, have a quick meal, and spend some time with MeeMaw. His aunt and uncle and his cousins hadn't said anything about it, but they couldn't be stupid either. If this was such a big family secret that everybody in the family (except, apparently, Matt) had known about, they'd know exactly why he was with her. Matt couldn't help but note that Uncle Donnie hadn't mentioned anything about working on the farm lately. (A reference to a very popular franchise that would be tempting to make here to describe what his time with MeeMaw was like could be made here, except we're worried that it would be a very *legally* actionable reference to an orphan with the glasses who played games at the magic school he was sent to that we sure as *hell* aren't going to mention here. Just like that, except with a sometimes surly 20 something, also it would be in West Virginia instead of that school we still aren't mentioning, also no glasses, or other schoolmates. Like that. We, of course mean, "Penn and Teller Get Killed.")

Today was medicine, or, in reality, it wasn't medicine at all. Joyce Anne Goins had come to call today. Her visit looked like a social call, which had annoyed Matt right on its face. How was he supposed to learn anything with all these neighbors pestering his MeeMaw by dropping off cookies and fresh bread?

His grandmother had taken him aside to "help me carry all this lovely food you brung and I can show him where to put it, Joyce Anne, just be a second." Once in her kitchen, she said to Matt quietly, "Now, you know those mint extract and sugar water bottles I made you fill?"

"Yeah, you called them medicine, don't see what's medicinal about liquid breath mints, though."

"Well, there ain't, to be honest. But that woman out there has got to believe it is. She's sick all right, but the people we take care of, well they won't believe enough in the magic to make it keep working if I don't give them a bottle of something and call it medicine. Science is all good and well, but it don't help none with faith. She talks like we're here to gossip over tea, and that is worth somethin'. Always keep an eye out on your own patch and all, but that ain't why she's here. While we is gossiping our fool heads off, you look at her and see if you can't look at her again. Look deeper, look to see what's there even if you cain't see it by just glancing. See what most people cain't see. Let's see how good your instincts are, my boy!"

His MeeMaw went out carrying a tray of cookies, with Matt in tow behind carrying cups of tea for the ladies. Joyce Anne took hers happily, setting it down before reaching over to grab a handful of cookies. She looked like a concerned PTA mother from an 80s movie, only how she'd look 25 years later. There would be a big scene at the school or church where some mother says, "But what about my Billy?" That was Joyce Anne. Polyester was much in evidence in her clothing choices, and Matt somehow suspected that this was very similar to how she dressed for church. The idea made him mentally chuckle that, in its own way, there wasn't much difference from church to what was going on here today. You prayed for miracles in both places.

"Anyway, Louise, I figured you'd want to know. Over near Odd, they're getting themselves a new preacher," the woman said, turning Matt's existence off completely and turning to talk to his MeeMaw (yes there IS a town in WV called Odd, it is right near Lego, this is in no way, shape, or form made up, look it up yourself, you go through Odd to get to Lego, no we're not kidding, this book thinks this is one of the most wondrous things imaginable and proof that the world is a truly beautiful place).

"What happened to Pastor Jeffers?" His grandmother's eyes lifted over her mug.

"I don't know if I want to say, what with your grandson being right here." The woman actually blushed.

"Oh, if that's what's bothering you so, honestly, he's a full-grown man." His grandmother sniffed before relenting. "Oh well, Matt, be a good boy and step into the kitchen to let Joyce keep her squawking among us hens. But if we need you, y'all can still see into the living room from there. I mean, you may have to *look twice*, but y'all should see fine. Joyce's dirt probably won't take but a minute to relay to me."

Matt was almost impressed with himself; he actually got the underlying meaning of what MeeMaw had just told him to do. He usually wasn't the first to pick up on subtlety and hints. You needed to tell him to even start looking for them in the first place, usually, and here he was pretty sure he got it in one! He grabbed himself a glass of juice from the refrigerator and took up a station where he could look right out from the kitchen across an empty dining room into the living room right where the woman was sitting. Matt had been taught a lot about things by his MeeMaw since he'd been here. Some of it had seemed to be about what he thought of as magic, she trusted him to be able to do this on his own now. It seemed a little unfair since he still wasn't sure what he should do here, but he was going to at least try.

He looked out, and at first glance, he saw what he'd seen the first time, a former PTA member who had moved on to the bingo league and church social set chatting away with his MeeMaw about what he could only guess at. Matt was certain that wasn't what his grandmother had wanted him to look for. That was all right there, plain as day, if you were observant in any way at all. His eyes bore into the older woman, and it still wasn't there. But then, his grandmother had said something about his instincts. Surely squinting at her until his eyes watered wasn't what she had meant when she had told him to "look again, but deeper." On a whim, he let his eyes unfocus a little bit, like a little kid experimenting with what it might be like to see the world needing glasses. It was hard to hold, and he had to fight to keep his eyes from refocusing when he tried to look at the woman again.

Looking now, he could see a pink glow with flecks of deep gray sparkling among it around the woman, which somehow surprised him not at all. Joyce Anne just exuded pink from every fiber in her being just meeting her, that she should glow that color seemed only natural. As he was doing this, he felt a tingling around his face. It almost felt like a burst of energy that was letting him continue to look at the glow around the gossipy woman. Before he could stop himself, he looked at his own hands. They not only glowed a faint blue, but strands of what felt like pure energy had attached themselves to him everywhere he looked!

It came to him that this was what his MeeMaw wanted! He saw how he could look to find the problem! With this energy, whatever it was, Matt could look again and far deeper than the surface using it! Better still, he could let his eyes focus again, saving himself from having a brutal headache in a few minutes! Matt turned his attention towards Joyce Anne. He made a mental note that he was looking for illness, something that seemed out of place, and poured some of this energy that was filling him to the task. He was startled for a moment to see that most of the woman vanished. Matt was completely grossed out to realize that what was left behind left him looking at the circulatory system without any other human bits in his way! When he mentally traced the pathways of her bloodstream, Matt could finally see what was wrong, where minute flecks of something alien flowed along with both the bright red blood of the arteries and the deep red blood of the veins. Flashes of it sparkled silver to him!

She had something in her blood that was making her sick!

It vanished the second that Matt realized completely that he had actually done something that could be counted as magic. It was like a lot of really good tricks—skateboarding, BMX, card tricks—the second you overthought it, it came crashing down around you. The blessing at least here was he didn't get any broken bones out of it like that one time he had been trying to learn how to do tricks on a skateboard. He had *finally* practiced to the point where he was getting good at doing an ollie, and his friend Matthew had asked him to show him how. Forced to think about it, he couldn't do it and instantly fell and broke a finger. Once his mother had seen that, he also no longer had to worry about learning skateboarding tricks. Her not killing him graduated to top of his list. But something told him there was something in what was happening here like how a skateboard trick got for people without overprotective mothers to worry about. Now that he had proven to himself that he could do something magical, even something small like this, it should get easier with practice! (Or at least, that was what Matt wanted to believe, so we'll leave him his small illusions as a kindness.)

He almost screamed when a voice said next to him, "So, how're the lessons coming along, boy?"

Turning to see the shade of his grandfather standing next to him, Matt had to take a deep breath before hissing, "We have company! I almost squealed like a farm animal, you scared me so bad!"

His Pa Pa actually managed to look a little contrite and apologetic when he replied, "Aww, now I am sorry about that. I know how much that woman likes to gossip with your MeeMaw and all, so I figured y'all could use the company."

"You almost got to talk to me all the time there, Pa Pa!" Matt gasped. "You almost gave me a heart attack!"

"Well, I did say I'm sorry. How are things? I mean other than the heart palpitations, that is."

"Well, I think I just did magic, so that's something."

"Y'all could see it? Her sickness?"

"I don't know what it is, but yeah, I could see it in her blood." Matt shrugged.

"Your MeeMaw'll be proud of you. Course, she probably already knows. Very sensitive woman to the workings of things like that. One of the things that brought us together; I was the sensitive one in my family and she was in hers. We had this great big thing that we could see and understand but nobody else could. Didn't feel so alone that way, I guess, having someone to talk to about it." The ghostly figure smiled softly at the memory.

"It almost sounds like you miss her," Matt replied.

"Well, not really. We talk, but she's got to sleep sometime. Maybe sometimes I just miss being able to hold her when she's sleeping is all. One day, hopefully, not too soon, though, we'll be completely together again," the older man said and sighed.

"I can empathize, if not completely. I mean, seeing how I ended up here and all," Matt replied, feeling like a goober the second he said it. This man was talking about the love of his life, and Matt was still whining about a roommate he had sex with when she wasn't busy banging a DJ behind his back!

"That reminds me, how you getting on, other than that? I've seen y'all deftly avoided working in the barn, like young Tyler managed, but other than that, how are you?"

That was a question, wasn't it? Was he fitting in here? Did he like it here? It was an improvement over the life he'd been kind of kicked out of; he used his SUV for driving these days instead of home sweet home, for starters. Matt thought that maybe he had been flirting with a girl, so that was something. He might even have a date coming up with her. Of course, deep down inside, Matt figured he was deluding himself there. What he really had was a friend of the female persuasion, and he knew it. Still, "what is life without fantasy?" was his motto, at least until he could get something other than fantasy, and a better motto, for that matter. Tyler made for a better buddy than anyone he was still talking to back home, as far as other friends went. But at the same time, this wasn't home. The mere thought that he still considered it "back home" and this place "his cousin's farm" told him that. How do you even explain all that?

Instead, he went with, "All right, I guess." This was a huge improvement in that it summed the general vibe up yet said nothing of any value that committed him to any opinion whatsoever.

"Ain't sure yet, huh?" his grandfather replied, showing an insight into the workings of the human mind that caught Matt by surprise for just a moment. The ghost added, "Well, you'll figure it out one way or the other, better to do it with a secure roof over your head and a meal in your stomach while you're thinking about it anyway. Looks like that old biddy is finally running out of steam while your MeeMaw still has an ear left to talk off. I better skedaddle, she'll be wanting to talk to y'all 'bout what you've seen."

Skedaddle? Who said skedaddle?

His Pa Pa was gone by the time Matt thought to comment on it. Just there one second and not there the next. Matt blinked a few times at the space he had been visible in—you really couldn't say he had occupied it, being a ghost. He was about to consider the implications of a ghost occupying a space further when that train of thought was interrupted by Mrs. Goins calling out from the living room, "Well it was nice to meet you, Matt, I'll be seein' y'all later!"

Matt dodged quickly towards the living room in time to say, "Nice to meet you too, Mrs. Goins." He was rewarded with a brief, brittle older woman polite smile and a closed door. Now it was just him and his MeeMaw in the room.

"Welp," she said almost as soon as the door closed, "did y'all see it?"

Matt turned and replied, "You mean in her blood, right?"

MeeMaw looked immensely pleased, but only for an instant. "Yep, she caught a virus, but it turned out was something more serious than just the flu. It would have attacked her brain if I hadn't seen it for what it was. As is, the poor thing gets headaches something evil. But it's being killed off now slow and sure, and that woman will drink that syrup regular thinking that's what's doing all the work, bless her heart. Well, that's a good start toward where y'all want to get to for today. But you're young, ain't you got some kind of a social life you need to get off to now?"

Matt figured it was a good idea to leave before MeeMaw started saying "Bless your heart" to him. Matt had been here long enough to know that "Bless your heart" was the West Virginia equivalent of "Did you tie your own shoelaces, or did you need help this morning?"

)O(

Matt was loathe to admit why, but he was looking particularly sharp for work today. He loathed to admit it because this was not a date. She had never said this was a date. She had said that she was showing him around the local music scene. It had certainly sounded like Madison was doing him a favor when she had said it, not some kind of mutually agreed upon date sort of thing. Madison had indeed sent him a friend request, which he had accepted, and he could see that she had more than enough friends online who lived in the area. Matt was just another face in the wash. Madison did not have to date Matt, or even the same person every night, judging by the amount of friends she had. So that made this clearly just a friendly gesture and not, he stressed to himself yet again, a date.

So, it was firmly established that he was not going out on a date, which made how she looked when he saw her walking up to the door kind of depressing. He had considered Madison a pal, but pal or, not she looked . . . she looked . . . well, she looked really good. She was wearing a tight skirt with a slit going up the side that showed off her stocking clad legs tantalizingly. She was wearing a leather jacket, but the t-shirt she had underneath it was cut and hung exactly right to give more than a glimpse of lacy black bra. Matt strongly suspected that he might be driving her to this show, but he most likely wouldn't be driving her home again. Odds were high that someone would actually try to spend romantic time with her, someone who was not him, someone who she ran into at the show itself.

"Look at you, all dressed up." She smirked as she sauntered in the door, eyeing up his tight black jeans and black dress shirt that he had cuffed at the elbows.

"I could say the same about you, you know."

"Naww, this is how I always dress when I don't have to go to work later." Madison shrugged and ignored the flush that bloomed on Matt's face. "You ready to go?"

Matt looked past Madison to see Jenny's rusting Ford SUV pull up. "Yep, as soon as Jenny punches in, we're out of here."

Jenny came in without a word, just a flustered wave.

She was a stay at home mom who filled in some for extra money, so that was how she usually came in. Children exist to make any perfectly normal human being look like they had just exited from some dangerous, potentially deadly situation, only more frustrating. Like a knife fight, but with a lot of hands on the hips toe-tapping while you waited for your opponent to tie his shoe, point out a pretty flower, and finally decide that he didn't like this knife, he liked his sister's knife better.

"Hey, Jenny," Matt said pleasantly.

Instead of responding, Jenny held up her hand and shook her head, flowing into the back room under full steam. A few moments later, she came back up front to the counter and let out an exasperated sigh. "Okay, hey."

"Tough day with the kids?" Madison asked. She knew Jenny from outside the store and figured this was the safest assumption.

"I come here for the peace and quiet," Jenny agreed.

"Do I even want to know?" Matt asked while raising his eyebrow.

"They should make childproof lids for jugs of vinegar is all I'm willing to say at this point," Jenny glowered.

"Well on that note, we will leave you to your well-earned peace, but I need to steal this boy," Madison replied, grabbing Matt's sleeve.

It didn't even dawn on Jenny to make a snarky comment until after they left. Kids took all the fun out of everything.

$$\mathcal{DOC}$$

Matt began to feel slightly uncomfortable. Since they'd gotten into the SUV, Madison was hammering away at her phone and had barely spoken to him. He knew this was a friend arrangement, but still, he thought he had the right to expect SOME conversation. Finally, Matt had to say something. "You know, if you wanted to talk to somebody, I know a guy close by."

Madison blinked at him for a moment and then chuckled. "Sorry, I was telling some friends where I was going tonight. Then they wanted to know with who . . . Then they wanted me to describe you . . . "

Matt groaned.

"Oh come on, how bad could it have been? Sorry . . . I mean I said good things!"

"I quiver in terror just to think," Matt replied, more or less meaning every word of that.

"Oh my god! I said you looked nice!" Madison lightly tapped him on the arm in mock outrage. She added a moment later, "Okay, now that I think about it, if I heard that I was being described to people I didn't know, you would already no longer own a phone and some turtle by the side of the road would be discovering the joys of Twitter."

The rest of the ride went better after that. Madison still couldn't resist responding when the phone dinged, as by a Pavlovian response, but Matt understood, at least they were talking between dings. (If you put a hundred people in a room naked and set off the message ding over a loudspeaker without warning, ninety-nine of them would have their hand on their hips to pick up their phone before it even dawned on them about the nudity part.) An often-interrupted conversation was better than no conversation at all. It was the best they were going to manage since Matt wasn't able to communicate by her preferred means. Not if they didn't want the SUV wrapped around a tree and their last texts being used in a "Don't Text and Drive" ad campaign, that was.

When they got there, it turned out "near Beckley" was actually "in Beckley." In the evening, the town seemed subdued to the point of being abandoned. Downtown always seemed kind of subdued for as large of a city as it was, but now it had added shadows caused by the larger buildings. Most of the shopping, and therefore people, happened on the edges of town in big malls, so traffic was always light, even in the afternoon. Coming here in the evening, it almost seemed foreboding. Like the scene from a horror movie where everyone has cleared out of the city, except the zombies or vampires or aliens or, in your higher class of film, the vampire-alien-zombies.

The one exception to the apocalypse plague movie feel was the little area around the bar, which was lit up like a beacon in the night. The building was on the thin side for a bar, some architectural fluke from a bygone era that somehow remained there, giving it a quirky feel that Matt was sure appealed to hipsters like mad. There were already people milling about in front of the place, a sure sign that some form of music and drinking was in the offing for the evening. Nobody was yelling at anyone or threatening to kick anyone's ass while being held back by a girlfriend, proof that it was still early.

"Crap!" muttered Madison.

"What?" Matt asked with concern.

"Could I ask a little favor?"

"What? What do you need?"

"Do you think you could ignore your cousin tonight? I just spotted Tyler out front."

Matt chuckled. "Okay, now I have to ask. What in the hell do you have against Tyler?"

Madison sighed. "All right, you'll find out sooner or later anyway. Never date a guy on the rebound from a divorce. They want you to 'Leave them the hell alone!' while at the exact same time expecting you to do every little god damned thing for them like a three-year-old."

Matt nodded sagely while staring straight ahead. Madison winced, waiting for the explosion for not telling him sooner.

Matt finally spoke. "I hang out with Tyler most nights.

He's my cousin and we live in the same house, so he's hard to avoid, but if it's any consolation, I don't care. We're here as friends so it doesn't matter, and I can totally see not wanting to date him."

"You can?"

"I'm in his room almost every night hanging out. I not only stay fully dressed, I keep my shoes on. I don't know what lives under the layers of clothing on the floor, but I think I saw a tentacle once. I couldn't imagine the risks you'd be taking if you took your clothing off in there," Matt said, his face completely serious.

Madison gawked for a moment before laughing, "Okay, you can talk to your cousin. But you gotta talk to me more, or I swear I'll pout. Anyway, I'm cuter. Now let's go have fun."

Chapter 7

"If you can't beat them, arrange to have them beaten."

—George Carlin

———————◆———————

MATT BARELY HAD time to even get a look at the place before Tyler spotted him.

"Hey cuz! What'n'thehell y'all doin . . . oh, hey, Madison,"

"Oh, hey, Tyler, didn't expect you tonight," Madison said with a smile that Matt suspected was so false, the rest of her face should sue it for perjury.

Tyler must have sensed the discomfort. "Well anyway, band's just settin' up, guess I'll see you up there." Tyler grinned, an out of place look of mischief on his face before he vanished back into the depths of the bar.

"C'mon, I'll buy you a drink," said Madison, as if that uncomfortable meeting had never happened. "What'll you have?"

"I guess I'll get a ginger ale."

Madison stopped dead in her tracks. "A ginger ale?"

"Well, I am driving."

"You definitely ain't from around here, and that is for sure. The day I hear one of these boys turning down free booze is the day I check for a pulse." She shrugged as she went for the bar.

She was back a moment later, pointing to direct Matt

102

to one of the few remaining open booths. As soon as they sat down, she pressed him for info. "So how many times have you been out doing something since y'all got here that didn't involve Tyler or bars?"

"So, since Tyler is here, and this is technically a bar, this doesn't count either?"

"Shit. Okay, other than watching your cousin drink, how many times have y'all gotten out? So, no, this doesn't count as watching him drink, because he's way over there and because we're here to see a band," she replied with a perturbed expression on her face.

"Oh, well this will make once then." Matt shrugged.

Madison stared at him hard for a moment before saying, "We need to get you out more, son. It's a fun state, but not if all y'all do is play video games and work."

"But what if I think it's fun to only play video games and work?"

Madison looked at him like he had just grown another head.

Matt relented. "Okay, I don't. I mean, I like doing other things too, but what if I did just want to do that? What would you do if I'd meant it?"

"Ask Tyler for a ride home tonight, for starters," Madison replied with an absolutely blank expression.

A squall of feedback drew their attention to the stage. (Which is the main reason for squalls of feedback at a bar. At least, you hope it isn't some alien or something about to devour everyone, that puts a damper on an evening.) Striding onto said stage were . . . well, they were four good ole boys at first glance, the kind of guys you expected to drive a coal roller with gun stickers on it. At second glance, you realized that all of them had DA haircuts and that the bands they had on their t-shirts had very little to do with country or western but quite a bit to do with blood and gore. It was an off-putting look because all of them were not only big ole boys, but all of them had beards that quite possibly had birds nesting in them. It was like Elvis and Charlie Daniels had a kid.

"Ummm, hey, we're It Came From Appalachia, hope you dig it," the bulky lead singer said quickly into the mic before turning his back on the crowd to look to the rest of the band—maybe for positive reassurance as to his lifestyle choices. A moment later, the drummer clicked his sticks a few times and the band launched into their opening number.

Matt wanted to like them; he really did. He'd boned up on the style of music at Tyler's insistence. He'd even found that he liked quite a bit of it. But these guys . . . Matt couldn't tell you what "it" was, that magical thing that went into a band that made them rock—probably nobody could, it was an indefinable, "I know it when I hear it" thing—but he could tell you one thing, these guys clearly didn't know what it was either.

It wasn't just one thing, there was a laundry list of reasons why this wasn't working. Thinking about it set Matt off on another brief mental journey . . . Why laundry list? Wouldn't shopping list or check down list be better? Why had society decided on laundry list? Also, who needed a list to do laundry? Whites, reds, darks, it was a short list, so who wasn't remembering this? The band's list was a bit more problematic. The singer, for instance, sounded like he was trying to sound like Elvis. Well, more like Glenn Danzig when he was trying to sound like Elvis, but his tone was just flat. There was so much background hiss from the size of the club's PA system that the lyrics were unintelligible anyway, no matter how he sang them. "Something something blood, something something heart, something something kill," seemed to be the gist of it. The bassist was slightly off-key to what the guitarist was playing, and the drummer often just missed a beat at a critical moment. Who knew? Maybe it was nerves.

It put Matt in a quandary. A girl asks you to take her

somewhere as a favor to you, it's her friend's band no less, what is the nice way to say "They kinda suck"? For instance, "Well they managed to stay on the stage!" seemed damning with faint praise, so that wouldn't work—even if, considering their size, that counted as an accomplishment. He was thinking, "They were better than I expected." That's a nice low wattage white lie, where it sounds like a compliment as long as nobody asks you what you expected. Being forced to say that you'd expected "Children banging on pans" would ruin it entirely, so best to change the subject quickly after that. You sort of relied on people being able to recognize those phrases for the well-meaning half-truths that they were and not ask any further questions. Society doesn't function otherwise.

Madison, of all people, saved him there when she leaned over and yelled to be heard over the din, "Don't worry too much about liking them! This is only their second gig! I just thought it would be nice to get you out of the house!"

"Oh, so if we talk to them after the show, I should be nice?"

"You can. I've known the singer since we were kids, I plan to be a total bitch!" Madison giggled.

As the band ground to a halt, the front of the bar slammed open. Mike turned to see what could only be described as a "big guy." Well, that wasn't entirely true. "Behemoth", "huge", "dear god", and "holy shit" would have worked there as well in this instance. He was kind of fat, he was very tall, and overall, he was massive. He was wearing overalls and a flannel shirt, which seemed out of place for tonight's crowd. For that matter, his blank expression also didn't fit with the idea of a guy looking for a good time seeing music. Usually, people hoping to see music have two faces: excitement and anticipation, or seen-it-all-before too cool for the room. Not this guy. He had the look of someone you'd just woken out of a dream before they figured out where they are but with a body striving forward with purpose. Matt had never seen anyone on meth that he knew of before, but he couldn't help but wonder if he was seeing one now!

Madison joined Matt in hulk watching as he lumbered past their table and towards the crowd in the front. Whoever he was, he had some kind of goal clearly in mind; there was no pause or even thought in his motion. It looked like he had either already found what he was looking for or wouldn't stop until he walked through the back wall of the place. Maybe there was a small city that needed to be trampled up there. People automatically cleared a path for him. It was that or be trampled, and nobody pays a cover charge for that.

The whole crowd froze when they heard him bellow, "HAWLEY! THERE GONNA BE ONE LESS OF YOU NOW!"

Matt was instinctively on his feet at the sound of it, just not fast enough. He got to his feet in time to see Tyler whirled around with his throat in the grasp of one of the monster's giant paws. Matt was already dashing forward before he had even given it a thought! This was his cousin, this was blood . . . this was *who he played X-box with*! This was not something that his instincts were going to let stand, even if he had more time to consider . . . well, maybe he'd let the bouncers handle it, assuming there were bouncers, of course. Instead, primal animal stuff was running this show! He'd want to have a nice and long talk with his instincts about this later, assuming he survived.

Matt rushed forward to make a grab at the hulk, really only hoping to get him to let go of Tyler, who, on top of choking, the giant had also punched in the face at least once! As the man-mountain pulled back his ham sized fist to drill his cousin again, Matt made a desperate grab at the guy's flannel-clad shoulder and yanked hard! The man-mountain didn't budge, but . . . something did! A ghostly figure pulled away with Matt as his hand slipped off the shoulder of the monster choking Tyler, causing Matt to fall backwards a few steps! That ghostly shape stayed clutched in his grasp and came away with him as he fell!

A cold blue face, one that could only be called a face at all because it had slits for eyes and a mouth, turned to regard him, the whole thing glowing in the dim light of the bar. Matt let go of it in a panic. Its voice hissed at him, "Thanks to you, Matthew Hawley, for my freedom! Now a warning before I'm gone from this place: beware of her!"

"Who?" Matt asked, wide-eyed, but he never got to finish the question, because in an instant, the apparition was gone!

Matt's attention was brought back to the real world by the solid sounding wooden thump in front of him. It turned out the noise belonged to Tyler landing on the floor when Gigantor let go of him. A moment later, other patrons and one of the bouncers (who was actually smaller than the guy who hit Tyler) had a hold of the brute and were dragging him out of the bar in a hurry. The particularly weird part of it was the dazed look of complete non-comprehension on the face of the guy as he was being force-marched backward out of the place.

"What in the hell is going on here? Where in the hell am I?" he kept bellowing as they rushed him out, only to be cut off as the door slammed behind him and his escort.

Matt couldn't help but stare after him as he was being bustled out the door. The guy really looked like he had no idea what in the hell had just happened here! Matt also couldn't help but notice that Madison was staring at him like she'd just seen a ghost. Which was kind of odd since if all of that had as much to do with magic as he thought it did, there was no way anyone else saw what had just happened there. She must have been just about stunned out of her panties that Matt had been fool enough to have a go at the enormous side of beef that had just been dragged out of there. In hindsight, Matt was actually kind of surprised at it himself.

He was about to ask her why she was gawking when he heard Tyler gasping and coughing. He was still down on the floor where he had landed. Matt rushed right over to his cousin to find him sitting upright at least, but only barely. His face wouldn't look particularly nice for a few days, judging by the busted lip and the rapidly closing eye the brute had laid on him before being stopped by whatever in the hell happened when Matt had interrupted the thrashing.

"Oh, hey!" Tyler attempted to grin at him, which only made him look more gruesome as it revealed the blood all over his teeth.

"So, what the fuck was that about?" Matt demanded as he helped Tyler to his feet. "Why'd that guy want to kill you?"

"No earthly clue, I've never seen him before in my life. And a big slab of fucking meat like that, you don't soon forget!"

"Good thing you didn't get killed."

"You'd get lonely without me, wouldn't you? Admit it!" Tyler flashed another gory grin.

"I guess, but mainly because *Overwatch* is multi-player, and I don't know a lot of people down here yet. I *need* you Tyler!"

Tyler looked crestfallen for just a second before letting his smile return to gross Matt out a bit. "That's possibly the nicest thing anyone's said to me in years."

Madison added over Matt's shoulder, "He's not lying, it probably is."

Matt decided that maybe sitting in on the rest of the poor band's set with the bloody mess that was Tyler in tow wasn't what the musicians needed at this point in their career. They just didn't seem competent enough to sing about horror while looking dead at it. So instead, he should drive his cousin home for the night. They could just come back if they wanted after he'd had a chance to clean himself up and they were sure Tyler didn't have a concussion—which might take a while, he said goofy things normally, so it would be hard to tell. They were just getting ready to go when Madison surprised them both by agreeing to come along.

"Why are *you* taking off?" Tyler asked as he was being directed by Matt towards the door.

"I was mainly here to provide moral support for those knuckleheads and get store boy here out on the town. Well, they've seen me, and Matt is leaving, so I might as well make sure I have a ride home."

"Cool, well we better get going. If I take him home late and busted up . . . " Matt said.

"Don't worry, the 'rents are used to it," Tyler interjected as he let himself be steered outside.

"One thing," Madison said.

"Yeah?" Matt and Tyler replied in unison, which they both instantly decided was not creepy in any way, nor an indication that they needed to spend more time with other people.

"Let's drop the pugilist here off at home first. You can take me home after that."

"Oh, okay, cool," said Matt, unlocking the SUV.

☽⊙☾

Tyler was deposited at home as quietly as possible. He had said he was fine, but Uncle Donnie would probably agree with Matt that it was best to drive him home anyway. Once word got around the family that the attack was unprovoked, questions would be asked, most likely at some point by MeeMaw. Matt had no idea what in the hell he would say by way explanation of the whole debacle and was hoping to put it off for a bit. How do you rationally explain any of that? He pulled a ghost that really wasn't a ghost—because ghosts are just dead people and not blue light with a face—out of a giant hulk of a human who was about to throttle the life out of Tyler? That was what happened, but it sounded screwed up every time he ran it through his head, and he suspected it could only get worse when confronted by his grandmother's raised eyebrow of doubt and suspicion.

There was nothing he could do about any of that right now and nothing other than dropping off his cousin that he wanted to do, so he barely even stopped the SUV to let him out when they got to the farm. As soon as Tyler was clear, he was already in gear and driving Madison home. It wasn't that he was mad about anything and driving off in a huff, although it did kinda look that way. Matt was more preoccupied with what in the hell he was going to tell his grandmother about everything, not to mention trying to figure out what in the hell he even thought had actually happened. Madison thankfully caught that he was a bit tight and just cranked up the tunes, saving him from making uncomfortable small talk.

They were just pulling up to the blocky, older building that held her apartment when she said, "So considering the whole beating up your cousin thing wasn't my idea, and I shouldn't be blamed in any way for it, you wanna hang out again?"

"Sure! I certainly wasn't going to blame you for anything my cousin got into. Like doing what?"

"Ever been to the Cascades?"

"I thought we'd already established that I need to get out more and haven't seen anything," Matt deadpanned.

"True. All right, it's a great big enormo waterfall in Virginia with, and I want to stress this is one of the reasons we're going there, a swimming hole at the base of it. How's that sound?"

"Well, I did buy the SUV with the idea of getting out to

nature once upon a time. Be silly to turn down a chance to do just that." Matt nodded.

Madison popped the door open and hopped out. "Great! Next weekend. I'm on your way to the falls, so you can just grab me. I'm probably bringing a friend, so . . . " she paused for a long moment for effect, "I suppose you can probably bring Tyler, so we've got an even number."

"Sounds good! We'll set a time when I see you at work." He smiled.

She gave him a thoughtful look, but only for a moment. It was so quick, if he hadn't been looking right at her, he'd have never noticed it. "Later Gator!"

The door shut behind her.

He would have said right then and there she was definitely fun, *even* if the only comparison to "fun" he had down here was Tyler, who mainly worked and played X-box. X-box was fun and all, but only if you weren't using it as a replacement for real life. Which now that Matt thought about it, was the entire extent of his life since he got here. He clearly needed to get some hobbies here, he certainly didn't want to turn into some weird shut-in just stacking up newspapers and cats eating out of tin cans among the stacks of yellowing paper and cat crap. Having a friend who was real-life fun like Madison could be his saving grace here.

Yeah, he absolutely needed someone to hang out with other than just Tyler, and Madison was fun and funny. Despite the massive amount of Tyler abuse that happened, Matt was willing to write tonight off as a win.

$$☽☉☾$$

Matt only had maybe a half an hour or so to drive back to the farm, tops. Knowing MeeMaw had been most likely assessed of the situation, and most likely by Uncle Donnie and Aunt Debbie, did not help. It made him want to go night exploring to see the sights, even knowing the inherent contradiction there. This all seemed to stir in him a newfound adventurousness, mainly because he *really* didn't want to explain things. Putting it off even further, of course, would only make people really want to hear his side of things, and probably the second he got there. He was fully aware he was only making this worse the slower he drove. That was the problem. For starters, he had no idea what in the hell had happened, so that put his ability to explain at a serious disadvantage. He was new to all this; maybe this crap was normal down here, with all the witches and magic and stuff. How should he know? Maybe they'd say, "Well god damn it, boy, how you gonna be any good if'n y'all don't know to stop a Womble Floop before it dun whupped on our poor Tyler?" He had no idea why the WV accent got thicker when he was imagining being yelled at, but it did.

He really didn't need this, he didn't want to go back to feeling like a total loser again. This morning when he'd woken up, he felt like he was finally getting some kind of mental handle on this magic thing. So, it went with that, that for the first time in forever, he felt like he was getting a handle on something tangible. He would even call for the local ghosts and talk sometimes; they made for interesting conversation. It was a part of himself he felt was kind of awesome; how could he not? Think of all the historical perspective you could get talking to ghosts! He had a job he at least liked enough to not be rushing to find something new, his savings were up to even past where they had been. And he had a nice get together with a new friend to look forward to. As he had stressed to himself repeatedly, Matt certainly didn't think of it as a date. He didn't think he was "cool guy" enough to be her type. But it was nice to have a friend of his own in the area, even if Madison had dated Tyler, which was weird. Now he felt like he was driving home to a dressing down. Worst of all, Matt didn't know *what* he had done wrong, but he had just dropped a busted-up Tyler off, and it felt like he had done something tongue-lashing worthy tonight. He just had no idea what it was, and that did not feel fair at all!

It felt like the longest drive of his life, and that included the drive down here. Coming down here, he didn't know what to expect, and tonight he had convinced himself as to what was going to happen. As he pulled in the drive, he saw there were still some lights on in both houses. It turned out Matt was wrong, the drive from dropping Madison off was the second longest drive of his life. The longest was going to be going up the driveway. This was even worse than the time he had the family car when he was 17 and fell asleep at his girlfriend's and had to drive home at 2 a.m. At least that time he was positive that his Dad had to keep him no matter what because of laws and stuff. Well, he'd been reasonably sure at least. Also, his Dad had seemed weirdly proud of him, probably thinking something had happened that actually hadn't happened, at least judging from the wink he gave Matt after he was done yelling at him.

Nothing he could do now but take his medicine. The Xterra crawled up the driveway, mainly because it was only in drive. Matt's foot wasn't even on the gas. As he parked it by the house and began to get out, the door burst open!

Crap! Here it came! Coming out in full flight was Aunt Debbie, followed by Uncle Donnie framed in the doorway.

Matt's shoulders sagged with defeat. Well, it was time to get this over with . . .

"Oh, thank god y'all are all right!" his aunt called out as she engulfed him in a hug, driving the air out of him since he hadn't had time to prepare for it.

"I swear I'm fine! Nothing happened to ME!" Matt said with astonishment after he got his breath back while extricating himself from the hugging woman.

"I'm sorry, sweetie," she said, regaining some of her

composure quickly. "When you didn't come in with Matt, well, we all got worried, honey."

"Everything's fine, I just had to drop off our friend Madison," he said, walking with her to the house.

As he stepped in, Uncle Donnie patted him on the shoulder. "Just wanna say thanks for looking after yer cousin. He may be a bit of a screw up some days, but we like him. Don't get too comfy just yet, your MeeMaw wants to talk to y'all." Seeing the instant look of horror on Matt's face, he quickly added, "Don't know why y'all look like that. Tyler isn't sure what exactly happened, so she just wants to hear it from you."

"Oh," Matt mumbled. "Okay, I'll do that before I try to settle down for the night."

Now that he was sure nobody was mad at him, at least some of the gallows feel had gone out of his life. Just not all of it. He had only been cleared in the secular court of public opinion here. MeeMaw and his dead relatives out in the family plot operated on an entirely different level, and that could still possibly be a hanging court waiting for him. For all he knew, he was about to be found guilty of "not being able to tell his head from a hole in the ground" with additional charges of "inability to find his ass with both hands and a map" in the court of magic and the supernatural, Judge Rod Serling presiding.

In theory, he shouldn't have been scared of the dark while walking the distance from Uncle Donnie's to his MeeMaw's lit up house. But as keyed up as he was, Matt swore that every twig on the entire hillside snapped under the foot of a serial killer and every breath of wind was masking the sound of someone hiding out there waiting to strike.

(A psychiatrist, at this point, would point out that Matt was manufacturing a fear of the dark in a way that he hoped would give him an excuse to run back to Uncle Donnie's and thus avoid a feared confrontation with his grandmother. But since we don't have a psychiatrist handy, why don't we say he was being a total wuss bag about the whole thing instead?)

The door was flung open, and there was the worried face of his MeeMaw before he even had a chance to knock. "There you are! I was worried sick about you!" she said.

"I had to drop off the girl I took to the bar!" Matt protested his innocence, which was weird, he was a full-grown man here. Taking a girl home that you took to a bar seemed pretty normal under most circumstances, but not in the face of his MeeMaw looking worried. It seemed decent manners to most people. He wished those people would stop by the house right now to explain it to MeeMaw for him.

His grandmother's eyebrow still rose a bit at the mention of a girl, but mercifully, she let it be, saying instead, "Well, never mind that, just come in and tell me what happened. I felt something odd tonight, and young Tyler's story makes me think that y'all might know why."

Matt did as he was told but felt compelled to say, "I really, honest and for true have no earthly clue what happened."

"Be that as it may, you go take a seat, and I'll get us some tea so you won't get parched while you tell me every single thing I want to know," she said and pointed to the couch before hustling off to the kitchen.

Matt groaned but knew it was pointless to argue exhaustion or even getting up for work tomorrow. The old woman could see his bedroom from her house. If he tried to beg off, she'd know if he was staying up playing X-box and drinking beer with Tyler. Considering that was EXACTLY what he planned to do, now that his night out was more or less ruined, he couldn't see much choice in the matter. If he wanted his normal night, he just needed to tell MeeMaw what she wanted to hear. Hell, she'd get it out of him sooner or later anyway, better sooner and back in the house and into a cold one.

She came back into the room and handed him a cup of steaming tea, then took her own cup and sat down across from him. "All right, we're settled. Now, how about telling me what y'all saw."

Matt told her every detail, stopping only occasionally for a question from her. When he finished his tale of the incident at the bar, his grandmother looked thoughtful before she barked, "That bitch! She ought to know better!"

"Who?" asked Matt, nonplussed by her outburst; he did not think of his grandmother as the cursing type.

"Oh, never you mind," she snapped before remembering herself. Composing herself by taking a deep breath, she smiled almost sheepishly before continuing. "I cain't even prove who did what yet, and already I'm throwing dirt on somebody's grave. But one thing I do think has happened . . . well, would you call the continued existence of your Pa Pa and those type of relatives a life in another existence from ours?"

"Yeah, I mean I guess so." Matt shrugged.

"Well, there's more to this universe than just other ways of existing here. There's other places *to* exist in. Someone, and I think it's obvious I have my suspicions as to who, has been messing with places she ain't got no business putting her fool nose. Now I s'pose I gotta prove the who and figure out the why later," she said by way of explanation.

"But what was the blue thing I saw?"

"Well, those places have things living in them. Powerful things, powerful enough to walk right over a man's free will, if someone be fool enough to give 'em a path here." She scowled angrily. As if remembering herself yet again, she concluded. "Well, cain't nuthin' be done about it tonight. I thank y'all for speaking honest, but no point in keeping you up any later."

Matt knew when he was being dismissed; it had been a recurring childhood theme when dealing with adults. He knew it when he heard it, even if he also technically counted as an adult in a court of law, he knew she felt she still had every right to use it. But as he left, he turned, "One more thing, is the guy who beat up Tyler going to be all right?"

"Well, as all right as y'all can be after waking up in a strange place with someone else's blood on your hands," she replied as she shut her front door.

$$\text{)O(}$$

That was that over with. Matt decided to go through with his original plan for the rest of the night. Which was to go back inside and play X-box with Tyler, who insisted he was fine despite the physical evidence all over his face. Matt was willing to admit that despite being run over by a cement mixer, Tyler did indeed act like he was as fine as he ever was. Which, come to think of it, was a damned lucky thing. That monstrosity could have easily made good on his threat of there being "One less Hawley." Hell, if the man-mountain had really put his mind to it, he could have gotten two for one tonight. He probably could have started hitting Tyler *with* Matt if he'd put any thought into his violent outburst.

"Whatcha doing next weekend?" he asked during a lull in the game.

"Well, I—"

"Wrong!"

"Wrong?"

"Right! Wrong, which is the opposite of right. What you're doing is going with me to a place called the Cascades," Matt said with some finality.

"I am?"

"Yes, you are. Madison is bringing a friend, so to keep it from being an odd number, she told me to invite you along," Matt replied, angling his body as if that would somehow affect the game he was playing on the screen.

"That's you asking?"

"Yep."

"Oh, well okay then." Tyler shrugged before continuing. "So anyway, what's with y'all and Madison anyway? You two dating or something?"

"No, we are not. But she is currently the only friend I have locally that doesn't involve pixels and multi-player in any way."

"Huh! Well, too bad. I keep hoping she'll find somebody she likes, and y'all aren't a total tool," Tyler replied before stealing a kill from right in front of Matt.

"Oh, such a compliment, and from a family member no less!"

"Don't let it go to y'all's head or nothing."

Chapter 8

"No man should marry until he has studied anatomy and dissected at least one woman."
—Honore de Balzac, famous author, and clearly a serial killer who got away with it.

———— ◆ ————

A **FEW DAYS LATER**, Madison finally reappeared at the store, her normal pre-work sunny self. Instead of her usual routine of scanning the racks for a bit, pretending that she was a customer and not just hanging out, she came right up to the counter, where she promptly planted her elbows. This forced Matt to come over to see what she wanted. It was like she had waited outside until there was no one else in the store and interrupting him wouldn't, well, interrupt him so much. But now that she had his eye, she intended to demand he give her his full attention.

As he made his way over to the counter, she immediately asked, "So, is your good for nothing cousin going to live?"

"That would be the general prognosis, yes. He was really just a bit roughed up, but he's fine," Matt replied, putting his elbows on the counter himself and beginning to bump hers.

She completely ignored him. "Good, as much as he can get on my nerves, I'd hate to see anything bad happen to him. So, is he coming this weekend?"

"He said he wouldn't miss it for the world," Matt said with a straight face while trying to see if he could use his own elbow to shove Madison's off the countertop.

"No, he didn't," she replied, delivering a counterblow with her own elbow directly to his funny bone, causing Matt to take his arm off the counter and try to surreptitiously shake some life back into his hand.

"All right, he didn't," he replied, wincing. "I told him he was coming, and he didn't put up too hard of a fight."

"There you go, tiger. Was that so hard?" She smiled.

"What, giving up my right to my own store's counter?"

"No, admitting y'all just told him he was coming, silly."

"If I had just asked him, and he really had been all enthusiastic about it, would you have believed it?"

"No."

"Well, look at all the time I saved then by just telling him he was coming and then pretending he was looking forward to it," Matt managed to reply with a straight face.

Madison huffed at that, withdrawing her elbows from the counter and turning to leave. "I know y'all are morally wrong for fibbing, but somehow, I can't fault your logic. I'm gonna mull this over and get back to you. So, don't think you've won. Fibbing about his enthusism for this weekend was reprehensible, and I'll prove it, just not today."

$$\text{)O(}$$

Saturday rolled around bright and hot. Not a humid hot, thankfully, but hot all the same. Matt loaded up his hydro pack into the back of the SUV, almost enthusiastic that he might actually finally need it for something. He had gotten it in a fit of self-improvement years ago, when he had sworn he was going to take up jogging and hiking. A week of jogging a little over a mile and one long hike had relegated it to his closet, where it had lived until it had been forced to move into the Xterra. It was only dumb chance that it had still been there and that it cleaned up all right. (This situation was what eBay was built on, the hopeful purchases of people pledging to finally do something who had yet to run smack dab into the reality of their own laziness. Faced with the truth of who they really were, they finally bowed to that hard set of truths and want to regain some closet space and maybe a couple of bucks, it gets sold off. Thus, eBay. A capitalist powerhouse built on the inescapable inertia of Americans.)

Matt had been feeling relatively happy and looking forward to the outing, but he was alone in his joy. Tyler, on the other hand, who had been out last night, had a very large travel mug of coffee in his hand as he trudged out to the SUV to join his cousin.

"Late night last night?"

"Uh-huh."

"Have fun?" Matt asked, secretly enjoying his cousin's misery, mainly because it wasn't him who was suffering.

"I think so." Tyler groaned.

Matt put a cooler in the hatchback before relenting, "There's orange juice and water in the cooler, there is aspirin in the glove box along with ibuprofen, and best of all, there is time enough for regrets on the drive down. But do us a favor and try and look semi-human by the time we get there?"

"I want a croissanwich, make a stop on our way," Tyler grumbled.

"You are just a health freak, that's what you are, my boy," Matt said, fighting to suppress a sadistic grin as he hopped in.

It took the promised fast food delicacy to make Tyler begin to approach human. He was approaching it cautiously and from a great distance, sure, but he was getting there. "So, who is this friend of Madison's? Do I know her?"

"Madison didn't say, and I didn't ask. I was just happy that after you went five rounds with Tyson last time she still wanted to hang out, "Matt said and shrugged.

"Hey, no fair; if it had been a fight with Tyson, I would have seen it coming," Tyler protested.

"Oh, and you think that would have helped?"

"Hells YEAH I do! I would have run like hell, or barring that, had a gun and shot the sumbitch," Tyler replied emphatically.

"Hmmm, considering the criminal charges, you might be better off now."

"Tyson? No jury on earth would convict me if I said it was self-defense."

"Well not now, I mean, they'd convict you NOW, he's old."

"True." Tyler shrugged. "You ever see his cartoon?"

"Funny as hell."

"They should give all former heavyweight champions cartoons," Tyler agreed.

$$☽○☾$$

Madison was waiting outside of her place when they pulled up. Tyler had texted her when they were close, so she'd known when they were going to be there and must have decided to not invite them up. Matt was unsure if he should read into that or it was just that she was in a hurry to get on the road. With her was a blond girl. They'd be almost identical if it wasn't for a few differences. The new girl had more tattoos, for one, and there were the aforementioned different hair colors. It was weird. Matt never met girls who looked like this at home in the "great big city," here, in what was supposed to be moonshine and bluegrass land, they apparently grew everywhere. Both of them were wearing khaki shorts and hiking boots, which clashed viciously with the tattoos and band shirts. It was hard to tell which fashion outlook was winning.

"Hey, guys!" Madison said, bounding up as they got out of the Xterra—which was unusual in and of itself, she usually slunk along in a manner that dared you to look at her hips when she walked.

Matt had worked hard to train himself not to do just that. Unfortunately, that meant he had been looking in the general direction of where other things had bounced as she came up, so it turned into a weird accidental win that would become a loss really quickly if she noticed him gawking.

"We're on time, right?" Matt asked quickly; he knew they were, but it was still the polite thing to say, and it distracted from the boob gawk faux pas.

"As on time as the clock is. This is my friend, Chloe," she said, thrusting the blond girl forward a bit.

"Hi, I'm Matt, and this is my cousin—" Matt began.

"Oh, I've met Tyler before," Chloe interrupted him. "He did a piece for me."

"I did?" Tyler snapped his head up.

"Yeah, but if you don't remember my face, it's fine, you didn't see much of it when you were working." Chloe giggled a little.

Comprehension dawned in Tyler's eyes. "Oh yeah! Sorry, I'm a bit slow this morning. Elsa Lanchester, Bride of Frankenstein on your—"

"Glad to see you remembered," Chloe cut him off.

They climbed into the Xterra with Madison calling out shotgun, which forced Tyler into the back with Chloe. Matt couldn't help but wonder if after his beating at the show, Madison had decided that Tyler needed a woman to take care of him and was engaging in a bit of matchmaking here with the seating arrangements.

"What's everybody want to listen to?" Matt asked once they'd settled in.

"Have any Demented Are Go?" Madison asked.

"Of course, I do, here, plug in my iPod," Tyler said, fumbling into his pockets for it.

Plugged in and turned up, Matt was happy enough to have his musical education expanded a bit, even if a song called "Cripple in The Woods" didn't really bode well for this particular trip.

$$\text{☽○☾}$$

"Dear God, is there anywhere to park here?"

"It's a popular spot. Look, there's a spot," Madison replied, pointing.

It wasn't so much a spot as an empty plot of grass next to lined off spots, but at this point, Matt wasn't going to argue and swung the Xterra in.

"Not quite getting away from it all, is it?" he remarked.

"Don't worry. It might be a little crowded at the falls itself, but you hardly see anyone when you're on the trail," Madison assured him.

"Speaking of which, how long is this trail? You never said."

"Long enough to get a good hike in." She shrugged.

Matt should have taken that as his cue to turn the SUV back on and pull out.

$$\text{☽○☾}$$

About halfway along the trail, he began to see why Madison hadn't given him a straight answer about the hike. First off, it seemed to involve a considerable amount of up. Matt was kind of surprised at how bad this hurt. He considered himself to be from the Northeast. They had some mountains up there; it wasn't like he was from the plains of the mid-west, for the love of God. This hike only seemed to have one consistent direction, up, steeply, and that was making his dogs ache. He began to suspect that what they called mountains back home were, in the context of the two Virginias, flatlands.

Tyler was still working through his hangover, and he would drop back often to where Matt was trudging along regularly to slum. Matt figured that with Tyler having grown up here, he needed the hangover to slow him down enough that Matt would have some company on this expedition. The girls, he noticed with disgust, did not even seem to be sweating much as they pulled ahead of them again. Worse, every few minutes, they'd start to giggle.

"You realize they're talking about us, right?" Tyler gasped as they trudged along.

"What makes you say that?"

"Girls giggle like that, it involves guys, and we're nearby. God, I'm afraid of what Madison is saying to her," Tyler wheezed.

"How bad could it be?"

Tyler just looked at him for a long hard moment with his eyebrow raised.

"Well, Okay . . . maybe she'll find it intriguing," Matt lied.

Tyler grunted and then started to hurry after the girls before they got too far ahead.

$$\text{☽〇☾}$$

They could HEAR the waterfall long before they could see any sign of it as they continued uphill (surprise!) along the stream that the falls fed. The way had gotten dark as the trees that had been well back from the stream began crowding out the sun. Slowly but surely, the sound of the approaching falls began to overwhelm the sound of the stream next to them. The rushing creek had numerous small waterfalls along it, but this noise was dwarfing any they had heard before. Matt was allowing himself some hope that they might actually reach their destination. He had given up on such a possibility ages ago, so he was now forced to struggle with this new concept.

Gasping and grunting, Tyler and Matt followed the girls around a bend in the trail. Matt stopped dead in his tracks to take it in. Finally seeing their destination, he figured this might actually be worth it. It took his eyes a second to adjust. Up ahead, the area was open and brightly sunny, while they were still standing in shadows. The falls themselves were enormous. Huge amounts of water just bucketing over a cliff onto the rocks below, where they spread out almost like a trickling fan of water! There were people everywhere, many of them swimming in the area directly in front of the falls, some clambering over rocks to get as close as they could to the water pounding down, and even more taking pictures from observation decks to the left. Something else Matt couldn't help but notice was that just about every ethnicity available was here taking pictures of the natural wonder, which made Matt wonder how in the hell had he never even heard of the place before. Clearly, somebody had mentioned it online, from the looks of things. The area they were in was populated by Ma and Pa Kettle, yet the people around the falls resembled the United Nations general assembly, but much younger and obviously not dressed in suits and ties.

It did go a long way towards explaining the parking lot, at least.

"Now what?" Tyler asked.

Madison dug into her backpack and brought out towels. "I came prepared! Now, we go swimming!"

It took a bit of effort to get over to where most people were swimming. Matt found himself feeling less rugged by the nanosecond as he carefully navigated his way over and along the wet rocks to get across the stream, hoping and praying the entire time to not slip and break his neck. To make matters worse, five-year-olds were flowing over the same terrain like it was a perfectly dry, non-slimy, non-algae-covered floor in their house instead of boulders covered with all that wet ick.

Once they were on the far set of rocks, Tyler and Matt stripped down quickly while the girls picked out a spot for their towels and things. The young men stepped into the shallow water with sensible fear and trepidation while trying to look manly about the whole thing . . . and failing. Matt could see that it was some kind of a rock shelf and that only a few feet past that it plunged into much deeper waters, so, image be damned, he was watching his step here. The water felt cold but not too terrible where they stood, but he had his doubts about the deeper water in front of them. He couldn't help but notice nobody was staying in it very long at all, and he had heard whoops of shock as they were approaching the falls. Matt considered that to be a really important observation. He wondered if he should share it with somebody.

Tyler came up next to him and read his mind. "It may be a hot day and all, and it's definitely a long hike, but y'all notice there ain't a lot of people swimming around out there?"

"Yeah, I had kind of noticed that almost everyone is in the shallows or by the falls," Matt agreed, both of them peering into the dark deep waters with trepidation.

"Maybe the girls will settle for standing here like this? Ya think?"

"Here's to hoping, because I don't want to—"

What Matt didn't want to do was lost to posterity as both of them were suddenly shoved violently forward!

The world went white for Matt, followed by blue—his eyes weren't open, those were just the colors that flashed in front of his brain from the shock. The water was not cold. You would have had to put a blow torch to it for an hour and then it would be cold. For a second, Matt didn't even do anything, he was so stunned by the violent change in temperature. The one brain cell that hadn't been frozen into incoherence did finally get itself heard by pointing out that if he swam up, he could get out, and if he got out, he could go to where the normal temperatures that humans needed to survive existed.

He burst the surface later, squealing, "Jesus Christ on a crutch that's cold!" Matt took in his surroundings and noticed numerous parents with children giving him the stink eye, but he also noticed that none of those people were coming anywhere close to where the water got deep. In his eyes, that invalidated any opinion they might have on how one should react. Matt also couldn't help but notice two pretty tattooed girls in the shallow water bent over with laughter.

Tyler and Matt both erupted out of the deep water at roughly the same time and headed towards the girls.

"Y'all pushed us!" Tyler accused.

"Only to see what the temperature was like," Chloe said, backing away, her hands in front of her.

"Yep, totally innocent," agreed Madison, keeping pace with her.

"Why don't you come in now for yourselves and find out?" Matt snarled.

"But that's what big strong men are for," Madison replied, giggling.

Tyler bent down and scooped up some water and threw it at the girls. "Here, it's a lot colder than this!"

We can probably safely leave it around there; if you have not been in a splash fight in your life, you will have to only imagine it. Also, you need to get out more and have some fun. Bring this book, it'll dry out eventually. It involves splashing (duh), laughing, and eventually getting water in your ear that will not come out for roughly a century, no matter how often you prod at it with a Q-tip or tilt your head to the side.

The Wild Witches of West Bygod

They pulled up to Madison's place as the sun was almost set. It had made for a brilliant and gorgeous view as they were driving over and around the mountains to get back from Virginia. Even Tyler had agreed, despite being still somewhat annoyed over the whole dunking incident. Matt was willing to blow it off. It may be sexist, but pretty girls had pushed them in, so that kind of got a pass. If Tyler had done it to him, he'd have been honor-bound to whip his butt for it. The rules of masculinity had spoken, and Matt was willing to listen.

Madison and Chloe got out; Matt figured they'd keep hanging out, so he got out too. Tyler, on the other hand, took his time about it. He called over to Matt, "Hey, I'm kinda beat, you mind heading back?"

Maybe Tyler didn't see it from where he was, but Matt saw Madison's elbow dove into Chloe's ribs. The girl actually grunted a bit before saying, "Well if y'all want to hang out, Matt, I got my car. I can give him a lift back; I live up there anyway."

Matt thought about it for a second. Maybe. He didn't get out much; he was frankly getting sick of spending all of his time at the farm. Not to mention that if he got home early, MeeMaw might dream up something for him to do that absolutely, positively had to be done right now. "Hey, that'd be great! Thanks!"

This was quick, instinctive thinking for Matt. He had just frozen Tyler out of the decision-making process entirely. His cousin probably would have hemmed and hawed about it, maybe come up with excuses as to why it absolutely *had* to be Matt who drove him home, but he'd never have a chance now. He was forced to just grunt, "See y'all back at the farm," before going off to follow Chloe. It would be good for him to learn how to talk to a woman again. Matt had noticed that while Tyler had lots of girlfriends over time, to go along with an ex-wife, he seemed to be in no hurry to reacquaint himself with the female half of the species lately. Just having to be civil for the car ride would do him good.

As he watched them go, Matt said to Madison, "So, did I just witness a bit of matchmaking on your part, or was I imagining it?"

"And why not? They're both single, they have a lot in common . . . "

"But if you broke up with Tyler, why would you hook him up with a friend?" Matt looked puzzled.

Madison turned to head in, saying over her shoulder, "Just because Tyler wasn't right for me don't mean I don't think he's a swell guy. I mean overall, in comparison to some of the chuds around here anyway. Him and Chloe should get along like a house on fire."

"Not right for you how?"

"The Peter Pan is strong in that one, young Skywalker." She giggled, unlocking her door.

"Oh, yeah, I can see that."

They went up the steps to her apartment. Matt was shocked as they went into her place. Not by the posters on the wall or the cheap furniture, he'd expected all of that. Nor that the place was kept tidy as a pin for all that it was decorated like a dorm room. No, what shocked him was the size of the place. The living room alone was probably as big as his entire apartment back home!

"Damn! How can you afford this?" he said before he could stop himself.

"Aww, rent's only four-twenty-five a month, pretty easy to pay for, even on my salary," she shrugged.

"Dear God, if someone had this place back home, they'd have to sublet it to afford the rent," he said, still in awe.

"Well assuming it ain't so big you get lost, fridge is over there, the Blu rays are there, and the game console is next to it. I'm taking a shower real quick, we've been hiking all day and swimming, and . . . well, I'm taking a shower real quick. Once I'm out, we can toss on a movie," she replied, sweeping off to parts unknown deeper in the apartment.

Matt watched her walk down the hall for a minute until she vanished in the gloom and considered his options. Well, beer and TV were the two on the table, so he wandered off to the kitchen to take care of part of that. Inside the older model fridge, tucked next to some leftover Chinese, was indeed beer. Matt was impressed. It wasn't a trendy IPA or an equally trendy bar beer like he'd expected, instead, she had an ample stocking of stouts, porters, and ciders filling up her bottom shelf. The girl had proper taste, not trend taste.

Flopping down on the couch, he set his beer down and turned on the TV while he waited. He was pleasantly amused that it had been left on cartoons. He was happy to let *Gumball* run, just to see if she'd come up with an excuse for why it was on. The show had plenty of adult jokes in there, and he didn't consider himself that much an adult, so it wasn't like he wouldn't have watched it on his own. He just wanted to see if she'd react. He half watched TV and half listened to the shower running down the hallway while taking sips of his beer.

Matt heard the shower turn off, and a few minutes after that, Madison re-appeared. Gone was her perfectly held in place hair, which now hung damp and wet to her shoulders, gone was the makeup, and she was dressed in pajamas. Matt gaped. She actually looked, if anything, cuter. She looked hot when she was dolled up, but au natural made her look, well, snuggly adorable, which he had not expected.

Seeing his facial expression, she said, "What? Do I have a spider on my face or something?"

"No sorry, it's the first time I've seen you without makeup," Matt said.

"Fugly?"

"No, pretty."

"Right answer. Anyway, assuming you don't want to watch cartoons all night, which would be totally fine if y'all did, whaddya wanna watch? I have Netflix. We could see something on there, but I warn y'all, it can get dicey," she said, perching herself on the couch next to him.

He was doubly impressed; she made no excuses for the cartoons.

"I don't know, you can pick something."

"*Return of the Living Dead* it is! Y'all are a stone-cold genius! How'd you know that was what I was in the mood for?" she bubbled, getting up and heading for the Blu-rays.

"Oh, lucky guess."

They had been watching the movie for a bit, Matt had seen it ages ago, and since Madison had it on Blu-ray, who knew how many times she'd seen it, so they felt free to talk here or there. Madison turned a bit where she was seated down the couch from Matt. "So, do you mean it?"

"Huh? Whu?"

"That I'm pretty," she demanded, her face serious and intent.

"Oh, c'mon, you don't need me telling you that, you're gorgeous," Matt huffed.

"Well, it's just, y'all never made a move on me. Why not? I mean, if I'm so gorgeous?"

"I don't know, just didn't seem right." Matt shrugged.

"I get it, y'all don't like girls with tattoos."

"It's not that at all, everyone has tattoos."

"Well, then why?"

Matt sat quietly for a moment before replying, "I don't know, a whole list of reasons. You're out of my league, to begin with. I really wanted a friend here, and when we got along so well, I didn't want to make you dislike me by being a horndog. I had just gotten out of a relationship, and the last thing I wanted to do to anyone was to make them be the bounce back girl who had to hear all about my ex. Not to mention you saying never date a guy on the rebound, which kind of automatically x-ed me out. Annnnd one day, we were actual friends, so then I REALLY didn't want to screw up anything." Matt rattled off his reasons on his fingers.

"Mmmm hmmm," Madison sat up straight. "That's all very, very adult. Mature, reasonable reasons, caring and nice even. But let me ask y'all again, do you think I'm pretty? And look at me first before you answer."

Matt turned away from whatever the zombies were doing to look at her. He'd been right before, of course, she was pretty, that was just a given. Why she needed him to say it was beyond him, but still, she'd demanded. "Oh come on, Madison, you are very pretty. You know I think that."

She leaned in very closely. Matt could smell her shampoo, it was herbal. "Okay, now what if I told y'all I was definitely NOT out of your league?"

)O(

"Oh, Christ! We have to stop," Matt gasped, removing his hands from Madison's breasts.

"What? Why?"

"I don't have . . . you know . . . protection," Matt panted.

"What kind of guy doesn't have a condom on him at all times?"

"Isn't it kind of piggy to just assume like that? I was celibate until twenty minutes ago, you know."

"Oh, y'all are just about adorable," she smiled, "Dresser drawer."

Matt slid out from under her and went to the drawer, pulling it open. He was shocked to see it contained DOZENS of condoms inside. "Umm, why is there . . . ?"

Madison laughed. "You know how I told y'all Chloe and Tyler would get along? This is her sense of humor. She thinks I don't date enough, so every time she goes out on a date, she tosses the rest of the box in there to remind me I'm turning into an old maid."

"Actually, when you put it that way, there aren't THAT many in there. Bunch of different brands, though," Matt replied thoughtfully.

"She thinks it's more colorful that way. Pick one and get back here, will ya? I'm getting lonely," Madison demanded.

Matt grabbed what he considered to be the right one and made his way back onto the bed. Madison noticed what kind it was. Now her curiosity was aroused, along with everything else. She pulled him back down to herself and ran a hand over the front of Matt's jeans, grasping him as she went.

"Oh! Good for you!" she breathed with a smile.

Chapter 9

"Insanity runs in my family. It practically gallops."
—Cary Grant

---◆---

THE TWO OF THEM were snuggling on the couch, watching a different movie but also one involving zombies, different zombies, obviously. This one was something that had been translated from Italian, so the voice-overs made it kind of unintentionally comical. First off, none of the voice actors could actually act, so it was this heavy zombie movie with the cast of your high school play doing the voices. To make matters worse, the translations were off ever so slightly, so it was common to hear lines like, "This thing we must do, is what we shall do." And, "Yes! That is the thing!"

Matt's head snapped up as his phone buzzed at him. Picking it up, he saw it was from Tyler, and he read, "So, I take it this means you aren't coming home tonight, young man?"

"Huh! He types better than he talks, go fig," Matt said out loud.

"Your cousin, I take it? Don't let him fool y'all, he's smarter than he looks," Madison replied, cuddling closer to him.

Matt typed back, "You take it right."

A moment later, the phone pinged again, "You have fun, you crazy kids."

Matt typed back, "You won't miss me?"

Ping! "No, no, I wouldn't be able to play tonight anyway."

"See you tomorrow."

"Ltr"

"I think you scored with your matchmaking. I'm pretty sure Chloe is with Tyler," Matt announced.

"I would like to think I scored much better a bit earlier on making my own match," she teased.

Matt thought about that for a second, then he asked thoughtfully, "So, what now?"

"Whaddya mean, what now? Now, we watch the movie."

"That's not what I mean . . . you know, after we saw each other's naughty bits, what now!" Matt protested.

"Do y'all like hanging out with me?' Madison asked, sitting up.

"Of course, you're my best friend down here that I'm not related to!"

"Do y'all like kissing me?"

"Very, very much."

"Did y'all like seeing my naughty bits?"

"Twice."

"Want to go condom shopping with me eventually, knowing we'll have had to use up the ones in there before we need to?"

"That sounds fun, and I could use the exercise."

"Well then, that's what," she said, kissing him lightly and snuggling back down.

Matt was quiet for a moment. "That sounds suspiciously like boyfriend/girlfriend," he said before adding quickly, "I'm fine with that, by the way. I just need to know where I stand here."

"Call it what y'all will. Anyway, you're sitting here, not standing. Now shush, there's a really cool scene involving an eyeball coming up."

Morning came. Whether Matt was particularly into the concept or not, it still got bright out, and his eyes opened, which were both tell-tale signs of morning. His first sight to greet the day was Madison's hair as she was curled up next to him. Guys can do a bit of soul-searching during morning afters too, contrary to popular opinion. Not as much, sure, granted, but still, they aren't only hormones with eyeballs. Mostly, but not only. It isn't all high-fiving and kissing and telling, or Netflixing and lying. Matt certainly wasn't like that, he hoped. For one thing, there wasn't another guy to high five here, that'd just be weird. He considered what he felt about this big life change and who it was with, like an adult human should. It just didn't take very long. After a moment's reflection where he thought about Madison, and not just about what she looked like without clothes on either, he smiled and decided to go with pleased and happy. That was ruined a moment later when he started to worry about whether or not she had regrets. Would this be a morning of cold shoulders, little talking, and hints that he should leave now? I mean, it wasn't like in the cold light of day he had any chance at her. She was still gorgeous. As soon as she woke up, it was just going to be one of those things that she was going to instantly regret and . . .

"Morning, handsome, want me to turn the coffee on?" she said sleepily, ruining his panic attack before it had really had a chance to get fully up to steam.

His self-doubts had just been forced to go sit in the corner and find some other opportunity to ruin his enjoyment of life, maybe something involving his chin.

"Umm, sure," he replied, befuddled. He'd had a really good "steeling himself up for the letdown" going, and it's hard to just switch gears back to a soft and easy lovers' morning from something like that.

She rolled over; Matt couldn't help but think she looked adorable with morning face. He leaned in but she put her hand up, stopping the approaching kiss. Seeing the worried expression on his face, she laughed a little.

"Morning breath, let me brush first."

Watching her slip off to the bathroom, Matt tried again to consider if he had any regrets about last night. Enjoying the view of her retreating out in the hall to the bathroom, the only thing he came up with was that he didn't have his toothbrush with him. That and he would have to get some kind of new non-related, non-girlfriend friendship going with somebody at some point. His current friendship had graduated to the big leagues, it would appear. Of course, a girlfriend and a cousin who were also his friends would work just fine for now, especially considering his girlfriend had been his friend first. Matt also decided he could probably make do with brushing his teeth with his finger and some toothpaste.

Toothbrush in her mouth, Madison ghosted by the door and held a finger up as she vanished in the other direction. Matt decided to take it as his cue to quickly pee and brush his own teeth, so he grabbed his shorts and rushed down the hall.

The bathroom, which he left open, was typical of an older building, lots of real porcelain, and like the rest of the house, kept neat as a pin. Matt made a note of that: clean freak, do not leave clothing everywhere. He knew he'd made mistakes with Ashley. It wasn't all her fault, nothing like that could be, and he was bound and determined not to screw this up too. He had no idea where he'd have to go to for another fresh start if he did. Maybe he had cousins in Alaska he didn't know about.

He was just spitting when she re-appeared to rinse her own mouth out. He was just about to leave when she called out, "Freeze, mister."

Matt froze.

The Wild Witches of West Bygod

She turned towards him and looked him directly in the eyes. "It's the cold light of day, so, rather than any evasions, or missed phone calls, forgotten texts, or anything like that. Regrets?"

Matt actually smiled at that, he couldn't help it. To think she thought *he* might be the one doing the "I just want to be friends" routine was hilarious. Out loud, he said, "You really are pretty when you're being ridiculous. I'm off today, whaddya want to do?"

She leaned in and kissed him, her breath a wave of mint overpowering his nostrils. "Well, we got some time to kill until the coffee is done brewing."

⟡

"Do you me a favor, son, next time y'all are gonna be out all night, text me," Uncle Donnie said when Matt walked in the door that evening.

"I did message Tyler," Matt protested his innocence.

"How much free time do y'all think he had last night?"

"Yes, sir."

⟡

"I may want to stay at your place for a night next week."

"Oh? Why on earth would you want to do that?" Matt asked her hair, since Madison's face was on his chest.

"My cousin is coming to town," she replied. "He's going to be staying here since it's cheaper than a hotel."

"Don't like your cousin?"

"Well, he's family. I don't really have a lot of family left, so . . . It's not even that I don't like Justin, it's just . . . " Madison drifted off.

"Just what?"

"You'll think it's stupid."

"Maybe I will, maybe I won't, but we won't know until you say," Matt replied in his reasonable voice.

"Well, Justin just seems to be cursed," Madison replied quickly, spitting it out to get it out in the open. Matt could see her shoulders tense up as she awaited his derisive laughter.

"Cursed . . . how?"

Madison sat up and looked at him with very serious eyes that tried to tell him she wasn't kidding here. "Do y'all know what our weather report said the weather was going to be this weekend five days ago?"

"No idea, I never look at the weather report, it's not like I can do anything about it." Matt shrugged.

"Bright and sunny. Now, we're expecting buckets of rain all weekend."

"So what? Weather changes, god, especially around here. Here, if you don't like the weather go one holler over and get something totally different," Matt said and shrugged again.

"True, but I swear, this happens every SINGLE time he comes here. And according to him, it's like that wherever he goes. He decided to become a long-haul trucker to prevent flooding in the spring and avalanches in the winter," she explained, her face completely serious.

Matt froze for a second. This was a conversational trap he was not expecting. She absolutely didn't mean it as one, which just made it all the more of a trap. Around here, he could *totally* see someone getting an actual curse put on them, but he was supposed to be a Yankee and therefore not believe in that kind of thing. Before he got here, he didn't believe in that kind of thing. Things had changed, but he couldn't exactly just come out and say why.

Faced with a looming panic attack, Matt said the only sensible thing, nothing really at all. "Huh, that's weird." *HOORAY BRAIN! GOOD TIME FOR PLAYING DUMB! Ummm, brain? You were playing, right? Right? Hello?*

She couldn't find any accusations that he was calling her crazy there, or mansplaining the impossibility of that, so she snuggled back down. "Anyway, I won't really stay over your place. I don't hate him. He's family and all, he's just gotten a bit depressive over the whole thing."

"Well, you could . . . I mean, stay at my place. I stay here often enough," Matt said, deftly changing the subject.

"You sure y'all's aunt and uncle won't mind?"

"Chloe has been staying over often enough, so no, I don't think so," he said calmly to mask his own discontent. In reality, he had no earthly idea how his aunt and uncle would react. For all he knew, they could be on the phone with his mom and dad in moments, or worse, they could . . . *tell MeeMaw*!

"I might have to consider that if we go to a show up your way. I guess we'll find something for Justin to do while he's here, maybe go to Blacksburg," she replied.

"You're shitting me about the weather stuff, right?"

"If it isn't raining or, worse, snowing when he gets here, I'll buy you dinner at that rib place we keep looking at out near Tazewell. Now hush, this is the part where they find the guy in the iron maiden," Madison replied, turning back to the movie they were watching.

☽◯☾

On the day Justin was due to arrive, it was indeed raining buckets, something Matt refused to remark upon. Nobody likes an "I told you so," not when there's a fully justified one waiting for you. Since he hadn't gone all "crazy kid" on her, it would be particularly uncalled for, in his opinion. The pair of them were driving in Madison's Subaru through town, going to meet Justin where he planned to park his truck cab, since he was between carrying loads. Madison was driving, which gave Matt time to do something he rarely had the opportunity for: people watching.

"You'd think they'd go to the mall if they wanted to

hang out, especially in this weather," Matt said, thinking aloud.

"Who?" Madison asked.

"Those three girls on the corner back there. The mall would beat standing around in the rain," Matt replied, explaining what he was talking about.

Madison started laughing. "You mean the three girls with Mountain Dew bottles, right?"

"Yeah, why?"

"Oh, you poor, naive thing. Those were hookers. They carry the soda to let people know they're on duty," Madison continued, laughing.

Matt tried to process the information, but his mind kept rebelling. They had certainly NOT looked like someone you would pay for sex, quite the opposite. If threatened, he'd have paid for them to keep their clothes on. "Those . . . were prostitutes."

"Yep, yep, you see them kind of often in the summer."

"Hun, one of those girls had both the build and a face that made her look like the enforcer in that Bugs Bunny cartoon with the Mobster who says, 'Okay, Boss!' a lot. The other looked like an after school special for why meth is bad for you. All of them looked like they were dressed for shopping at Wal Mart, which is not a sexy look. People are paying money, *American money*, not crystal meth, to have sex with them?"

Madison, still laughing, replied, "Just goes to show, there's somebody for everybody in this crazy world, even if y'all gotta pay for it."

The air practically vibrated as possibly the largest truck Matt had ever seen rumbled down the opposing lane. It had chrome everywhere chrome could be stuck, along with a variety of macho looking stickers all over the window declaring things about machismo, guns, very macho guns, how great the truck was, and something obscene.

Matt shook his head. "I always wondered what possessed somebody to drive something like that."

Madison shrugged. "I feel bad for whoever he convinces to date him."

Matt gave her a shocked look. "Stereotype much?"

Madison chuckled. "Name me another reason for paying that much for gas every week if y'all ain't using it for work or for off-roading, and noting again that thing is cleaner than a hospital."

"Well, but it could . . . "

"I've just assumed they gave you a lifetime supply of the male enhancement pill of your choice when you put down the down payment. Come on down for our low, low, prices that will make up for something else being short, short, short!" Madison said and giggled.

They pulled into the parking lot of the local Wal Mart, and as expected, towards the very back of the lot, a tractor-trailer cab sat parked and dark.

"So, why's he up to visit? I mean, family and all, but any special reason?" Matt asked as they were pulling into the parking lot and heading towards the waiting vehicle.

"He's waiting for a load in Wytheville. Seems there's a tropical storm in Florida, and they always give the treacherous loads to Justin now. He's become a total expert in driving in them." She shrugged.

"What if it only seems like he's always in the rain because they always send him where it is?" Matt applied logic to the situation hopefully.

"Nope, wish it were true, but that's the cart before the horse. He became a long hall trucker after he and his momma had to move from next to the Tug when he almost flooded the place. They experimented with it for a while. Sent him away to visit some distant relatives up North and then a friend of his in North Carolina. Both times, clear skies for weeks while he was gone, day he came back, pissing rain. Rained everywhere he went. Last time he stayed at the old family home, it was coming in the basement. It ain't come within a foot of the bank since he's been driving. His momma lives in town now, but she sold the place to a friend cheap, and she still talks to who she sold it to," Madison explained.

"I'd say I don't believe it, but . . . "

"Buuutttttt," she goaded him.

"West Virginia doesn't seem to operate like back home, it's a bit weirder." He shrugged.

"Honey, y'all ain't got no idea." She snorted at the notion, incorrectly it turned out. Matt had a very good idea indeed.

It could have been the rain, but the man who was supposed to be around Matt's age that got out of the truck cab looked crushed and old, defeated and beaten down, and now he had been washed past that through to the still, calm waters on the other side of indifference. His bearing and facial expression were like the dog in the fire cartoon saying, "This is fine." It was almost amazing to Matt that he was still alive. A week of rain and Matt found himself looking for razorblades longingly. If what Madison had said was correct, that was her cousin's entire life. Like living in Seattle without the really good coffee and music scene to soften the blow some.

Justin gave Madison a hug before turning to stare Matt up and down for a second. He simply nodded his head and said, "Hey, how y'all?" Somehow, he made even that simple phrase sound world beaten and forlorn.

Staring at Madison's disconsolate cousin as he plodded along to the car, Matt's eyes had to squint, and they went unfocused for just a moment as he tried to clear water out of them. Automatically, without him asking whatsoever, the other sight that he had kicked in and he could see the problem right there in front of him. There, bobbing along behind Justin, was something that almost looked like a cloud. Grey and nebulous, it trailed right behind the man as he sulked along. Matt was pretty sure that it was something far worse than a cloud! Clouds don't usually have sinister-looking eye slots, for one thing, so he considered that a clue. Why Matt knew they were eyes, he couldn't really say, but he was absolutely sure that it was something similar to what he'd pulled out of the barroom pugilist before the guy could kill Tyler. The monster was lashed to Madison's cousin by lightly glowing threads around his limbs and around his waist! Holy crap! It wasn't "like he was cursed," the poor guy really was cursed!

Of course, it left Matt wondering what in the hell he could do about it. Like, on different levels. There was the *he wasn't sure how to break the threads holding it to Justin* level, for starters. Then there was the *did he really want his new girlfriend to see him doing something else that was weird and miraculous* other level. Not to mention there was the *MeeMaw might get mad if she hears about me doing magic without her knowing* level, which was where the real fear hid. This problem had numerous sub-basements, and it needed an *I don't feel like taking the stairs* elevator of a solution. He was going to need to table this one until he could think it through, or just ask MeeMaw, but probably just think it through. She might tell him not to do anything, which seemed downright mean. The guy looked like he could really use a break.

Justin barely talked as they drove, and Madison didn't seem inclined to press him. Matt had no idea what, if anything, he should be adding to the situation. He wasn't really a take-the-lead-in-a-conversation sort of guy. Not to mention, if Justin didn't want to talk to his own cousin after who knew how long on the road, he sure as hell didn't have anything to say to her boyfriend.

Justin finally broke the uncomfortable silence to say quietly, "Mind dropping me off at Momma's? I can walk to yer place from thar."

"Sure, no problem," Madison replied evenly.

☾◯☽

"Well, hi! How are you?" Matt said as he slid into the front seat while Justin was vanishing inside another apartment building.

"Oh, I'm fine, why?" Madison replied, instantly seeming like his girlfriend again, not that silent person he'd just been sitting in the vehicle with for the last ten minutes.

"I'm not used to you being quiet that long. If you hadn't been driving, I would have checked for a pulse."

"Oh, sorry. Justin just don't talk much, and I don't like to push him about it. It's more for his benefit than anything." She shrugged and then smiled at Matt. "Anyway . . . enough about my depressing cousin, we have an hour or so to kill. Anything in particular y'all want to do with that time?"

"I can think of one thing, but there's just a small problem."

She looked surprised and asked, "What's that?"

"It has yet to take me a whole hour."

☾◯☽

Justin was . . . well, you couldn't say he was objectionable in any way. Quite the opposite. He was quiet, he cleaned up after himself, he understood that when her door was closed, Madison and Matt were playing House or Doctor or The Postman Always Rings Twice. He was the perfect house guest. Justin was also depressing, indefinably so, but he was nonetheless. He was quiet and withdrawn, but that wasn't what made being around him make you long for Zoloft by the fistful. It was more that he was the living embodiment of a sad, resigned sigh on a boring Sunday afternoon when you were a kid and all of your friends had to go out with their parents and couldn't play.

It was getting to Matt, and the fact that he couldn't really complain because there was nothing you could specifically point to to complain about made it worse. Not to mention they had made plans to go hiking in the gorge on Saturday before Justin had come. With a normal guest, it wouldn't matter; but with Justin's undeniable, permanent rain cloud, it would be miserable to even try the hike. It would probably be deadly too; parts of the gorge certainly did not play around with the unprepared hiker. Well, it did, but more in the same manner a cat plays with a mouse as it's killing it.

By Friday, Matt had had enough. It had become an irritant under his skin, something you will do anything to fix or get rid of, even if you have no idea what you're doing. This was a magical, otherworldly rash. This had become the sort of impetus that down through the ages has made men everywhere think, *How hard could plumbing even be?* Matt began to let himself look at the nebulous monster strapped to Justin more and more often with every waking hour. More importantly, he found himself studying the strands that bound the thing to Madison's cousin. Maybe he could just snap them, he began to consider after a while. He'd been able to pull that whatever-the-hell-it-was out of the goon that was pounding Tyler, right? As far as he could figure, the only reason the weather was following Justin was because of the thing strapped to him. Maybe he could just break the bonds and the thing would float off on its merry way, the same way the monster had run off after he had freed it from King Kong Bundy at that show.

The two of them were watching TV. Matt had come over after work to wait for Madison, who was still working, so it was just him and Justin for a little while. This actually worked better; once Madison got home, he would be expected to snuggle with her. There'd be almost no way to hide what he was up to. With it being just him and Justin, it was fine if he just hovered behind the couch a bit with his arms resting on its brown plaid back, which was exactly what he was doing. He continued to study the strands, which he had decided quite a while back were gossamer thin and should snap easily. At this point, he was steeling himself up to actually trying to do it. Sort of like jumping into a pool on a hot day, but with more magic and less water involved. (We are willing to concede that analogy might need a bit of work.)

Finally, trying to control his breathing so as to not draw attention to himself, Matt reached out carefully with both hands and grasped one of the strands. There was a tingle to it; there was definitely power there holding this magical creature to Justin, yet it wasn't what he'd expected. Here was this creature from somewhere else, powerful enough to affect the weather, and he was touching what bound it. Yet, it only tingled. Matt gave a slight inhalation of air, summoned up all of his strength, magical and muscle, and tugged with both hands, trying to snap it.

He almost succeeded in knocking himself over when it just fell apart easily!

Hearing him stumble, Justin whirled his head towards Matt. "Y'all all right?"

Matt blurted out with shock, "Yeah! I mean yeah, I was just trying to scratch my leg and I slipped!"

Justin looked at him for a long moment suspiciously, spurred by wondering what kind of itch could knock you back like that. But seeing nothing that looked out of the ordinary, he just shrugged and turned back to the TV. "Well, all right then."

Matt considered for a moment that Justin's friends growing up, assuming he had some, must have been boring as heck. If the tables were turned, Matt would be looking everywhere for any kind of instrument of a prank about to be played on him after something like that. Anybody behind you who had the expression on their face that Matt had on his had to have at *least* concealed a water balloon on their person. What could be considered worse didn't even bear thinking about. It had taken Matt a *month* to get the nail polish off of the back of his neck.

To cover his tracks, he went into the kitchen like he was fussing over something in the fridge before coming back to watch over Justin's shoulders. Justin was more or less oblivious to what was going on behind him. Matt looked at the ghostly thing tied to Madison's cousin, and oddly, he thought he could see a change in the facial expression of the shape of the nebulous creature. It was crazy, but he thought he could see hope there!

It took multiple passes, but Matt had finally managed, between pretending to busy himself in the kitchen and rushing back, to snap all but the last strand. He had gotten his hands on it and was just beginning to pull when the door burst open, framing Madison, who was staring straight at him. The surprise made Matt jolt, which completed his task but made him look incredibly weird standing there with his hands in fists spreading out waist high.

He ignored the ghostly "thank you" that floated away from him.

"Oh hey!" he spluttered. "You're home early."

Madison stared at him wide-eyed for a second, almost as if she'd seen a ghost, which struck Matt as odd. Catching your boyfriend not doing anything but standing there looking stupid should be perfectly normal for a girlfriend. At least she hadn't come home to find him in her underwear, she should count herself lucky. Finally, she recovered and smiled.

"Jan covered so I could come back to my boys. How'd it go today?"

Matt decided he was going to take the smile on face value and said, "Well, TV, so not exactly excitement city."

He couldn't be sure, but he could have sworn her eyes narrowed for just a moment as she headed to the kitchen with a bag of groceries she was carrying.

The rest of the evening was fine. They just hung out watching movies, like normal. Something that should have been normal, but hadn't been lately, also happened. Matt found himself glancing out the window a few times and was pleased to note that the storm clouds seemed to be moving away. It had been a massive rainstorm, so the odds that it was just going to instantly become sunny were slim to nil. Still, it seemed like Justin's perma-storm had finally found other places to be and was anxious to get there.

Around eleven, Justin was snoring in his chair when they decided to tiptoe off to bed and stream a movie from Madison's desktop. She opened up the screen and ran through a few streaming services before finally putting something on. Just as Matt was settling in on the bed, she turned back to him, her face serious.

"What in the hell was that?"

"What in the hell was what?" Matt demanded, bewildered by the sudden change.

"When I walked in tonight, y'all were doing something to Justin!"

"You saw that?" Matt said, so shocked to find anyone could see it that, like an idiot, he out and out confessed.

"Yeah, and it was the same that night at the bar. What did y'all do? This is twice now you cut some big cloud from someone."

"It's . . . " Matt threw up his hands and leaned back on the bed's headrest. "It's just something I can do. I'm not very good, and I don't always know what I'm doing . . . Look, you were the one who wanted me to believe that there was weird stuff in these mountains, why do you think I didn't argue?"

Madison's face looked calmer when she sat down on the bed. "Well, what did y'all do?"

"Let me put it this way. We'll probably stay dry if we all want to go up to the gorge tomorrow. I predict sun, and I would consider Justin un-cursed," he said.

"Oh, so a "powers for good" sort of thing. Well, all right then," Madison replied with a ghost of a smile on her lips as she curled up next to him on the bed.

A few moments later, something that had been nagging Matt's subconscious was finally able to make itself heard. "You seem to be taking this pretty well, and also, you were able to see that?"

"Uh-huh," she replied, her voice soft as she was already getting sleepy.

"Ummm, how do you feel about meeting my MeeMaw? I'm beginning to think you ought to."

CHAPTER 10

"My feeling about in-laws was that they were outlaws."

—Malcolm X

---◆---

THE NEXT DAY dawned bright and sunny. By the time Matt was awake enough to toddle out to get himself breakfast, poor Justin almost looked hunted and panicked. If Madison was right, and he saw no reason to think that she hadn't been, it had been years since Justin had seen the sun in its full, shining glory. It would be like living your life in a cave and suddenly finding the entrance to the surface. But still, Matt wasn't particularly worried. If Justin had been able to get used to it raining everywhere he went, he could learn to deal with normal, boring, unpredictable weather just like everyone else.

It also meant that their trip to go hiking in the gorge could go off as scheduled, even if Justin had to wear sunglasses. So that was a positive.

☽☉☾

The gravel snapped and popped as the Xterra came to a halt in front of the farmhouse the next day.

"Probably best we came up to visit anyway, they'll start to wonder if I've eloped. Well, except for Tyler; the bastard almost got us killed on *Fallout* last night, so he'd know different," Matt said, trying to keep it light.

Even without all the magic weirdness, on the face of it, the situation still called for a light touch. She was still about to meet his family down here—except, of course, for Tyler— so it was kind of a big thing. Worse, Madison would be meeting the family matriarch, which had to make her nervous—it made him nervous and he would hate to think she was getting off light here.

"Tyler never brought me up here. Wow! This is a really nice place. Been in y'all's family for long?" Madison asked.

"I guess since before it was even West Virginia," he replied, inwardly happy that she was taking this well.

She was quiet for a moment before saying with a noticeable pain in her voice, "Our family just moved off our land a few years back. I wish we still had it."

Matt didn't know what to say. He was spared having to think of something when the front door banged open to emit Tyler, who came straight for the vehicle. Matt got out quickly and called out, "What's up with you? Didn't expect a meet and greet."

"Well, I thought I'd warn you. The folks will be happy to meet Maddie in a bit, but you're supposed to go talk to MeeMaw right now, ASAP," Tyler warned.

"Oh shit!"

"Yep, that is the normal response when the old lady demands you get yer ass out there. I'd be going if I was you, don't want to give her any more time to stew."

Matt's brain froze, and he started walking to his grandmother's house. It would have made more sense to drive down the road a bit, but he was already out of the car and his normal, logical brain had just locked up and went in to shut down, leaving full-blown panic brain in control of operations. Before they'd made it even halfway down the lane, he could see MeeMaw coming out on the front porch.

Crap! His panicked, animal brain started looking for

an escape route before his logical, reasonable brain woke up and stepped in to inform him that there was nowhere to run to. He lived here; it wasn't like he could avoid her for long, at least without hiding in the woods like a hermit. Matt had no idea how to herm. He'd be dead within minutes, and even then, he had to consider for just a moment if it might not be preferable. He wasn't even sure what he was about to get yelled at for, but there was no getting around it now. (Resignation to our fate, even when we have no idea what we've done, we've all been there.)

Madison must have picked up on his worry. "Are we in some kind of trouble or something?" she asked.

"I don't know why we would be, but MeeMaw is the boss around here, and I'm not totally stupid, despite some of the looks she gives me," Matt replied, moving faster.

When they got closer, MeeMaw peered at them intently for a moment. "Well, I only asked for Matt, but I wouldn't mind meeting y'all too." She squinted for a moment at Madison and tilted her head before nodding and saying, "Yer an Armstead, ain't ya?"

"Yes, ma'am," Madison replied with flustered formality.

"I'm powerful sorry what happened a while back. Well, come on in, like I said, wouldn't mind talking to y'all either after I'm done with him." With that, the old woman turned around and headed back into her home.

"Well," Matt said, "I don't think you're in any kind of trouble, but I'm pretty sure I'm fucked."

When they got inside, MeeMaw was standing, waiting. Her toe was tapping a steady rhythm and her arms crossed in front of her. Matt wasn't a rocket scientist as far as reading body language and didn't need it here either. He figured that his earlier assessment of the situation had been spot on. MeeMaw's grim countenance broke into a brief smile, which she directed at Madison. "Look, dear, I know you know what I am, what with your Ma and

MeeMaw. Well, he's one of them too. I want to talk to him 'bout what he's been up to that I felt all the way up here."

"What?!" Madison and Matt said in unison.

"Oh dear, young people just don't talk any more. Well, we'll get it sorted in a bit. Why don't you go out to the living room and watch some TV? I'll bring out some milk and cookies in just a moment," MeeMaw said, still smiling, but with a brittle quality to it that spoke volumes about how she was just managing to maintain pleasant, and only for Madison's benefit.

"I don't know what the big deal is, I just broke a curse is all," Matt protested, showing the survival instincts of a moth at Burning Man.

MeeMaw's jaw visibly clenched before she sighed, "Bless your heart, that's what we need to talk about."

"TV and milk and cookies you say? Good luck, Hun'!" Madison replied quickly before leaving for the living room. She was mountain born and bred and knew immediately that when a grandmother is calling her very own grandson an idiot this soon after getting home, it was time to find another room. (The book has noted previously what "bless your heart" means, and it takes a lot out of a woman to just outright say about her grandson, "You were dropped on your head as a toddler" like that.)

They could hear the TV turn on from where they were standing, staring at each other. MeeMaw's face softened only slightly, but it still looked stern when she said, "I think you might have done better there with that girl than you realize, my boy. But we ain't here for my opinion of your lady friend. I felt it up here, so what in the hell did you do with magic, and don't sass me by saying 'Nothing'. I still got the wooden spoon I used to keep your daddy in line."

"What? I just broke a curse, like I said!" Matt fumed. He was frustrated. He'd done something good, all on his own, and now he was getting yelled at!

Something in MeeMaw finally broke a little bit, but

maybe not totally. "I know y'all meant well, ain't in yer nature to mean different, but . . . But sometimes those curses, when y'all let them go loose in the world, they still got power here. They can still do things, and sometimes bad things!" She let out a gusting sigh. "Maybe y'all should tell me what kind of curse and how you done broke it then."

"Umm . . . Madison's cousin, wherever he went, the weather was always terrible. I could see what it was, it reminded me of the thing that was in the guy that was pummeling Tyler. So, I just snapped the strands that were tying it in place. I swear that was all I did."

"Simple as that, huh? Y'all just reached out and snapped them strands?"

"Well yeah, it wasn't that hard." Matt shrugged.

MeeMaw's eyebrow shot up at that a bit, and then she sighed yet again, which either meant high-level exasperation or she had sprung a leak. "All right, if that old biddy is gonna play with demons and the like, I guess I'm gonna have to teach y'all to recognize them. There's different ones. In this particular case, other than making her sore angry, it most likely won't hurt anything much. Those things drift along with the winds and work their mischief wherever they blow, almost like normal weather, really. But who knows what y'all might take it into your fool head to set free next time."

"MeeMaw, one other thing I should probably mention," Matt said tentatively before taking a breath and just spitting it out. "Madison could see it when I did it! Both times."

MeeMaw didn't even blink at that. "Bein' from these parts, that surprises me a lot less than y'all, I'd wager. Guess I'm going to have to have a bit of a talk with her as well." She threw up her hands and called out theatrically, "Oh, Curtis, where did I go wrong to deserve this?"

Matt's Pa Pa materialized beside her. "Now, Lou May, I don't think it's gone so far wrong at all yet," he said, smiling calmly.

MeeMaw jumped, clutching her hand to her chest for a moment. After she'd had a moment to compose herself, she muttered darkly, "Bless your heart, Curtis, you never could figure out when a question was rhetorical."

☽◯☾

MeeMaw brought in some milk and cookies as promised and turned off the TV. Madison was gnawing at a Milano with trepidation as MeeMaw regarded her.
She gave Madison a long once over before saying, "I'm awful sorry for what happened to your Ma, let me start by saying that."

Matt could see Madison's face tighten when she heard that.

MeeMaw continued, "Your Ma ever tell you much about the gift?"

Madison looked down for a moment and replied, "No, I don't think she wanted it herself, really. She tried not to have much to do with it for most of my childhood. It wasn't until towards the end she ever did much at all, and even then, I don't think it was 'cause she wanted to, more that she felt she had to."

"No, no, she probably didn't want to at that. I'm gonna guess it probably wasn't until your MeeMaw, rest her soul, had passed away, was it?"

"Right about then, yeah, I guess," Madison's eyes narrowed a little.

Matt, on the other hand, was watching this whole conversation with shock. He had barely gotten his head around the idea that he had any powers along these lines, or that there were any powers of any kind for that matter, and here it was that his girlfriend came from witch blood too? Was the whole state hiding some grand witch conspiracy like in the *Weekly World News* or something on Infowars? It was the kind of coincidence that made him question whatever higher power was writing the narrative of his life (As that higher power, the narrative would like to apologize for that)!

"Y'all come from the hills past Cucumber, right?" MeeMaw asked (yes, there IS a Cucumber, West Virginia, and NO, we did not make that up. They have a teeny small post office. We've been there, unlike some people that we could name who doubt the veracity of books).

"Yeah, but I ain't been out there much since MeeMaw passed on. My Ma was trying to live in Welch when the fire happened. She used to travel out there to take care of MeeMaw's place, but I don't remember it all that well," Madison replied.

"Well, I don't like to think the worst of people, it ain't nice, but I'm beginning to suspect that your Ma's death t'weren't no accident," Matt's grandmother said, putting her hand softly over Madison's.

"I know damned well it wasn't!" Madison hotly replied suddenly. "I know it was that summbitch Billy Baldwin! He wanted my MeeMaw's land, and Ma wouldn't sell. Suddenly the Welch house just got a short in the wires, huh?"

"Well, that kind of confirms what I been thinking, dear. But it wasn't Billy alone, I'd wager. If you'd ever met him, you'd know he ain't near smart enough to do somethin' like that and get away with it as well. His own grandmother, Beatrice, had some hand in it, I'd almost promise y'all." Matt's grandmother nodded, as if satisfied with Madison's response.

"Well anyway, I've been more or less done with the county and all that mountain folk talk since then. Took some classes at Bluefield State, got a job, got a place, moved on." Madison shrugged as if that statement put some finality to the whole topic.

"Well, not quite. Nobody ever totally moves on, do they? Y'all been out to yer family plot in county? I know y'all have one," MeeMaw said quietly.

Madison's face blanched a bit at that. "No, why should I?"

MeeMaw made a little tsk noise. "Let me ask you something else, then, how well do you like our young lad Matt?"

Matt was almost amused to see Madison's face go from white as a ghost to red in an instant. She did that shy shrug of the shoulders that girls do. "I don't know, quite a bit, I guess; I mean, if I'm meeting his family and all."

"So, we've settled that then, and y'all can see what he does, and you're still here?"

"What do you mean?" Madison's eyes narrowed.

(You will note here that Matt has not said anything for a while. That is because Matt is not an idiot, no matter that he acts like one sometimes. When two women want to "have a talk" about something, almost any interjection a male of the species could come up with would be the wrong one. In the case of your Grandmother and your Girlfriend, the odds are so astronomically against you not saying anything that would anger either party that even the sleaziest, most low-down odds maker outside of Vegas in a strip mall would not take your bet out of pity.)

"I know why y'all don't go to that graveyard and why y'all can see what he does. Whether y'all like it or not, girl, you're the one who done got the gift in your family. Just a question now of whether or not y'all want to learn how to use it any," MeeMaw replied with a soft smile on her face.

"I don't know . . . I . . . "

"Well, y'all should at least take a visit to the family plot; I know your family misses ya."

"I don't know. It's just that it's all too . . . "

"Tell you what, let me bring in an expert on the topic," MeeMaw cut her off, before yelling, "CURTIS! COULD Y'ALL COME IN HERE FOR A MOMENT!"

Pa Pa was there in an instant. "Good lord, woman, y'all ain't got to shout. I'm dead, not deaf!" Seeing Madison's gaping, shocked expression, he softened his face. "Pleased to finally make your acquaintance, miss. Our Matt thinks quite highly of y'all."

Madison whirled to gape at Matt.

Matt had the decency to look contrite. "Look, I was going to tell you at some point . . . but that's a hard thing to just come out and blurt out, don't you think? I like you so much and didn't want to screw it by telling you I have weird mountain backcountry witch powers I don't even understand. I figured I could work you into it, 'Hey look at this neat trick I can do, and by the way, after you meet my live ones, how 'bout I introduce you to my dead relatives!'"

Madison looked for a second like she was going to yell at him, but then she took a deep, shuddering breath. "I know y'all mean well, but this is all a bit much. No, no, I take that back, this is all a LOT much."

Pa Pa smiled kindly and said, "I know it is, girl. I think Lou May just wanted you to see fer yerself, so you'd understand some. Y'all's family is there tied to that land, that's where their heart was and where their spirit lives on. They miss you, I'm sure enough of that. If you visit to say hello, I'm sure they won't mind the absence, and who knows what y'all might learn from them."

"Like I ever learn anything from Mungo," Matt muttered.

"Did Ah hear someain caa mah nam?" came a voice from the kitchen.

"Why don't y'all . . . " MeeMaw said to Matt's Grandfather.

"Yeah, why don't I get him back to the plot right now," Pa Pa replied, moving quickly.

Turning back to look at them, MeeMaw clapped her hands together. "Well, I'm sure you two have lots to talk about. You won't get a chance at the main house; lord knows Donnie and Debbie will take up all your time once y'all are up there. I think I got some gardening that needs tending to, so why don't I leave the both of y'all be for a spell?"

"Thank you, MeeMaw," Matt said gratefully.

Once they were alone, for lack of anything better to say, Matt just said, "So."

"So," agreed Madison.

"You know, if you want to just ignore this . . . I mean, I'm learning and all, but I never promised I'd ever even do this for good and always. I mean, you don't have to learn anything if you don't want. I just . . . I just don't want you to break up with me over this," he admitted lamely, his head down.

Madison laughed at that for a moment before her face turned slightly more serious. "Y'all kidding? I'm from here. If I refused to date everyone who might have a little bit of witch blood, or in your case, a lot, I'd be damned lonely. It's like Cherokee. Everyone claims they got some in them here. Well, if y'all get 'em drunk enough, everyone claims they got a bit of witch in them too, or they know someone who's got a lot of it. Some girls would even consider you a catch *because of* it, not in spite of it. No, my problem right now is I don't know what it is that I'm going to do about myself."

"How do you mean?" he asked, sitting down on the couch next to her and slipping his hand into hers.

"I mean . . . I guess I've been running away from who my Ma and my MeeMaw really were 'cause of how it all ended. I'm starting to wonder if that's fair to them, or their memory. Here's your MeeMaw offering to help with that . . . I don't know. I want to say yes, but I'm afraid to," she replied, staring straight ahead.

Matt reached up and brushed a tear that had formed in her eye while she was talking. "Well whatever you decide, just please keep sleeping next to me. I get cold otherwise."

Madison started to laugh. "I don't know whether to hit y'all or thank you for trying to cheer me up."

"How 'bout kiss me to say thank you? And hit Tyler later if he's available?"

"That just might work."

However Matt might have responded to that was interrupted when something caught his interest out of the window over Madison's shoulder. She saw him peering intently at something other than her and was forced to ask, "What in the hell are y'all looking at?"

"Somebody coming up the drive . . . it looks like Mrs. Goins, but why in the hell is that old biddy coming up the drive hell-bent for leather?" Matt could see his MeeMaw walking to the front of the house, her gardening tools in her hand as she went out to meet the woman.

The local woman got out of her car and practically ran up to Matt's MeeMaw. She talked frantically at his grandmother, whose facial expression neither of them could see (Mrs. Goins, who they could see, was demonstrating the difference between *talking at* and *talking to* quite admirably and with lots of hand gestures). Matt could see MeeMaw nod a few times at her, but that was the extent of her reaction. He could dully hear their voices, mainly Mrs. Goins, but the windows were just soundproofed enough that the words were unintelligible to them sitting inside. He was just about to see if his grandmother needed him for anything—a tranquilizer gun for starters, from the looks of things—when MeeMaw turned around and started walking towards the front door with Mrs. Goins hot on her heels.

The door banged open; MeeMaw didn't even break stride. "Matt, umm, Madison? Could I talk to y'all out in the kitchen? Joyce Anne, why don't y'all take a seat. I'll brew up some tea while I'm talking to the youngsters, okay?"

Mrs. Goins nodded gratefully, and Madison and Matt got up to complete the "talk to MeeMaw" changing of the guard.

The Wild Witches of West Bygod

As soon as they were in the kitchen, Matt began, "MeeMaw what's this about that you need to talk to us?"

His grandmother carefully put a couple of cups of water in the microwave and said, "Well, if I was to guess . . . and seein' how it's me doing the guessing, we got us a similar situation to what you ran into with Tyler. Couple of men showed up at their property, said they wanted to talk to her husband 'bout buying up the mineral rights. Well, Jimmy ain't the brightest bulb out there, but he knows what side his bread's buttered on, and he knows we have final say on that. He told them to get the hell offin his land. They said they could wait until he was ready to talk, and they were very good at waitin', and went back to their car at the end of the Goins's drive and just stood there. Jimmy took out his shotgun and shot over their heads a couple of times, figurin' that'd scare anyone off. Joyce Anne swears up, down, and sideways they didn't even blink. She says they were still standing there by the road when she come here down the back lane."

Matt let out a long whistle. "So you think that's like the same thing I pulled out of the guy who pasted Tyler?"

"Honey, now think for a moment. What kind of sane man, working for the mine companies or not, don't even blink when a shotgun gets fired at 'em?"

"Okay, I can probably see that," Matt replied sheepishly.

"I'm going to need y'all to drive me to see for ourselves what's goin' on out thar'. Y'all got some learning you need to do today, my young man. Of course, the next question is to you, young miss." MeeMaw turned immediately to look sharply at Madison.

"Me?"

"Yes, you. This is all coming very fast, I know. But if you want, y'all can come along and you can watch me teach my grandson how to not do anything stupid with what power he has. Or if you want instead, I figure Joyce Anne won't mind the company while she waits here," she said quickly.

Matt wanted to let the "not do anything stupid" thing go as just nerves.

Madison's face became a riot of emotions. This really was all coming too fast for her. She had spent years trying and had almost convinced herself that in the really real world, there was no such thing as "Granny Witches" and her Ma and MeeMaw had just picked the wrong fight with the wrong people. Yet at the same time, she had seen what Matt could do with her own eyes, and whatever other sight beyond 20/20 she had going for herself was getting harder to deny. With this context, it was hard to write that off as a trick of the light. It was a question being put to her again: was she denying her own birthright and her own heritage by pretending it just didn't exist, or was she protecting her sanity by avoiding all this? Not to mention, if she bailed on the whole thing right now, how many other gainfully employed, decent looking, nice guys was she really going to even find out here? Matt was her buddy and her boyfriend, like, both at the same time, and that wasn't easy to come by.

"Does whichever ghost that made those horrible noises in the kitchen a little while ago have to come?" she said at last.

"No, dear, we can leave Mungo at home. Actually, it would probably be better if we did, he's not exactly good at handling things with tact. And Jimmy is waving the gun about, so maybe a little bit of tact is in order here," MeeMaw said.

"He'd still be here then?"

"Yes, dear."

"So, are we taking Matt's SUV, or do y'all want to drive?"

"We can take the SUV. This is probably for the best, dear. Joyce Anne is a sweet woman and all, but she can be a horribly boring old gossip if she gets y'all alone."

Matt let out an audible sigh of relief. As MeeMaw smiled and went back to working on the tea, he leaned over and whispered in Madison's ear, "So does this mean I'm not sleeping alone tonight?"

She whispered back with a smirk, "Well, I suppose it depends on how y'all do out there today. A girl does like to be impressed by how big and strong and magical her man is, after all."

Chapter 11

"He who would learn to fly one day must first learn to stand and walk and run and climb and dance; one cannot fly into flying. Unless of course, one has a plane, in which case going straight into learning to fly would probably be for the best."
—Frankie "The Neetch" Nietzsche

———— ◆ ————

BILL WAS SWEATING like a stuck pig in the office today. In his mind, he felt like he was already above this punch-the-clock crap, and that meant he was definitely above being in this particular office. He was going to be a senator, god damn it; he shouldn't be having to come out here to these damned mine shacks to go over the paperwork anymore. It couldn't be helped, as far as he could see, no matter how hard he tried to find a way out of it. If you wanted the best, the hardest workers, that meant sometimes you had to deal with the fact that their brains were a bit slow. Because maybe their brains weren't all there. That meant that if you wanted the paperwork to shine like a diamond in a goat's ass, you had to come out here and go over it your own self. What he needed was a paper pusher he trusted enough with the secret to his success. The problem there was that he didn't trust anyone at all with that. He barely trusted himself with *that*.

If he knew one damned person he trusted enough with everything he knew about who was working in this damned hole in the ground, his ass could be inside a real office, sucking up real air conditioning today. Instead, it was stuck out here, with crap air conditioning that barely worked, sitting on an uncomfortable seat and going over numbers and trying to figure out how to fudge them convincingly. Bill wasn't good with numbers, but he'd learned to get good enough to pretty them up for OSHA and MSHA. Man wanted to make real money in this business, he knew that the numbers had to look right and survive more than a casual prodding. Profit ain't profit if y'all are getting fined.

He couldn't let it be known that the reason his payroll was so low was that almost everyone on it at this mine was pulling double and triple shifts but getting paid like it was all single shifts being done by red hats. The truth of it was that almost everyone employed here anymore were all working the absolute maximum a human body could work before it broke and, most importantly, that they were doing it without pulling overtime and at starting salary. It was a lot of work finding that many fake names and SSIs to report to the government, but he'd been able to. Maybe one day, those men out there would be free to do something else but work in the mine, and maybe they'd get to spend the sizable amount of wages they'd been racking up on the books, even without the overtime they weren't getting. It'd come as a pleasant surprise to them. Bill figured when they finally got through all the confusion of the lost time and thought to check their bank accounts, maybe that money would buy them some peace of mind about the whole thing.

Maw Maw had made the men like this for him, which was why he wasn't saying anything. She had gotten a lot of the working types around here for him, and he knew to not ask too many questions, just cut checks for the amount he was telling the government they were paying them and direct deposit it. They didn't give a good god damn about time off, or much of anything else, the perfect employees.

You told them what to do, you showed them how to do it, and they damned well did it until the body just couldn't take no more of doing it. They didn't complain, they didn't unionize, they didn't talk to no damned press, not a word. They didn't say much of anything at all unless you asked them a direct question. It was spooky; he'd briefly met some of these same men working these same mines before Maw Maw had done something to them somehow, and they hadn't been like that then. He might like the money better, but he certainly didn't like being around them better.

Bill was starting to get nervous. He'd sent two of those goons off to go shake up those damned Goins people hours ago. Maw Maw had warned him off doing anything to the Hawleys for now, she'd flat out forbade it after whatever had happened before that made her so all-fired mad. She said she'd tell him what to do and when, as far as putting pressure on. So, if he couldn't touch the Hawleys, the Goins were the next best thing to putting a hole right down the middle of that whole community. Get the Goins land, you could start picking off the ones around the edges. Make 'em feel isolated and alone, offer good money, put on the pressure, and they'd sell eventually, well, usually, at any rate. Some people were just accident-prone, Bill supposed, even if they didn't know it yet.

He told those idiots to make an offer. If the old man turned it down, to hit him around a little bit if they had to, but not to come back until they did. The only other thing he had said was to not do anything that would get themselves hurt in any way. Maw Maw got awful bent at him when he had to ask her for another of these zombies because he'd broken one; no way did he want to deal with that on top of everything else he had on his plate right now.

"Pull over here!" MeeMaw said suddenly.

"But why? We aren't there yet, are we?" Matt protested, pulling over in a wide spot you got on these one-lane country roads in case two cars tried to use it at the same time.

"Well if those goons of Baldwin's is just a-sittin' at the end of the drive, how welcoming do y'all think they'd be to us, for starters! Second off, I don't want 'em to see us coming. It's easier if they don't know to fight it," MeeMaw replied in exasperation. The old woman got out of the SUV, shutting the door quietly. "Don't hurry up and come along then, y'all might learn something."

Matt sat there quietly for just a moment. "I think my grandmother just dissed me."

Madison replied while getting out, "I think y'all can forget about thinking about it, Hun, she definitely dissed you. Y'all got totally old person dissed, sweetie."

Matt sighed and got out as quietly as he could. He caught himself, but only just, from hitting the keyless to trigger the alarm. He had it in his hand and everything. Nothing says "stealth" like the alarm chirping away to tell you it's armed. Worse, Madison saw it and smirked as they both hurried to catch up with MeeMaw, who had already moved a good distance down the road from the vehicle.

They had parked in one of the wooded patches of the road, with the road itself continuing up a steep incline. Matt was embarrassed to find himself panting a bit as they went; worse, his grandmother didn't even appear to be breathing particularly hard as she marched determinedly up the hill. Matt almost gasped with relief when she held up her hand, signaling that they should stop where they were.

She pointed to Matt and waved him forward to join her, standing on the wide gravel berm. As soon as he was close, she whispered, "See the bright spot ahead, that's the Goins land. If'n yer eyes are good enough, y'all can see the vehicle them thugs come in and them as well standing around like real ugly lawn ornaments."

Matt squinted a bit, his eyes narrowing automatically. He felt foolish a moment later when he found that he didn't have to and decided his grandmother had a poor opinion of his eyesight. It was understandable since many parents and grandparents assume their progeny must be blind, as evidenced by the fact that they can never seem to see a mess around the house, no matter how large and disgusting. MeeMaw, having raised two sons, also probably assumed that none of her offspring could smell either. Even without squinting, and even with bad eyesight, the vehicle of the intruders would have been hard to miss. It was an enormous black SUV, the kind you usually see driving near the President's limo when he came to a city to snarl traffic. The men it had been carrying around would have been equally hard to miss. Both of them had to be at least 6'5", 280 pounds, easy. Men who missed their calling in life as NFL offensive linemen aren't exactly easy to miss, even with the glare from the open sky up ahead and congenital male offspring vision disease.

"Well, what are we going to do about them?" Matt asked.

"Might as well use this as a time to teach, it's as good as any other. That way, if y'all screw it up, I'm right here to fix it," MeeMaw replied, showing the kind of confidence in him that Matt had come to expect the world to offer. She turned to Madison, who had already settled into the role of passive observer. "If you don't mind, young lady, y'all can just watch this time. The boy has already started with messing with things he shouldn't; he needs to learn how to do it right 'for he hurts someone. But maybe y'all can just watch and see how you feel about it after, all right?"

"Sounds like a fine idea to me, ma'am. I wouldn't even know where to begin."

Matt found himself almost shocked by Madison's quick

acquiescence and sudden burst of demure manners, but he was willing to concede for a little old lady, MeeMaw could intimidate with the best of them.

"Now, sweetie," MeeMaw suddenly broke out her best grandmother 'who's my little trooper?' voice, "remember how y'all saw those threads holding that thing to your Madison's cousin?"

This automatically worried Matt. That was the voice she used when she assumed he was an idiot child but was obliged to let him try anyway. Like when he had been down for a visit and asked where the bathroom was for the first time

"Yeah, the ones I broke," he winced as soon as he said it. She'd been annoyed about that, and he'd just reminded her.

She gave him a flat look for only a moment before returning her face to its "Patient Grandmother" position. "Yes, like that, dear. Well, those type of lines of power are just about everywhere if you know how to look for them. So that's what we're going to do first."

"Aren't you afraid about those two getting away or doing something?" Madison asked.

MeeMaw smiled at Madison. "No, dear. Trust me, they had a job to do, and ole Jimmy waving the gun around has put them in a position of waiting for other instructions. Now they *might* get other instructions, I grant you, but in a lot of ways, they're just like a machine. If y'all point a machine in a direction and tell it to do something, it will keep trying to do it until y'all tell it otherwise or it breaks. Our job here is to break the machine a bit."

"But how do I find the lines? I mean, I don't normally just see a bunch of threads floating around," Matt pointed out in what he considered a reasonable manner.

He found out that MeeMaw did not find it quite so reasonable when she let out a big gusting sigh. "How did y'all see that woman was sick? Or that there were some of those threads tied to Madison's cousin? Just look, then look again, and you'll see them."

Matt suppressed a sigh of his own. His grandmother might be right; he was fumbling around trying to learn this. He was more than aware of that, but she didn't have to treat him like she did when he was a child and found out that the bees nest was dangerous all on his own. Of course, he had to admit that in her mind, he probably was still the little boy who started crying when he didn't know where his personal potty had gotten to and he had to "GOTTA POOP NOW!" when she had guests that one day. He thought that was a sign of full-blown adulthood, instead of the numeric kind, not being able to notice height changes in those younger than you despite them having grown taller than you. He was grateful; if that was the case that he hadn't reached adulthood yet.

He let his eyes and mind go a little unfocused and tried not to try too hard. Which was still contradictory in his mind, but it seemed to work, at least. At first, there was nothing but the blur caused by his eyes watering. Matt had to force himself to not get frustrated, which would make whatever closeness he achieved to pulling it off to vanish in an instant. It seemed easier this time. He guessed the old saw of practice making perfect was working in his favor. Shortly after he started, he began to see the threads his grandmother had promised, like they were fading into existence. They were multi-colored, and the more he let his mind slip into an almost trance-like state where magic actually existed, the more of them he could see stretching out in every direction and in every hue imaginable!

"Do y'all see 'em yet, boy?" MeeMaw implored.

"Yeah, yeah I do," Matt sort of whispered, as if whispering would make it like he wasn't talking, and if he wasn't talking, then he couldn't lose the tenuous grasp he felt he had on this other world.

"What color do y'all see?"

"I see all kinds of colors," Matt almost whined with frustration at having to converse while trying to keep seeing them.

Madison noticed that Matt's grandmother's eyebrow went up a bit at that, even if Matt wasn't aware of it.

"Okey dokey then, guess I'll have to be a bit more specific than that. Do y'all see any red ones? The darker the better. See any of them NEAR you?" MeeMaw said after a moment, putting extra emphasis on location.

Matt looked around himself carefully and deliberately. Yes! There were some crimson ones right at hand. "Okay, yeah, I see a few of them."

"All right, I want y'all to grab one of those."

Matt did as he was told. He could feel a light tingling, like he was holding the lightest charged electric wire you could imagine. "All right, I've got it."

"Good, now imagine a lasso on the end of it."

"Umm, I don't know how to tie a lasso," Matt said quickly.

He could see out of the corner of his eyes that MeeMaw's shoulders slumped. She let out a long, put upon breath before she said, "Well imagine it with a loop on the end, about as big around as those corn-fed hunks of beef up the hill."

"Imagine it how?"

There was the sigh again. "Look, just tell it what y'all want, picture it in your mind. The strand is a mindless thing, but it can obey a simple command." He was only grateful she didn't add, "Unlike some people."

Matt buckled down and attempted just that, thinking, *Okay, strand, make a loop!* as loudly as he could. He didn't even realize at first that he had closed his eyes when he did it. But when he opened them, being careful to maintain his view of this world of magic, nobody was as shocked as he was to see that there was indeed a loop at the end of the strand now!

He looked at his MeeMaw, who actually looked pleased with him. He turned to look at Madison, whose eyes were wide.

"Do you see this too?"

"If I say yes, do I have to do magic today? I mean, I just admitted for the first time I can see these things . . . I don't think I'm up for joining a coven or anything. I saw *The Craft*, and it did NOT end well," she replied, not taking her eyes off of what they were doing.

"No, no, you're being brave enough just coming out to observe, dear," MeeMaw said pleasantly, which made Matt wonder why her own flesh and blood was not getting the kindly grammie gram routine nearly so much.

"What do I do now?" he asked.

"Just tell it to loop itself over one of the big goons up there. Take the one on the left, I'll take the one on the right," she replied, turning her face to look back up the hill where the men stood as if waiting for something behind their own SUV.

Not knowing what else to do, seeing MeeMaw was concentrating on giving her own loop some kind of order and realizing that no more help was forthcoming, Matt turned to the task at hand. He was just getting himself ready to let the strand free when something flashed in the sky above the road that caught his eye. A falcon whisked by, looking for prey, silhouetted perfectly against the blue sky. He had been getting ready to tell the strand what to do, and before he could stop himself, he thought, *Man, wouldn't it be cool to have a falcon?*

Matt almost wanted to slap himself in the face immediately. He could feel the strand and the loop jerk, instantly diving upwards towards the drifting raptor. He could also see MeeMaw's strand flying straight and true towards the big thug on the right. It looped around the corporeal body of the man, but when she tugged just a little, the loop came away with another of the blue specters like the one he had seen at the bar! She had just started to drag the thing towards them when there was a brief squawk above. Like, just maybe, he didn't know, a sound remarkably like that of a real live bird who had briefly felt something like someone walking over its grave, who, without the mental capacity to deal with it, flew off in a panic. Not that Matt knew anything about the noise, no sir, and his wincing at that exact moment was just a pure coincidence, you betcha!

MeeMaw stopped her own reeling in of the specter that had occupied the now befuddled man up the hill. "What in the hell happened, boy?" she demanded, glancing sideways at him.

"I got distracted!" Matt protested.

The other thug, sensing that something was happening, turned his attention away from the Goins farm and looked down the hill at them. While his ability to reason might be minimal, he clearly saw something was wrong, because the brute gave an inarticulate bellow and set off down the hill at a run! Worse, Matt could see he was pulling a gun from underneath the coat he was wearing! The man pulled and drew in stride, and the boom of the firearm disturbed the quiet of the mountain lane!

"You best un-distract yourself damned quick, boy. I cain't let this'un go to get that one!" MeeMaw yelled, which Matt wanted to point out wasn't helping his concentration any but wisely decided to refrain.

To his surprise, he found that despite MeeMaw yelling at him, and despite an armed zombie hurtling down the hill at them, finding the lines again came much easier this time. They leaped into vision like a hidden picture, once seen, always available for future viewings. Matt quickly grabbed one of the scarlet strands. As soon as it was in his hand, he gave it marching orders and released it.

He was shocked to see that another scarlet strand flew at the thug alongside his, and it was coming from Madison!

This time, both of them, his strand and hers, looped around the giant; and without even thinking, they both yanked! The spirit, or otherworldly creature, erupted from the body of their soon to be assailant so violently that it flew several feet before coming to a stop.

Another gun went off, this time from up the hill and to the right of where they were, roughly where the Goins farm sat. "Either of y'all got a phone?" MeeMaw demanded quickly.

"Yeah," Matt and Madison chorused in unison.

"Y'all got signal?"

"I do," Madison said quickly.

"Good, hand it to me, I got to make a phone call as soon as we take care of this."

Madison dutifully handed over her phone, asking, "Who do you have to call right now?"

"If I don't get his fool self on the phone, and now, Jimmy Goins is gonna end up in jail for murder," she replied, taking the phone. "First things first, we got to put these things somewhere safe until we figure out what to do with 'em," MeeMaw added, heading back to where her big over-sized hemp bag was in the Xterra. The spirit, or being—Matt couldn't decide what he thought of them as—that MeeMaw had roped bobbed gently down the hill at the end of its tether she still held. "Oh yeah, take some of the slack out of your line, please, don't want the damned thing to get any ideas about going right back into the body it came from."

Madison and Matt instinctively pulled on the strands they held at the same time. They probably didn't both need to be holding on to the thing like this, but neither of them wanted to let go of their strand, just in case it might have some awful and unforeseen consequence. MeeMaw might yell if something terrible happened now, and that was the first and foremost worry in both of their minds at the moment. The situation had been saved, unsaving it . . .

would have horrible consequences, and MeeMaw was sure to deliver the vast majority of them.

MeeMaw was back a moment later. She set the bag down quickly and took out two things that, for all Matt could guess, looked like expensive booze containers. They looked ancient and dusty and unlike anything you ever saw at a state store, at least not the parts Matt shopped in. They looked more like what got served in mansions in a film. They had crystal stoppers in each bottle, and the bottles were wide and belled out at the bottom and made of green glass. She opened them both, leaving them on the ground.

"Now, I'm going to want y'all to start drawing in your lines all the way until the thing is right on top of you. But first, I want y'all to pay attention to how I do this. Matt dear, I need you to pay extra special attention to what I do once I get the thing close. You're going to have to do this yourself soon enough."

Matt watched as if his life depended on it, but somehow more seriously—because if you were to ask him which he'd prefer, a quick death or another tongue lashing from MeeMaw today, he would have asked, "How quick are we talking here?" He watched as she took her end of the strand that held the nebulous being and wrapped it around a small stone. She looked deep in thought, but for only a moment, before she dropped the stone inside the bottle with a clink. As they watched, the line between the nebulous entity and the bottle began to contract.

The creature, whatever it was, had been watching all this powerlessly. You could see eyes floating in it with an almost bemused and passive look before the line started to contract. It had looked almost as if it was wondering what would happen next before that. Once the thing saw the line dragging it towards the bottle, it began to struggle and twist, trying desperately to get loose from the strand of power that held it. Its thrashing increased like the panic of a trapped animal as it was brought inexorably towards the bottle.

All of its fight was for nothing. The thing was drawn in and trapped inside the glass. The bottle would look empty to the naked eye, but to their attuned vision, somehow it now contained all of the previously sizable spirit inside of it. MeeMaw rapidly conjured another thread, a blue one, into her hand. With the other hand, she slammed down the stopper in the bottle. Her eyes closed for only a moment before the strand that she had held leaped from her to wind itself rapidly around the stopper, effectively sealing it in place.

Once it was finished, MeeMaw turned to them and said, "All right, now y'all do yours."

"Do *what* with ours? What did you even do?" Matt protested.

MeeMaw gave him a long look but didn't immediately comment. After a moment, she said, "It's simple, reel the thing in until it's close but can't reach you. Then you take a bit of your line and wrap it around a stone, drop it in the bottle with an order to pull the creature tight. While that's happening, grab another strand, a blue one will work best. Once it's inside, put the stopper on and wrap it around, telling it to seal up the bottle."

"Oh, so, easy as that, huh?" Matt said quietly and with not only little conviction, but more like anti-conviction. The sort of tone of voice that says, "I'll do it because you're making me, but I hope you realize that I'm going to get us all killed in a horrific manner even attempting this." (That's a lot to read into a tone of voice, but sometimes, you can just tell.)

Matt did as he was told anyway, first scouting around until he found a small enough rock in the gravel by the side of the road. Then he commanded the strand he was holding to latch itself on to the tiny stone, which, thankfully, it did with ease. Throughout all of this, he was relieved to see that Madison kept a hold of her own loop around the entity as a failsafe against his own perception of incompetence here. Finally, he carefully dropped the stone into the other bottle.

"Ummm, why isn't anything happening?" he asked after a moment of nothing much really occurring.

"Did you tell the strand to pull itself in?" MeeMaw replied with a knowing twinkle in her eyes.

Matt sighed. Looking up the hill a little, he saw what he was positive was the ghostly entity giving him a look that surely meant, "What a god damned amateur." He reached out quickly to re-grasp the strand, trying to maintain an expression of "I meant to do that to test you," and gave the order.

When the ghost—which was what he was thinking of it as because it was the only thing that worked mentally—was safely tucked in the bottle, Matt went looking for another strand. He made damn sure to look for a blue one. He was not getting another look from MeeMaw over this. Finally, he sealed the bottle as he had seen her do before. This earned him an appraising glance at his work and a sniff of what he could only take as "Good enough."

"Now what?"

"Well, it would probably be a good idea to tell those men up the hill that they have the keys to that big dumb vehicle and maybe they should get themselves out of here 'for they get themselves kilt," MeeMaw replied, picking up both bottles and tucking them in the SUV.

There was another explosive gunshot that rent the air, followed by the sound of a motor turning over.

A moment later, MeeMaw said, "Nope, never mind, the big ole boy closest to it is figuring it out."

They watched as the vehicle sent a shower of gravel behind it as it sped away. As it fled the scene, Madison pointed out, "Of course, that does leave the one who was coming down the hill."

MeeMaw sighed. "Let me call Jimmy and tell him the war's over and he can stop shooting. You two see if y'all can't corral our innocent victim there."

179

It was hard to conceive of the man-mountain that stood there dazed as an "innocent victim," but orders were orders. As Matt moved forward to go get the lost and frightened looking man from up the hill, he heard his grandfather's voice right by his ear.

"Don't you mind her nit-picking, boy, you done good today."

When Matt whirled to say something back to him, the old man was gone already.

MeeMaw already had Madison's phone and was waiting with it to her ear. After whirling to find no one talking to him, Matt got a good look at her perturbed expression. A moment later, she said loudly, "JIMMY GOINS you know DAMNED WELL who this is! I have it under control, and if you fire that damned gun of yours one more time, I will give you a wart so large you'll need a wheelbarrow to carry it! Am I understood? Good, we'll be up in a little bit. Unload the damned thing and get yourself a beer while you wait!"

As she handed the phone back to Madison, Matt's girlfriend was wide-eyed. Madison swallowed, "Can you really do that?"

"Do what, dear?"

"Give him a wart that big?"

MeeMaw smiled softly. "Well, I don't rightly know, never tried. But if that idiot fires that gun one more time, we're all going to find out together. Now, why don't y'all run along with Matt and help him fetch sleeping beauty up there while I make sure the bottles are secure."

$$\mathcal{DOC}$$

"Hey!" Matt called up to the man. "Believe it or not, it's going to be all right." The, we're going to go with man here since mountains aren't mobile and bulls don't wear suits normally, was enormous and looked strong as an ox, but suddenly waking up somewhere you've never been before to the sound of gunshots would be enough to throw anyone off their game. He looked lost and confused. Matt actually found himself feeling bad for him, despite him waving a gun in Matt's direction only a short time earlier.

"Who . . . who are you?" the former goon asked with some fear in his voice, which Matt thought was almost amusing, considering that same man had Matt almost pissing himself so recently.

"Well, as soon as you tell me your name and come with us, hopefully, we can figure out where you need to be. My name's Matt. What's your name?"

"Ballard, Ballard Snap. I'd 'preciate the ever livin' hell out y'all if someone could tell what in the hell I'm doin' here and who died, since I cain't figure no other good reason to be wearin' a suit."

"Thankfully, ain't no one died, honey, but if that Jimmy Goins gives me an ounce of lip, that may change," MeeMaw replied for Matt before heading up the road past Ballard under a full head of steam.

They took him to the Goins farm, letting MeeMaw go in first to explain some of what happened and to tell Jimmy himself what would happen to him if he wasn't the picture of Appalachian hospitality while she was working this all out. It must have been a very good explanation because their host's thin face was quite pale, all the way to his mostly bald head, and his thin hands had a noticeable palsy to them by the time Matt and Madison brought Ballard inside.

She must have gone well past warts, Matt figured.

Mister Goins had found some chores he absolutely, positively needed to get done at this exact moment, leaving them all alone in the Goins' sitting room drinking some sodas he had brought out. MeeMaw did almost all the questioning of their guest. Madison and Matt were happy to let her. They had learned that the man lived out near

Wolf Pen alone in a trailer, for starters, which meant someone was going to have to drive him home. Madison blanched when she heard MeeMaw promise that they'd give him a ride. Matt made a note to ask about that later, but no way in hell was he contradicting her.

"What's the last thing you remember?" she asked the man, who sat there still looking completely befuddled as to how he'd ended up this far from home.

"Well, ma'am," he replied with a deep, rumbling voice, "I was doin' interviews. A few of the mines out that way had been taking applications for red-hats, and I got my certs and all. I was doin' one for a mine that 'sposed to pay good money, even if'n it were a scab mine. Last thing I remember was gettin' up ta' leave and the feller who was interviewing me sayin', 'Boy, you is a big feller, ain'tcha?' Next thing I know, I'm standin' in the middle of the road out har!"

MeeMaw nodded before getting up abruptly. "Well, y'all enjoy your pop for a minute, I need to go talk to Jimmy real quick."

As soon as she left the room, the silence that followed for the three of them sitting there in the pristinely decorated sitting room was heavy enough to cut. Matt found himself groping for things to say, but what did you say in a situation like this? "How did you enjoy being possessed by a nebulous creature from beyond this dimension? How are the hours? Medical benefits? Would you recommend it to a young man looking towards a career?" It didn't help that the room was decorated in *Ye Olde Fussy Old Lady Knickknack*. You couldn't even point to something interesting as a conversation starter. It just wasn't believable to say, "Oh look, a little china dog and little boy fishing, how interesting." People would know you were faking it immediately if you were under the age of 50, and even if you were older, they'd suspect it.

MeeMaw came back in a few moments later. Matt

could see Mr. Goins hovering over her shoulder, looking chagrined about something,

MeeMaw said sweetly, "Mister Snap? Why don't we give y'all a lift back to your place, if you'd like that?"

A look of relief creased the big man's face. "Thank ye' much, ma'am, I had no idea how I was even gonna get home today 'for y'all said sumthin'.'"

MeeMaw turned to Matt. "I'm sorry, I should have asked. Is that going to be all right for you and Madison? I could see if maybe your uncle could do it if you're busy. This has already taken up a lot of time already."

Madison shocked Matt by answering for him. "I think we can make time for something like this." She turned to look at him. "Don't you think, Hun?"

Matt knew he was outgunned here, so he didn't even try to fight it off. "Sure, I guess, why not," he said.

Madison leaned in and kissed him on the cheek, whispering so only he could hear, "I'll make it up to y'all, and y'all *know* I will."

Matt did the only thing he could do in the situation; he blushed.

CHAPTER 12

"We live on a placid island of ignorance in the midst of black seas of the infinity, and it was not meant that we should voyage far. But no matter how hard you try to avoid it, sometimes you end up waking up on a ship deck with a lump on your head and the smell of rum on your breath."
—Harry Petey Lovecraft,
"The Call of Cthpaulie the Parrot"

———————— • ◆ • ————————

ONCE EVERYBODY HAD piled into the SUV, the full weirdness of the situation began to settle in some. Here Matt was, with his MeeMaw and his girlfriend, who it turned out had as much a witch background as he did, driving a man home who just an hour ago had been possessed by an out of this world entity who had been trying to bully a local farmer. Not the kind of situation that normally happens to, well, more or less anyone, really, and certainly nothing his life back home had prepared him for. There was really only one way to deal with all of it: not deal with any of it right now, break it down to smaller parts for later, and, for now, try to be enthusiastic about seeing the parts of the state west of Beckley, which he had little experience with at all. It was the only sensible thing to do at the moment because everyone else was dealing fine and would look at him weird if he started screaming. (Politeness and a positive outward appearance often hide the unrelenting terror behind a person's eyes. Remember that the next time you're tempted to punch an overly perky salesperson; their manager could be some dread terror from the lands beyond the stars, for all you know. Actually, that would explain a lot of chain store policies.)

What became readily apparent to Matt was that this part of the state seemed poorer than what he was used to. Few parts of West Virginia looked opulent, but this looked especially roughed up. Longer stretches of nothing along with more abandoned buildings—as well as cars, for that matter—were heavily on display. Which didn't make a lot of sense to him; this was where the coal was. Shouldn't this area, if anything, be *more* well off than those east of it? He'd have to ask about it later to understand it better; he somehow suspected he wasn't going to like the answer much.

As they were driving along, they went through another worn down little town. Buildings were boarded up, and what stores there were that hadn't been actually boarded over were left to exhibit dusty, empty pane glass display windows with no wares behind them. The houses themselves varied wildly in quality, from rotting abandonment to some actually very nice white picket fence type places. It made it hard to gauge in any way how a place like this was really doing. In the north, neighborhoods didn't usually have that kind of disparity right next to each other like that. If it's a poor neighborhood, it's all poor, and vice versa, not this situation of having the nice little American dream next to a war zone after the fighting's moved on.

As they rounded a slow, long corner in the road, an enormous stone building swung into view. It was real cut stone, not a cheap facade over wood and plaster like you expected to see these days. It was large, to begin with, but the relatively small almost suburban surroundings made it appear massive. Matt immediately felt a prickling on the back of his neck as soon as he saw it, like that unexplained feeling that something's right behind you, only turned up to eleven. He glanced over at Madison just in time to see her eyes go a little wide. A look in the rearview showed that MeeMaw's eyes had narrowed and the wrinkles at the corners of her mouth had hardened with displeasure at the feeling of whatever it was they were coming up on!

The feeling only intensified the closer they got, making it almost too much to bear. Matt looked into the rearview again, only to see MeeMaw looking directly back at him. Before he could say anything, she said softly, "Matt, my boy, I need to talk to y'all about something after we drop poor Mr. Snap off at his house. It can wait until then, but be a dear and remind me."

Matt knew he'd been told to stow it until they were in private, but it was easier said than done. The feeling was almost like an itching rash that was rapidly spreading! It reached a fever pitch as they were passing the vaulted stone walkway that connected the two halves of the massive, foreboding structure together.

Ballard noticed them all casting glances at the decrepit creepy place. "That's the old company store. Since it closed, ain't nothin' been able to stay open in thar. Seem a shame, pretty, old building like that rotting away empty the way it is. People keep on hoping the state might do sumthin' to preserve it, but so far, ain't nuthin' happened. Guess they don't care what happens out har, long as the coal usage taxes keep showing up in the budget."

"Oh, that is a shame, such a grand old building," MeeMaw said obligingly; but Matt could see her face in his rearview, and there wasn't an ounce of sincerity behind that statement. She was just being polite.

The further out they got into these mountains, the more Matt began to think long and hard about when the last time he'd had the Xterra serviced was. It was one thing to break down in Beckley, or Bluefield or Princeton or even all of the natural "sights" that Madison liked to show him, but out here was something else entirely. This was deep country, which consisted of places that were barely towns, when there even were towns. They had gone where he could barely even tell anyone where in the hell they actually were located anymore to come tow them if they broke down. "Somewhere in Wyoming or Raleigh or McDowell County or maybe Canada" barely counted as directions. That was, if he could get a signal; there hadn't been much of that out here either. On the plus note, that meant he'd stopped getting texts from Tyler demanding to know what in the hell was going on, so every cloud had its silver lining.

Matt was beginning to try and remember how some of the scenes in *Deliverance* went when Ballard called out from the back seat, "I'm gonna be up har on y'all's right. Just pull over and I'll walk up."

As they slowed, the only house that Matt could see was originally a neglected-looking trailer. It had at some point been worked on extensively to hide that fact—a patio had been put in, there was new skirting—but it looked like it hadn't been cleaned or looked after in months. The grass was getting unruly and overgrown, and a large truck sat in the driveway looking like it hadn't budged in months either. It all looked like someone had just walked away from the place.

As Ballard got out, MeeMaw stopped him and handed him a slip of paper. "Things might be a spell confusing for you, dear; who knows what happened that y'all don't remember right now. If y'all need sumthin', you be sure to give me a holler, okay?"

Ballard stood there for a minute looking down at his trailer solemnly before he rumbled, "Thank y'all kindly, I may just have to do that."

As they turned in the drive and began heading back home, MeeMaw said quietly from the back, "Y'all felt that by that big building, right?"

"What was that?" Madison asked, turning in her seat. She didn't specify the "that" in question, she really didn't need to.

"Something very wrong. Every action has a reaction," MeeMaw practically spat, her eyes locked on the foliage as it flew by.

"What do you mean?" Matt asked without looking back. He had been here long enough to know that the man who takes his eyes off a road in West Virginia for too long is a man who doesn't live long enough to have children. These roads were a man-made Darwinist adventure park ride. (In most places, texting while driving is a bad idea. In these mountains, it marked a desire to suddenly see if your car can fly by hurtling it off a cliff.)

"Think, children. If that fool woman who I think is behind this can reach into another world for what she can find there . . . Look at it like this: if our world has magic, who's to say theirs don't? Who's to say they might not have a few witches of their own got curious as to what they could find hereabouts?"

"You mean . . . " Madison said slowly.

"That I would bet there might be some unexplained disappearances 'round that old company store recently," MeeMaw replied flatly.

☽◯☾

The gravel seemed extra loud as Matt pulled into the parking lot of the abandoned gas station across from the huge foreboding structure. He was grateful for the bigger shocks on the SUV as it bumped and danced among the potholes until he parked it, but even with the beefy suspension, he winced a couple of times. Matt still had no idea what MeeMaw planned to do here; he was barely positive where *here* even was. He was sure that if you told him to find the place on a map, he'd most likely get it wrong, he'd only hope he put his finger down on the right state.

So that was the situation: Matt and his girlfriend were going to help his grandmother go into a massive abandoned stone building that looked like Dracula's castle from the old Hammer horror flicks. They were doing so to fight an evil from beyond the stars. Cool. Sleepy, quiet West Virginia . . . hah!

The building itself wasn't really a single building, it was more two buildings connected by arched over walkways circling an enormous courtyard. The kind of place where he fully expected to see Dracula's carriage waiting in the open area. Matt could not help but consider that other grandmothers offered you inedible orange peanut candy while they reminisced about people who were long dead, doing things you didn't care about, and occasionally asking you how your schoolwork was going. That was called "earning the birthday card with the five dollars in it", and that was what normal grandkids dealt with. This, this was a bad movie on late-night TV you watched for a laugh after you'd had a few.

But, in for a penny, in for a pound, that was how the saying went, right? Welp, time to pound one ou—

No, wait, that was bad metaphor mixing if ever there was. Try again.

Time to buckle up and fly right . . . all right, that one almost worked. Matt was still mixing his sayings, but at least this one didn't involve masturbating in front of his grandmother, so there was definite improvement there.

Clear in the metaphor he was going to use to convince himself to do this, Matt took a deep breath and said, "Well, now what?"

"Well, now we go in. We might be able to see some of what's what from here, but we won't see all of it. Be careful, and remember to check with your second sight some," MeeMaw replied, getting out of the vehicle.

"Won't someone call the cops?" Madison asked as she unbuckled herself.

"Nope, most folks what lived in these parts long enough will see me for what I am. If things have been happening like I expect they have been, they'll be happy to see us go in there. They'll either hope we're gonna fix it or figure nobody messes with a witch's business that got any common sense at all." MeeMaw smiled knowingly

Matt got out reluctantly; the chirp of the alarm being activated sounded forlorn and lonely out here. A light breeze blew down the road, and it only accentuated the empty quality to the town. It felt like people were hiding indoors, looking out through drawn shades, wanting to see what would happen next, like in a B-Movie western. Looking at the massive stone structure across the street with the signage left behind, all that remained of numerous attempts to use the place for something new now sadly flapping in tatters, Matt knew one thing: he didn't want to go in. In fact, what he really wanted to do was go visit the nice normal people hiding behind their shades, maybe ask how they liked the view. He also knew it didn't matter what he wanted once he saw MeeMaw start marching with determination across the road.

As MeeMaw marched directly for the door on the left side of the building, Madison couldn't help herself. "What? We're just going to walk right in? Won't it be locked?"

MeeMaw was already halfway up the steps; she stopped and turned. "It might have been once, but y'all can be sure it ain't now. Only police out here are state troopers; they ain't gonna come running out here for kids partying or someone needing a place out of the rain to sleep."

As promised, the door swung open easily enough—the only hitch was the pneumatic door latch sticking a little—letting MeeMaw march purposefully into the gloom inside. Both Madison and Matt froze up for a moment. They looked at each other before looking at the door.

Finally, Matt said, "She might be able to magically kick both our asses, but I can't let my grandmother wander around an abandoned building by herself. What if she trips?"

"Well, I can't leave you wandering around either. I need someone to shove my butt up against in bed when it gets cold," Madison quipped to hide her own worry while pulling the door back open to follow.

Matt stepped inside; he could see MeeMaw's back retreating into the shadows. Looking around, he wondered if he could call her back and maybe they could forget the whole thing. Madison was right behind him; he could hear the pneumatic hinges letting the door close slowly, haltingly shut.

"Whoa, creepy," she said quietly.

Matt wanted to say something manly at this moment, something to show how little fear an empty building held for him. Instead, he replied quietly, "I know, right?"

They were in a hallway lined with ancient-looking woodworking and tiles. Their feet clacked on the tiles below them, causing a slight echo down the hall. What paint there was on the walls was beginning to peel away in huge chips, making the decay around them more obvious. It probably had more to do with improperly preparing the painting surface and less to do with eldritch horrors spreading corruption; but for Matt and Madison's money, they were betting on corruption at this exact moment. It was easy to see that once upon a time, these had been offices, which is not your normal eldritch horror setting; but considering how boring offices were, that would probably be an improvement. Near each door was a large window that had been made in a kind of frosted glass that Matt had never seen before. It looked like a cross between shatterproof glass after a car accident and a window with actual frost on it during a brutally cold winter. The whole place created a surreal feeling, the kind of dark imagery you liked as a photo or meme on Facebook and Pinterest because creepy stuff always looks cool in a picture, not because you wished to be standing in the middle of it.

Hearing their faltering footsteps, MeeMaw turned and looked at them. At first, her face was stern, and Matt automatically winced, expecting a tongue lashing, but then her expression softened, and she smiled in a reassuring manner. "Look," she said, "I know. Trust me, this is a bit bigger than I'd want for either of y'all at the moment. This ain't what I'd have wanted for me neither, if it were up to me. 'Cept it ain't up to me, or y'all. Normally by now, I'd have Matt working on maybe helping someone get over a cold. Young lady, I'd have you observing him while he did it. I figure for the moment, that and being able to talk to your relatives what stay around to watch over you'd be plenty for y'all to do. But that ain't what we have to work with at the moment, so I need y'all to be strong. People are probably gettin' themselves hurt through no fault of their own from whatever is hiding away in here, and we got to put a stop to it. Just remember to keep your seeing open to more than what normal eyes can see, and I'll be right here, so yell if y'all need me. Now if y'all can check the left side, I'll check on the right and see if we can't get on with it."

Madison and Matt looked at each other for a moment before nodding in unison.

MeeMaw's smile widened a bit. "Thank you, dears. I know it's a bit much, but we'll get through it together."

The door opening as she left them in the hallway made both of them jump a bit. It sounded enormously loud in this space, empty of any furniture or people or anything at all that might buffer it. Both of them just stood there for a moment, letting the silence—except for MeeMaw's footsteps retreating to their right—settle back in. Left with no choice, Matt tried the door on the left, part of him hoping the entire time that it might be locked. He was disappointed when it swung open, leading to another hallway running parallel to the first with more doors opening off it. Where peeling paint had been noticeable in the first hall, here it was the main feature. Even the varnish on the wood was peeling off.

"They must not have prepped their surface first," Matt pointed out (not realizing that the narrative had already beaten him to that observation).

"Well, why bother if these guys rate even smaller offices than the guys across the way?" Madison retorted, but Matt couldn't help but notice she did it very quietly.

They swung open the first door in this new hall and peered inside. Matt had to remind himself to look both ways, first with one sight, then the other. Not that it mattered, it was just as empty, no matter which sight he looked with, nothing but dust and faded carpet.

"You know what I never had a chance to do up north?" he asked as he pulled the door shut.

"Date someone as cute as me?"

He paused for a second. "Well, that's true, but I was going to be snide and bitter about this, and dating a cute girl would be a real positive and ruin my vibe entirely. No, what I was going to say was, I never had a chance to skulk around abandoned doom castles looking for terrors from beyond the stars."

Madison was silent for a moment as they checked the next room before she said, "Well, two problems with that."

"Being?"

"Well, it's an old company store, for one; and aren't they from a different reality all together?"

"Point on the alternative reality, I still say this place is a doom castle, though," Matt replied as he pulled the door shut on another blissfully empty room.

The last door they opened was to a room with almost no light at all inside. If there had been windows, they were blocked off. Matt went in; Madison, on the other hand, was smarter and waited by the door where there was nothing to trip over. Matt did try to scan the place with his second sight, which discovered nothing.

Finally, standing in the middle of the darkened room, he called out, "You know what I bet MeeMaw has in her bag that we don't?"

"What?" whispered Madison.

"A flashlight."

"Probably. Wanna go back out to the main hall now?"

"Yes, please," Matt exclaimed with relief.

MeeMaw was waiting for them when they came out. "What took y'all so long?" she demanded.

"We stopped for lunch on the way, they put in a Chipotle," Madison responded before she could stop herself.

Madison and Matt froze for a second. MeeMaw had been petulant and annoyed over this whole business today. Both of them tensed, awaiting the chiding they had coming. Instead, MeeMaw chuckled.

"Good for you, I needed a joke today. Well, come on, we gotta check upstairs, and if that ain't it, we gotta go to the far building."

It turned out that upstairs wasn't it either. But on the plus side, it was more pleasant than the downstairs had been. The rooms of the upstairs got good light from large windows without all the woodwork creating deep and, most importantly, frightening shadows. The paint was mostly a light blue, and despite the fact that it was peeling off in huge flakes just like downstairs, it was still really hard to get completely worked up and terrified or spooked at in a room that's baby blue on a bright sunny day. (The killer never waits in the nursery when it's well-lit with no shadows, it would look silly. Just standing there in the middle of the room holding a knife like that, you'd almost be laughing until he stabbed you.) Matt felt his heart rate plunge back to something approaching normal as they wandered around the dusty empty rooms. He kept hoping that whatever they were looking for *was* up here because this was the part of the building that he most thought he'd be able to keep a clear thought process working in.

Hope was dashed and forlorn when it turned out there was nothing there. They could all still feel that tingling that said there was something nearby, but it just wouldn't be here. Matt looked out the window towards the rear of the building to see if anyone had come out of any of the houses sitting tucked on the hill above the town to see what they were doing. Not a soul had moved, not a person stirred, but he could still *feel* them out there, hiding behind their curtains, waiting to see the outcome of all this.

"Now what?" he asked.

"Well, we still got another building and whatever kind of basements seem to be opening up from down in the courtyard to look into. Don't worry, I know y'all can still feel it, we'll find it."

"Problem," Madison said, joining Matt at the window. "There's no way to the other building from this one, we'll have to go outside."

"So, we'll go outside. Everybody in town knows we're here, ain't no point in skulking around. There'll be a way into the other building too, so no worries there," MeeMaw said before heading downstairs.

Well, at least she'd confirmed Matt's suspicions about the townspeople. He wanted to feel smart about that, wanted to, but how smart can you be when you're the one in danger and they're the ones inside watching *Maury* reruns? Still, with sensing the presence of the town folk, at least that way he could feel smart about at least one single solitary thing they'd done today; before this, he'd spent the day fumbling around completely out of his depth.

MeeMaw was, of course, correct. There was another way in, it just wasn't through the other front door. That was locked, and they were already heading around back before

Matt could even consider suggesting they just magic it open. He wasn't 100% sure they could do that, but he considered that if they could, MeeMaw certainly would have thought of it and had deemed it a bad idea.

They stood outside of a partially open back door while MeeMaw fumbled in her bag. Madison turned to Matt. "Abandoned building 101 in this state: check the back door, *somebody's* broken in at some point just to get the wire."

MeeMaw turned to look at them. "So where's your flashlight?"

"We didn't bring any because we didn't expect to be doing this today?" Matt replied.

"Well, there's another lesson for today: put together a travel bag for when you have to be steppin' out. A flashlight ain't never gonna do you wrong, good thing to keep in y'all's vehicle regardless," she replied.

"We can use our phones," Madison supplied.

"Well, one of y'all is thinking at least," she huffed, pulling the door open and going in.

Matt couldn't help but once again feel he was losing ground in the family business to his girlfriend, the way today was going. It was like if you had belonged to a family of chefs, you were the heir to the family restaurant, and you brought home a date who proceeded to make your chef mother and father cry tears of joy with a souffle she whipped up on the spot. Actually, the way today was going, he was beginning to wonder if he might just cede the whole thing to Madison and go back to looking for normal work.

The door opened into what looked like had been a storage area for lawn cutting equipment, judging by the green stains and gas smells. It was impossible to see much of anything past that by the dim pathetic light of the door and their little phone lights. MeeMaw, on the other hand, seemed to have a distinct idea of exactly where they were going, most likely because she actually had brought along a real flashlight. She strode off resolutely to their left, mostly ignoring the dirt-encrusted room they were in. Almost as an afterthought, Matt thought to look the room over with his second sight. Upon seeing nothing, he felt kind of silly. MeeMaw had probably done it while walking in the door.

MeeMaw pulled a door on the far side of the room open, letting glorious light flood in from the main building. She turned and said, almost apologetically, "I was here a few times when I was a girl. This leads into a stairwell. Might as well go check the upstairs first."

MeeMaw wasn't that spritely heading up the stairs, which suited Madison and Matt fine. Even though we know logically that moving more slowly into an unknown only makes the tension worse than it needs to be, even though we know if there is something where we're going to be afraid of, our reactions will be more fear-fueled and uncoordinated if we have too long to think about it, even knowing all that, everybody becomes Shaggy and Scooby in this situation and moves as slowly as possible. Matt could only consider the cold beer he had waiting in his mini-fridge back at the farm to be his scooby-snacks for going through all of this today. "Gee, Scoob, would you do it for two lagers and a porter?"

They stepped out to what looked like an empty open floor, except for a few offices toward the back that were separated from the rest of the floor by the same woodworking as in the other building. The empty space ended in a railing looking out over the lower floor. They slowly took a few steps forward, then MeeMaw stopped suddenly and turned, pointing towards an area tucked away next to one of the offices. Matt and Madison could see what she meant immediately, a dirty mattress with a blanket piled at the foot of it and some books stacked next to it.

"And that's where they found their first victim," she breathed.

CHAPTER 13

"But as soon as one is ill, as soon as the normal earthly order of the organism is broken, one begins to realize the possibility of another world; and the more seriously ill one is, the closer becomes one's contact with that other world, so that as soon as the man dies, he steps straight into that world. He usually doesn't want to, I mean it's icky there, but you know, things happen. Look, sometimes, you know, earthly order and all. I mean shit happens, amIright?"

—Fyodor Dostoyevsky,
discarded first draft of *Crime and Punishment*
entitled "Russian is the New Black"

———— ◆ ————

BEATRICE BALDWIN SCREECHED with rage, sending a napping cat hurtling for the hole in the wall it came and went by. Again? How could this happen yet again? She kept loose tabs on her creatures, a weak mental connection that let her know where and how they were. She knew when they went free, and now two in one day? It couldn't be that Hawley woman, that hippy almost never went out, and Beatrice was certain that her own idiot boy, Billy, never sent anyone to her farm. He damned well better not have. She had told him specifically to leave the Hawleys be for now, and he couldn't possibly be dumb enough to outright disobey her on that.

Somebody was coming into their powers; someone was tampering with her work out there! She doubted it was one of the Hawley grandsons, the two of them she knew had never shown the slightest inkling towards the art. The one was nothing but a farmer covered in cow shit, and the other might dress himself up in the otherworldly with his tattoos and all, but he was only in it for the music and to look cool, like young people do. So, who? Who was doing this?

Beatrice felt like one of her chickens was coming home to roost. Not for the first time, the thought came to her that it had to be that Armstead girl! Had to be! Beatrice wasn't going to waste her time firing up the truck for a little girl, she hated driving if she could avoid it. Instead, she figured there might be other ways to get to her, there always had been in the past. Just ask the girl's mother if there was anywhere you could hide from Beatrice when she was looking for you. Well, you could ask, but only if you could talk to the spirit world, that was.

She was going to think on this, maybe ask her friends that were supplying these fine slaves if they had some ideas, but it wasn't time to just rush off and act the fool. No, she would get her hands on the girl all right, it was just a matter of how and where Beatrice wanted this to happen.

☽◯☾

MeeMaw more or less ignored their horrified expressions and went right over to the mattress and began examining it and the books next to it. Finally, she said, "You two, come here a moment."

Begrudgingly, Matt and Madison unfroze their feet from the spot and went over to join her. She pointed to the books.

"Look at those and tell me what you see."

Matt could see the books were worn, and he sort of recognized a few of the titles, but he just wasn't getting it.

There was something important here that MeeMaw wanted them to see, and he was missing it entirely. Apparently, that only made one of them.

Madison let out a low whistle. "Some hitters in here, Baldwin, Camus, Vonnegut, Kerouac, these aren't thrift store books. Worn copies too, these have all been read more than once."

"An educated man." MeeMaw turned to look at them, a righteous indignation burning in her eyes when she spoke. "It happens. 'Specially in these parts where a man's brawn is considered worth more than his brain most days. Man falls down on his luck, finds a place out of the wind, maybe keeps a PO Box and hopes to scrabble together enough for a security deposit on a trailer or something. Sometimes, well, maybe he'd just given up on the world altogether. But there it is, a man who thought about the nature of the whole world was up and snatched away from this one just to be a slave in some other one! Just like is happening to those spirits that we got in the car. I just want the pair of you to consider this a bit, so you know the kind of evil we're trying to get rid of here today. 'Cause trust me, if they are willing to rent out slaves from there to some power grubbing witch, anyone they take from here's fate cain't be any better."

Matt hadn't realized it fully until then, but he really had been viewing this as some grand adventure. He hadn't been able to really view any of this as real; it was all just too fantastical. So instead, he had made it some game to play at, like when he was a kid and he went adventuring with his friends in the woods. Just like a game in the woods or in a backyard, he expected somewhere deep down inside that they would all turn around and go home when and if it stopped being fun. Something for him and Madison to joke about later, "I wasn't scared, you were!" He couldn't tell how he knew, but he knew that his grandmother had been absolutely right in her assessment of what had happened here and who that empty throw away mattress had belonged to, he was positive she was. That knowledge changed everything. This had been a real person, and his life was not a thing to be devalued as an amusement for Matt and his girlfriend!

The upstairs was empty, both of other belongings and of any of the otherworldly signs of magic they were looking for. Just the open floor, an office that proved empty, and the remains of the elevator. Somehow, the thing had been ripped out of its shaft and toppled onto the dusty floor. The whys and the wherefores of that had no explanation, but considering it was an abandoned building, Matt figured it must have seemed to be a good idea to teenagers at some point or another. Major but stunningly stupid vandalism in an abandoned building usually has that explanation to it.

The three of them were subdued and silent as they made their way to the rail overlooking the downstairs. Where the other building's first floor had been closed up and dark and oppressive from the variety of offices crowding in and blocking the light, the front of this building was wide open. Matt had to guess that this had been the part that had been the actual company store. It must have been some kind of store in its last iteration as well, probably a thrift store, judging from all the tatty and dusty furniture down there almost piled up in tight little rows of couches and chairs that even college freshmen getting an off-campus apartment for the first time would turn up their noses at. There was a set of stairs leading down right from the balcony, so that at least was a blessing.

"Well, I suppose we go down." Madison said what everyone was thinking.

This part of the building, while it was open and airy, really drove home the point that this building had sat abandoned for quite some time. Chips of paint hung from all the walls in such profusion as to almost create a stucco effect. The chips and plaster that had already fallen coated everything with a thick layer of white dust and grime. How somebody could even live here at all was beyond Matt. The amount of dust must have played merry hell with breathing.

"I hope they didn't use lead in this paint," Matt muttered as he moved gingerly down the steps.

"Oh god, me too. If you got brain damage, it would be like dating Tyler all over again," Madison quipped behind him, engaging in a time-tested pastime of women everywhere, ripping their exes.

"I'll take shallow breaths then, shall I?"

They weaved their way through the derelict furniture to the front of the building first. Leading off to the left, there was another side room, which they approached with additional trepidation. This was a room that truly looked like it should be the home of some eldritch power from another universe. Tiles had fallen off the roof above, and years of water had poured in, turning the filing cabinets and desks hunkered down in there into a misshapen, twisted mass of metal and paper. This room had no windows, so all light came from the doorway and the hole in the roof. The lack of lighting and the smears of rust everywhere made the whole thing look nightmarish, like something out of a horror game! At least with first sight, it looked like something horrific; with second sight, it only looked as mundane as the rest of the place. It was a poser fake horror room but not the real thing, the Hollywood stage for a horror movie, not the crime scene.

All of them had to hide their frustration as they worked through another set of rooms that opened off the showroom back towards the way out. They had been through both buildings and had nothing to show for it except for the aftermath of a tragedy and dust on their clothes. Something was here, but even MeeMaw, with her far superior magical senses, had found nothing of any mystic note in the rooms they'd been through. Only the more mundane lack of a human being where one clearly had lived only recently stood as a physical testament to there being anything more than rot here.

Giving up on this building as well, Matt couldn't believe how overjoyed he was to be back in the open air. He hadn't even realized how stifling being inside those buildings had been or how tense it had made him until he was free of it. He could see why. In so many ways, the buildings were enormous crypts, covered in mold in some spots and dust everywhere else. Being inside them was walking through mausoleums of the people who lived here when this was all a thriving town with what it mistakenly thought was a bright future ahead of it.

Matt's happiness was short-lived.

"Well, I was hoping it wouldn't come to it, but I guess we have to go in the courtyard and check the basements next," MeeMaw said, already striding off towards the front of the building.

Speaking of crypts . . .

They came around to the front of the building again and headed into the courtyard. If the front of the building reminded one of a horror movie, the courtyard and the soft echoes of their movements bouncing around drove the point home completely. The doorways that led to the basement areas were black holes. All of the doors had been broken open at some point, and what windows there were, were all smashed out, leaving nothing but inky depths to be explored beyond. Nothing about the picture it presented was at all inviting, more anti-inviting. Not that it mattered, inviting or not, here in the courtyard, the buzzing feel of magic in operation that had told them all to look at this building was practically reaching a fever pitch.

"Ummmmm . . . " Madison said quietly, which Matt was glad for, since that little noise encapsulated his own feelings pretty successfully, he thought. Matt was just glad to know it wasn't just him.

"We'll check the one on the left first," MeeMaw cut off that avenue of discussion. She was going in anyway, so she wasn't going to let either of them have room for doubts about it now.

Matt jogged ahead, trying to catch up with his grandmother. Just before they entered the darkened basement, he noticed something sitting on the windowsill below the shattered panes. Perched there like some kind of weird omen—for what, he had no idea—sat a small, ancient angel doll, the kind old women like to have on their shelves. Matt could only hope the little guy was going to be on their side here as he stepped into the dim twilight of the doorway. Whatever the other side that they were up against consisted of, it probably didn't need the help as much, so that seemed only fair.

Matt could hear the broken glass crack under his feet as he stepped further inside. He could see from MeeMaw's flashlight bobbing and weaving in front of them that there didn't seem to be much of anything but dirt and support columns past the shattered glass. He also knew that was just the parts you saw with your eyes; the tingling he was feeling told him something else. Matt took a deep breath and looked again. Seeing the basement all over again told a completely different story! There was an area dead ahead in the furthest section of the basement that seemed to consist of something that was definitely there, something that somehow managed to be blacker than it would be just from lack of light. Looking closer, Matt could see with his second sight that off a little to the right in the back was a spot where the tendrils and swirls of color that were all around them normally were as dark as the grave instead. Even as he watched, he could see the occasional black line dart out, questing from the mass it sprang from!

"Umm . . . MeeMaw," he whispered in fear.

"I see it, boy," she replied shortly. "Just trying to decide what in the hell to do about it."

"Shouldn't we have thought about that before we got here?"

"Boy . . . " MeeMaw growled in a low voice.

Matt suddenly discovered the self-preservation instinct at that point to shut the hell up in case she decided what to do about it was to feed him to it.

They all stood where they were while MeeMaw pondered a course of action. Matt still thought she should have had one in place before getting them all so close to the thing, but he had to concede, how often did something like this even come up? He was sincerely hoping very rarely. Never would be pretty good as well, way better than rarely, if you thought about it. The concept that an alien race was just creating waystations where they could reach into our world and pluck us out of our life for a new life of multiverse slavery made the whole world an almost unforgivably frightening place. What with all the magic and stuff he'd already been taught, it had only seemed occasionally frightening before, more so if Mungo was about. The thought of something like this being commonplace was outright "I can't sleep without a night-light anymore" terror levels.

Matt didn't notice anything especially threatening at first, just an overall terrible presence emanating from the corner. By the time he did, it was already too late!

A tendril of all black—like the strands they used with a purpose after they had been given an order—snaked out of the black mass in front of them! It would have looked like it was only probing again if Matt hadn't watched it the entire time. It was flashed out like it knew something was there but was trying to discover exactly where it was, like it had done this before! As Matt was about to say something, it darted out across the distance between them and twined itself around Madison's leg!

"Madison!" he yelled as she fell to the ground next to him, an exhale of pain and shock erupting from her as she hit the hard floor!

Whatever the tendril was, random magic or a sentient thing, no longer mattered. It was already dragging Madison toward the black mass looming a short distance from them!

Matt's mind immediately recalled the empty cot in the other building. How far that man must have been dragged to be pulled through this . . . gate? It must be a gate! Matt sure as hell wasn't letting that happen to Madison! MeeMaw called out something, but he couldn't hear it. It was like he had tunnel vision on what was happening! In his panic, he came up with what his panicked brain perceived to be the easiest solution; he needed to find more powerful magic!

Matt reached out into the ether instantly. He wanted the most powerful line of magic he could possibly get his hands on. (When Jason is running at you through the woods, you don't want your weapon to be a nail file, you want high explosives, right? Well, he didn't want any little strand of magic, because this was the scene where Jason drags the girlfriend away). In a moment, Matt's mind could sense a major line of power floating nearby! As he came in contact with it, he had a brief second where he forgot what he was doing this for, he was so shocked when he didn't encounter the resistance he expected from something that big! The massive strand just came easily, almost like it wanted to help!

Matt's mind was a confused jumble of images of what he wanted, at first. Madison was scrabbling at the floor, trying not to be dragged into the mass. He certainly wanted the line pulling on her to let the hell go, for starters. But he wanted more than that; he wanted whoever was grabbing people from their world to not only stop, but also to suffer for what they did! He wanted all of that, and he wanted it now! Before he had truly formed even a coherent thought, the line of magic itself seemed to get the gist of it. With a show of almost doglike sentience, it jumped free of his hand and dove away from him.

After the blinding flash of light that came immediately afterward, Matt and MeeMaw suddenly decided that it would be a fine idea to join Madison on the ground, and maybe also cover their ears to muffle the enraged screaming that erupted from where the tendril had been coming from! It wasn't anything formal or planned, where one person had said to the other, "Hey wouldn't it be great if we both rolled around in the dust for a moment?" It was more one of those waves of force driving them off their feet that lent a more informal "What in the hell just happened?" atmosphere to the whole thing.

After allowing his eyes to adjust a moment, following the return to inky darkness, Matt whispered, "Is everybody all right?"

MeeMaw was already regaining her feet with a rapidity that belied her age. She brushed off her sundress and sniffed. "Well, it might not have been how I would have done things, but that gate sure as hell's gone all right. Congratulations are in order, I suppose. Any idea what in the hell ya done?"

Matt was helping Madison to her feet when he replied, "Honestly, I had to do something; what that was that I managed to do? No idea."

MeeMaw nodded solemnly. "Well, probably for the best not to do it again then, I suppose."

$$☽☯☾$$

As they were dropping MeeMaw off back at her house, she turned and leaned in the Xterra's window. "We'll, y'all have had a mighty busy day, s'pose. We can talk about everything soon enough. This all took a lot longer than we could have expected, best to head on up to the main house, they'll be wondering after y'all."

As MeeMaw moved off to her own house, Matt turned to Madison and grabbed her hand. "Look, umm, with everything . . . you don't have to meet the rest of my family tonight if you don't want to."

Madison smiled, one of those big natural ones she showed off when she thought she was about to be clever. "Oh, come on, I've dated the biggest reprobate of your family and met the most interesting member. At this point, I'd like to meet the rest, just for contrast and comparison."

Matt smiled back. "Thanks, I really do appreciate it. Everybody else is pretty normal, I swear."

"I texted Justin. He's going to be out trying out his new affinity for dry clothing tonight anyway. If you want, we can just stay here tonight, I mean if y'all think it'll be all right with your family," Madison replied.

"Well, they've let Tyler have a girl stay over. I think with the whole grunge thing back when they were young and everything, they're pretty mellow about stuff like that." Matt shrugged, pointing the Xterra down towards the main house.

To Matt's surprise, Aunt Debbie was out the door to greet them the second they pulled up. As he was getting out of the SUV, she said, "Well there you two are! I was afraid you'd miss dinner. Y'all have a bit of time yet, so why don't you get upstairs and get yourself cleaned up. Edwin and Adrianna are going to be up in a bit with the kids; we'll have ourselves a nice sit-down meal all together."

As soon as Aunt Debbie whirled around and headed back inside, Madison said, "So, y'all's family are scoping out the girlfriend, ain't they?"

"Eeyup."

"They never did when I was dating Tyler. I don't think I ever met his folks."

"I think maybe they have high hopes for me," Matt said with a shy smile and then winced internally for dissing his cousin like that. It becomes a habit when your girlfriend drops subtle slams at her ex. He needed to remember that her ex was still his cousin.

Madison grasped his hand as they stood side by side, just a soft, natural boyfriend/girlfriend movement. "Well, so do I. Let's go get a shower and let them check the teeth on this horse."

☾☉☽

Beatrice Baldwin was not having a good night. She had made arrangements with the other side, she had made plans with them, and things were not going according to plan. They had a working agreement; she had even recommended the store to them, because frankly, who in the hell gave two good god damns about those people what lived there already? Not Bill, and he hired them, and not her, and she was supposed to be their Granny Witch in these parts. Not that she particularly wanted to be, but she'd managed to drive off every other person with an ounce of power that could be a threat to her. When the land fell to her, by default, so did the people, whether she wanted it or not, and *not* had always been the answer to that question. She viewed that whole agreement that herself and her benefactors on the other side had come to as having an added bonus of thinning her herd down a bit. She wanted the land, it was just an unfortunate side effect that it came with people on it. Thanks to those beings she communed with, there had been fewer of those people all the time.

Someone had come on her land and done magic. Worse, they'd done MAJOR magic. Apparently, the spirits on the other side could die, and a few of the ones that were working that crossing did just that in the blast its closing caused. According to her contacts, everything was set back now. Worse, they hinted heavily that there might be someone out there slinging better magic than she had, and maybe they should consider finding out who that was and working with them instead. One of the ethereal things had even hinted that whatever that better witch had going, they might not demand something so ridiculous as being made young again as part of their final payment. Well, they didn't say it in so many words, but she could tell that's what they meant.

Beatrice knew one thing; it wasn't that insufferable Hawley hippy. She was absolutely sure of it now. No, she'd never do something that might be considered that destructive, or for that matter, as un-directed as all that. She was like that back in the sixties, all peace and love and the like, and no way she'd have changed that much over the years. No, it took the impetuousness of youth to act like that. She'd checked years ago; Donnie's boys didn't have that kind of magic to work with in both their bodies combined. She had a strong suspicion who it was before, but this was just driving the point home to her.

Beatrice berated herself. She should have left the possibility open that it wasn't the cousin she'd driven off, that boy Justin, who had the skill. She should have had Bill keep track of the girl in case she'd guessed wrong about who had gotten the power in that family. It could be that boy Justin, it wasn't impossible, but last she'd heard, he was driving long haul to prevent flooding and probably hadn't been anywhere near here both times. Maybe for one, but not both. No, it had to be the same person doing all this. And how could it be the boy Justin? If he had the power at that kind of level, why hadn't he gotten rid of the curse years ago, and Beatrice would have known? No, it had to be the girl.

She should have killed that damned girl when she killed her Mamma.

Better late than never, Beatrice supposed.

Dinner was pleasant, even if Tyler slouched the entire time. Uncle Donnie and Aunt Debbie were on best behavior, which was helped by having Edwin and Adrianna on hand. The nice, polite farm couple served as a counterweight to Tyler's rocker tattoo artist hipster personality. They had probably made a point of inviting Edwin and Adrianna up, same as when Matt first arrived, to prove that their live-at-home son was more the aberration than the rule of the family. Which was kind of funny. Madison had dated him, and Matt spent most of his time hanging out with him, so who knew who it was his aunt and uncle thought they were fooling here. Not to mention, apart from the divorce driven living at home, Tyler was doing pretty well for himself, all things considered. He had a good job that paid well, he had a real talent, Matt had seen his work, and he now had a girlfriend who was cute. He could be doing worse.

Nothing was said about Madison staying the night, everybody just made small talk while cleaning up after dinner. Finally, Uncle Donnie and Aunt Debbie excused themselves to go off to TV, leaving just the younger members of the family with Madison. There was a long, uncomfortably forced bit of small talk until the baby started fussing, then both Adrianna and Madison vanished to wherever it was people went when children were fussing in public. Somehow, they managed to get little Noah to join them, trailing behind his mom, informing her repeatedly that he "wanted a tookie."

That left just the three cousins alone to try and build some kind of conversation up. Tyler took the lead. "So, what in the hell happened with y'all today? Y'all go over to MeeMaw's and then we don't see hide nor hair of any y'all for hours."

Matt considered it for a moment. "How much do you really want to know MeeMaw's doings?"

Tyler looked thoughtful at that, but Edwin laughed. "Naww, I think I could live without knowing too much about any of that. Better y'all than me that it got passed on to, cuz. I like my life nice and simple, feed receipts, bills of sale, and manure, you know where you stand with manure."

"Yeah, in cow shit," Tyler said with a slight smirk before turning to Matt. "You know y'all are telling me eventually, right? I need to live vicariously through y'all's magical adventures and shit."

"I figured I would, but hey, you know where I live."

"And I can hassle y'all through the internet if we multi-play Destiny 2, and trust me, I will."

"You will not interfere with X-box time with nattering questions," Matt replied firmly.

"Maddie staying tonight?"

"Yes, but if she hears you calling her Maddie, *you* might not. She hates that nickname."

"Aww, that's what I called her for years!" Tyler protested.

"And notice how you're dating Chloe now?" Matt pointed out reasonably.

Tyler's face froze for a second. "Okay, point, but y'all are going to have to remind me not to. I always wondered why she kept smacking me in the back of my head when we were dating."

"And knowing is half the battle, GI Jackass."

They were interrupted by Adrianna and Madison returning, trailed by Noah, who had a cookie in his mouth, proving that persistence is everything when working over a parent.

Adrianna was holding Harper; she said quietly, "Well, cowboy, I hate to break up cousin time and all, but I think our little ones are about to drop off."

Edwin nodded and got up. "Well, that's all for me. If you two layabouts ever decide to do an honest day's work, come down to the farm and say hi."

"As soon as I see a pig get airborne, I'll be sure to do that, brother mine," Tyler replied.

"Depending on whether or not that one boar Dad keeps out in the south pen starts acting like an asshole again, y'all just might. I think I can work out the logistics of heaving that bastard quite a ways, he tries to bite me one more time."

As soon as Edwin and Adrianna had left, Tyler turned towards Madison and Matt. "All right, spill. I want spine tingles, I want magic, I want all the stuff I have to watch movies for. If y'all think I'm going to have my ex-girlfriend and, frankly, my best friend doing this shit and not get deets—"

"Who says deets anymore?" Madison cut him off.

"The inquiring mind that is not going to be put off by having his slang criticized," Tyler replied.

Matt sighed. "You know how I told you there was some kind of fucked-up spirit thing inside the guy who beat you up?"

"Yeah, and I told y'all you were full of shit and walked y'all into a trap on Halo for lying to me."

"Well, the day STARTED with two of them inside some big old boys outside the Goins' farm and Jimmy shooting at them."

"No shit? Then what happened?"

"It got a lot weirder after that," Madison answered.

☽◯☾

Once Tyler had been told everything, at least enough that he was satisfied enough to let them go, they headed up to bed. Matt was happy to finally be alone with Madison, even if his room could have been cleaner than it was. He was also a little afraid. They should probably talk, but talking would give him ample opportunity to say something dumb and break that very fragile balance they'd achieved during the day. After everything that had happened, he really, really didn't want to say something dumb here, and understanding the distinct possibility that he might was giving him panic sweat. Madison was the best thing that had ever really happened to him. They weren't just boyfriend and girlfriend, they were more than that, she was his best buddy who laughed at his jokes. If he screwed anything up here, he'd be losing twice.

No point in beating around the bush though. "You all right?"

Madison pulled off her shirt and tossed it on top of his dresser. She looked thoughtful for a moment before answering, "I think so. I think long term I might be even better than okay for it, if y'all can believe that. Even as weird as it was today."

"How so?" Matt asked, patting the bed next to him.

Madison sat down and shucked off her jeans before putting her head against him. "Well, you can't run away from who you are forever. You might want to, but it isn't healthy. If you're tall, y'all can slouch all the time, but it just gives you backaches and it don't fool anyone. This just sort of forced the issue a bit. I've known, I've known for a while that I'd have to stand up straight eventually."

They were silent for a bit, just enjoying snuggling before she said, "Hey, want to go somewhere with me in the gorge tomorrow? I can show y'all how I've always known?"

"Ummm, yeah, sure."

"We better make sure to bring extra water, it's a hell of a hike. Hey, that reminds me, y'all got beer in that fridge?"

"Unless Tyler's been sneaking in here, in which case, I'll just return the favor, why?"

"Well, thinking of sweating reminded me of wanting something to drink. Which made me think of fun ways to get sweaty. By the way, you're overdressed."

Hours later, they both slept. The moonlight played across the bed where they lay spooned up next to one another, Matt's arm draped over Madison. It also shined on, as well as through, the shape of Mungo, who stood at the foot of the bed in contemplation. He looked just about to say something when the shape and form of a beautiful woman appeared directly behind him. She wasted not a moment before smacking Mungo directly across the back of his head!

"Wa did ye gang an' burst me fur, hen?" Mungo hissed.

"Och ye a bampot cheil, wa ur ye appearin' haur noo?" she demanded, her china-like face wearing a stern expression, not unlike a mother dealing with a wayward kid.

"Ah needed tae gab tae th' loon abit something," Mungo protested.

"Cannae ye see they ur in a lover's embrace? Anythin' ye need tae gab abit can bide until morn, ye auld rockit!"

"But . . . "

Mungo saw her hand begin to pull back for another strike. He muttered, "Ye ur a harsh hen, Wynda." Seeing her facial expression harden, he quickly added, "But Ah can see ye ur completely correct!"

A moment later, all the moon shone down on in the room was Madison snuggling back tighter against Matt.

$$ \text{)O(} $$

"So, where the hell are we going?" Matt asked as they drove up the turnpike.

"Place called Kaymoor. I've been afraid to go back there for years, but now, well, I've got y'all with me, don't I?"

"Not that I would count on me to be any great help. Now if we had MeeMaw . . . "

"Doubt she'd want to do the stairs. Anyway, y'all saved me yesterday, didn't you?" Madison replied with a smile.

"Sort of, I mean, I'd take more credit for it, but I have no idea what in the hell I did," Matt admitted.

"Well, it certainly worked. Y'all do more when you're screwing up than most people do all day," she laughed.

"I THINK that's a compliment, but yet . . . "

"Oh, it is, ya goof. Y'all out magicked your grandmother, which is impressive," she said and lightly tapped him on the shoulder.

"Well . . . all right then."

CHAPTER 14

"In the main, ghosts are said to be forlorn and generally miserable, if not downright depressed. The jolly ghost is rare."

—Dick Cavett

———◆———

MATT WAS PLEASED to see that the remote parking lot they pulled in to was pretty much full to the brim. He had to admit to himself that with everything Madison had said, his imagination had been completely getting the best of him on the ride here. Matt had no idea what to expect when they got to where they were going— a haunted castle, evil demons, a haunted wood, an abandoned campground, a haunted amusement park with a castle and demons next to a campground in the woods, what have you. He had blown this up into something Scooby and the gang would have to investigate instead of what they found: a lot full of hikers and mountain bikers. His visions had been full of guys with an amazing collection of blades and overbearing mother issues, and his best-case scenario ended with pulling a mask off a tied-up villain. Instead, it looked like today involved dodging rock climbers, which wasn't quite as dangerous, not to mention fewer masks.

"Get your game face on, sweetie, we got a heck of a hike in for today," Madison said, swinging the door open.

Okay then, it could just be the convenient parking to

hike to the haunted woods with the evil demon castle and the guy with mommy issues, he made a note of it.

Matt grabbed a backpack with water and snacks in it and trailed after her. "So what is this place anyway? You were kind of short on details last night."

"Well for one," Madison called back as she marched along the gravel parking lot with determination, "it's an abandoned mine and mining town. But we'll see a lot of people while we're on the trail."

"Are we staying on the trail?"

"Course not."

"Figured." He sighed as he hurried to catch up with her.

Matt could see it all, and he knew there was going to be fleeing today, he had known it deep in his heart when he woke up. Well there it was, the scenario all laid out, and he was still walking right into it like a dopey teenager. Cool. He blamed evolutionary hormone issues for this since he couldn't blame his parents, who both would have agreed that this was pretty dumb.

At first, the trail seemed relatively gentle; relatively being the optimum word here because this was still the gorge. Gorge being the optimal word *there* in that sentence. Matt wanted to believe that it would last. He knew it wouldn't, but it didn't stop him from repeating a mental mantra of *This isn't so bad* as they went along. And it didn't even seem so bad for the first big drop down; hey, it had stairs, nothing is all that bad if it has man-made stairs, right? (This would prove to be an *amazingly* ironic thought, showing that we are dabbling in the high-minded literary conceit of foreshadowing here, and you should respect us for it.) It even led to a small waterfall trickling down a rock face, and further along, they could see rock climbers taking advantage of the non-waterfall-y parts of the face to do whatever it was they did. Chalk seemed to figure in heavily, so maybe they had to climb the rock faces to draw art installations or something and the chalk was so it wouldn't be permanent and they wouldn't get yelled at for it.

After the waterfall, the path kept on, only significantly steeper and significantly more directly downward instead of following switchbacks. Neither of them talked much, mainly because of the exertion but almost as much because it was a nice day in a quiet wood in a stunning, beautiful part of nature. It seemed somehow dirty to be chattering away, filling the still air with small talk; something felt far more right about trying to blend in rather than to call attention to yourself. Well, that and Matt kept a steady mantra in his head going of *Jesus, I don't want to have to come back up this, that is gonna suck!* So, his silence maybe wasn't all of the communing with nature type.

As they began to round a bend, Matt was stunned when he could actually see the roof of a building right below them and asked, "What in the hell is that?"

"That was the explosives building, we're almost at the mine," Madison explained.

"Mine? You mentioned mine before. We aren't going into a mine, are we? That's where the monster always grabs Shaggy!" (Matt watched a LOT of Scooby Doo as a kid; this book didn't, this book was busy with important intellectual pursuits, like Looney Tunes.)

Madison laughed at first, but then her face got serious. "It's gated, but mark my word, only idiots go into old mines. They have bad air, rock falls, not to mention getting lost or turned around. Only dipshits and meth heads hoping to steal copper wire for scrap go into abandoned mines."

"I would like to think I am neither of those." Matt shrugged.

"I wouldn't sleep next to you almost every night if I thought you were, I've got major league standards," Madison replied with a smile.

They came down another set of steps to a plateau of sorts—more of an expanded roadway than anything—with more steps leading down from there. The view out across the gorge itself was stunning. They could easily see the huge cliff faces of "Endless Wall" from where they stood, with the cliffs looming up on the other side of the expanse. As pretty as it was, it wasn't what really captured the imagination the most. Tucked against the cliff was the mine itself along with some ruins and, improbably, the safety board listing accidents at the mine. To get closer to the sign, they had to walk under a large gate made of heavily rusted I-beams. Painted on it was the message, "Your Family Wants You To Work Safely." Matt couldn't say why, but it put a chill right up his spine; it almost sounded threatening.

"So, were there a lot of accidents here?" he asked quietly.

"Injuries, deaths . . . mining isn't a safe job today, back then, they didn't have the government breathing down their necks as much, so you can only imagine. The government can only do so much now, before that, they were way more obviously on the owner's side. Old joke is, if there's a collapse, send a person in to see if it's safe for a mule, damned mules cost money," Madison replied, her face unreadable.

They stood there for a moment, staring at the pitch-black low entrance, which was closed off with large metal beams. Finally, Madison broke the silence. "Now for the part that this hike is famous for, the steps."

Matt looked down at the steps; he, did not like the view. Any thoughts he had about steps meaning "easy going and leading to and from civilization" were vanquished by what he saw. There were an awful LOT of steps going down. In fact, he couldn't see the end of the steps from the top, which boded like all hell; specifically, it boded poorly. He was kicking himself for not looking this place up before they had come here; it would have taken him less time than the five minutes he spent on the can this morning completely unproductively watching last week's SNL skits on YouTube (not even particularly good skits). He sighed gustily, reminding himself that the journey of a thousand miles started with a single step. He also didn't want to walk a thousand miles either, but he stepped anyway.

He could feel Madison getting tense as they walked down the steps. Matt stopped on the first landing. "You know, we don't have to do this if you don't want to."

She smiled wanly back at him. "Yeah, I think I really do have to do this. Thanks for coming with me, Hun. I appreciate it. But really, I have to get over this."

Well okay, that was something; he was making good boyfriend points here. With everything that had happened in the last 24 hours, it was probably a damned good thing to be making some ground back if he didn't want to become single. He gave her a reassuring hug before they started down again. Despite her saying she was fine, Madison looked like she could use a hug—boyfriend 101: knowing when they need a hug. He was learning here; he was showing the kind of growth that might have kept him out of West Virginia in the first place if he'd had it months ago. Of course, if he hadn't ended up here, he'd have never met Madison, so maybe he should call it peaking at the right time instead.

The first indication that there might be something down here except a hike straight down an enormous gorge was when they passed a massive rusted water tank to the left of them.

"There used to be a tram running up and down the mountain," Madison said. "It would take people to the mine and back down again to where there was also a road leading to civilization. But even with that, they were pretty cut off here. People stuck in housing the mine provided and isolated from everything but the mine bosses."

Matt tried to take that in with his modern view of the world. "Why did they even take the jobs?"

"A lot of times they were immigrants right off the boat. Sounds good, doesn't it? Y'all just got here from famine or oppression in Europe and a man is waiting right there to say, 'Want a house and a job today?' Course, they were signing on for an all new oppression, but it sounded good. Tucked way out here in the mountains where reporters didn't want to come, who was to say any different about how they were treated?"

Matt didn't even know what to say to that, so he just kept quiet and kept walking. Even the endless stairs showed signs of ending before too long. Matt made a mental note that down always seemed faster than up, so maybe he shouldn't be too happy. Eventually, the ruins of the place came into view. Ruins were the optimum word for them. Everything was what was left of something and barely recognizable as the thing itself. There were the remains of the tram, a huge tin metal construction that tilted dangerously over like it was the most slow-motion collapse ever, and a few enormous stone buildings missing part or all of their roofs.

Madison led their way confidently down into the ruins. Once the trail began to move in around the edge of the larger ruins, she suddenly stopped and left the most traversed area. Their way from there went turning and twisting through the wreckage before, finally, they came up to one of the larger stone ruins. Madison turned and winked before hopping through a stone window.

"Come on down," she called back. "We should probably be left alone in here."

"Is it safe?" Matt asked before he could stop himself. Now he felt like a total rube; he'd just watched as she hopped on in there without saying a peep, but the second his own safety came into question, oh, now he had a concern. "Never mind, be right down," he added, trying to keep the annoyance with himself from sounding like annoyance with her.

He had to slide his way down into a dank open area rather than jump the way she had. The building was mainly just one massive room, and he was coming in halfway up a wall, down a jumble of tin. Years of water and vegetation coming in had reduced most of the floor to a dark mud that squelched just a little as his feet landed on it. The place still had most of its roof, which created a feeling that they were in some kind of vast indoor cave. Large pieces of track, possibly for the tram, were stacked to one side, left where they had been tossed one final time and forgotten, as well as numerous other less identifiable bits of ancient machinery. This place, Matt concluded in the spirit of the open-minded attitude he had taken towards this trip, was a total dump. No wonder Madison was confident that they'd be left alone here; who in the hell else would want to come in?

"Not much of a going concern, huh?" Matt asked when he rejoined Madison.

"Most of it burnt down at some point, but still it's a tourist stop. I think that's mostly for the steps really, people want to say they've done them," she replied.

"The steps you didn't mention," his voice weighted with accusation.

"Oh shush, you're young and relatively fit, and it's not too hot today. Think about being able to brag about it when you go back home."

"Huh, I kinda thought I was home."

Madison looked at him curiously and then said, "Well I suppose I should show y'all the big deal. Look around, but you know, like really look. Y'all know what I mean."

Matt did know, so he let his vision drift into the middle world where magic lived. He saw what she had been alluding to immediately, the swirls of light and almost shape that were everywhere around them! He wasn't sure exactly what it was he was even seeing until he watched a man glimmering in the sun outside walk by one of the doors to the building they were in. Ghosts!

"Y'all see 'em?" Madison asked quietly, her voice tight with tension.

"Yeah," Matt breathed, "they're everywhere, but how?"

"It's a mining town, Hun, people died here. They died here and they didn't leave, that was kind of what I was warming you up to when we were coming down," she explained almost tearfully, her eyes watching the show just as much as him.

He figured she was probably relieved that he was seeing it too.

"So down here, was this the first time you saw anything like this?" he asked as he watched another man walk right through the wall of the building. None of the ghosts seemed to notice them at all, they just went about their business like they weren't even there.

"Yeah, when I was a teenager. Me and some friends snuck down here to take shrooms. Don't say anything," she added, putting up her hand, "I know what a dumb idea that is *now*. Kids do dumb stuff. I kept asking my friends if they were seeing it too, but they just assumed I was tripping. I knew I wasn't; I knew they were real! I mean, why in the hell would I trip create normal people in old-style clothing just walking around? I knew what it was, but what with my mamma and all, I just pushed it away, didn't want to talk about it or think about it after that. Until now. That's why I wanted to come down here, to prove to myself after all this time that it was all real."

"Well I'm sure as hell seeing it too, and I'm stone-cold sober, "Matt confirmed.

"I wonder why most of them are all fuzzy? Just swirling lights and shapes, a lot of them."

Matt thought about it for a second, but then he knew. He didn't know how he knew, but he knew it anyway.

"They've never had someone to talk to, to keep them focused," he breathed.

"Hey, GHOSTS!" Madison yelled impulsively.

This proved to be a bit of an error in judgment on her part, no matter how well-meant it was.

(Have you ever seen what happens when a group of preschoolers wants to get an adult to talk to them in the middle of playtime? Probably not, no sane human being would ever subject themselves to that, which is why preschool teachers should get the kind of hazard pay that is usually set aside for NFL defensive ends or members of the secret service. To boil it all down, the little snot factories haven't really developed the idea of "taking turns" yet and all want to talk at once. What happened next was like that, but more Stephen-King-ey and less Chuckie Cheese during a rush—"Stephen-King-ey" is a word we just made up, and you should use it in your everyday life as often as possible. If you can find an occasion to use it to Mr. Stephen King personally, you will get major points from this book.)

The cacophony that instantly erupted when every ghost in a ghost town realized that they had company that could see them was almost instantly deafening. At first, Madison and Matt were at least able to make out individual spirits, ghosts who still retained their mortal form as they flooded into the building—miners, children, mothers, some disfigured still by whatever killed them because there had been no one there to tell them they could look however they wanted. Within moments, it became impossible to discern one from another; all of the spirits that existed here became an insane swirl of faded colors and ghostly white around them! A very loud swirl at that.

Matt said loudly, "I think we should leave!"

"What do y'all believe?!"

"NO! LEAVE! AS IN GET THE FUCK OUT OF HERE!" he yelled at the top of his lungs

"GREAT IDEA!"

They began to scramble up out of the building only to discover that it was indeed a lot easier down then up. Gravity had been on their side, for one thing, and also nobody performs best in a panic, for another. Eventually, Matt gave up and boosted Madison up before dragging himself up after her. From there, they bolted as best as they were able through the rubble and undergrowth of the former mine town and to the stairs out of there! It wasn't until they were at least a third of the way up that the ruckus had settled enough for them to finally collapse on a landing, gasping for air.

"Maybe . . . yelling . . . was a bad . . . idea . . . " Matt pointed out reasonably between gulps of air.

"Ya . . . fucking . . . think?"

Matt took a deep shuddering breath. "I didn't want to be rude."

Madison shook her head, replying, "No, on this one, y'all would have been within your rights."

Matt sat there for a moment, sweating, occasionally staring up at the roughly 5 million stairs above them (there are only about 821 total from the bottom, and he's being a weenie here). Finally, he looked over at Madison, whose head was down with her hands on her knees. "I'm even more sure I'm right now."

Madison's head came up. "About?"

"Nobody to talk to, nobody to keep them cohesive. People go mad in a room by themselves. The ghosts down there might not even know they can talk to each other," Matt reasoned.

Madison was very quiet for a minute, just staring at Matt in a way that made him wonder if he had a spider on his face or something. Finally, she said, "Matt, Hun, I know we've put each other through a lot lately . . . "

"Forgive me if I don't like where this is going."

"But could y'all come with me to the family plot out in county?" she finished.

Matt stared blankly for a minute and then chuckled. "Oh, thank god, I was afraid you were going to suggest coming down here again or something."

Madison smiled. "No, but it would be nice if we could do something for those trapped down here. Don't y'all think?"

Matt thought about it for a moment before nodding. "Let me ask my Pa Pa when I get a chance. Who knows, maybe we can send Mungo down here on occasion to keep them company. They'd probably start thinking more clearly just being forced to concentrate."

"On what?"

"On what in the hell he's saying. I can barely understand a word of it, and he's my ancestor. Hey! Maybe we might convince them to keep him!" Matt brightened considerably at the thought.

They had to stop again around step five billion seven hundred and two so Matt could get another breather (around step six hundred, and Matt was really being a weenie about all of this). He didn't say anything, that would have been a precious waste of oxygen that he desperately needed to somehow sieve out of the humid air lest he die. Funny, it hadn't seemed that humid on the way down, but now he'd be willing to swear that shoals of fish were out there somewhere, floating by the mountain gracefully in the afternoon light.

"Not much further now," Madison said cheerfully.

Matt was looking at her with newfound respect; sure, she was a little sweaty, but not the least bit worn-out from everything. He, on the other hand, would have been perfectly willing to die right here, except for the fact that only recently he had seen what had happened to everyone else who had died here.

"I think I need to jog or something. I mean, assuming I don't expire here on the mountain," he replied eventually.

Since life has a funny sense of humor, an older couple,

looking to be in their sixties easily, came into view coming down the steps almost as soon as he said it. They looked light and easy, like they did this kind of hike all the time. They smiled and said hi before passing them by. Great, now he was getting fitness dissed by the senior-circuit.

A glacial epoch later (ten, fifteen minutes tops, we're talking major king god weenie here), they made it back to the mine. Elation over having not died coming up the steps overcame Matt's desire to lie in the grass and whimper for a while. He was happy for that, considering he was with his girlfriend and it's behavior like that that would inspire her to reassess her opinion of Tyler if Matt wasn't careful. Sure, he might be all kinds of cool and magical, and might very well have saved her very existence, but he was pretty sure that Tyler wouldn't have collapsed to a puddle over some steps. It wouldn't have looked cool and kick-ass; it totally wouldn't have been Tyler's style. Complaining about it but doing it in a cool kick-ass psychobilly ironic manner, that's how Tyler would have handled it, Matt was sure.

Letting elation win meant looking out over the gorge. If anything, he appreciated the open air and the view even more now that he'd suffered to achieve it. He turned to look at Madison, but in doing so, his eyes fell squarely on the mine itself. The source for all the endless upset and tumult down by the river below them. His face hardened a bit, thinking on that.

"What's up, Hun?" Madison asked with concern.

"Yeah, maybe I do need to talk to Pa Pa about this a bit," was all he said by way of reply.

"Well, cheer up," she smiled, "we're a little past halfway there now!"

Matt wanted to stop himself, he truly did, but it was something deeper and more primal that forced the groan of misery at the thought of more hiking through his lips.

☽○☾

They were staying at Madison's place that night. Justin was leaving tomorrow, and there was just no way to stay up at the farm that wasn't rude to him. Now that the perpetual storm was off his head, Justin was a changed guy anyway. He still didn't talk much. Matt didn't ask, but he kind of suspected he had been kind of quiet even before the doom of being perpetually damp and squishy had been laid upon him. But he smiled more and was just an overall more pleasant person to be around. While they'd been having takeout and streaming movies, he'd even mentioned that he might want to consider finally settling down somewhere, somewhere he could achieve more permanent female companionship than the kind afforded him by truck stops. Seeing him like this actually made Matt swell with a feeling that he had a sneaking suspicion was pride at having helped the guy out.

They were in the bedroom, having said goodnight to Justin, watching some dumb—like, truly idiotic—horror film involving zombies, as the cheap ones often do, when Matt turned to look at Madison. He couldn't help himself, a grin spread over his face.

She noticed; her eyes went wide. "What?" she said, feeling self-conscious under his scrutiny.

"Thank you," he said softly.

"For what?"

"Putting some joy into my whole bizarre life."

She pulled back a bit to look at him better. "How so, may I ask?"

Matt smiled. "I was raised up north. A few short months ago, I was a suddenly single loser being banished off to West Virginia because my dad had converted my bedroom into a den and didn't want to give it up. Then, I had to get a job and had to get a kind of loser job to avoid cow shit. Suddenly, I'm the scion and heir to an ancient magical tradition rooted in the very mountains, but with a loser job. There were no Granny Witches or anything like that when I was a kid. If you said there were, you went into a special place until they could get your meds sorted. So, this is all deeply over-the-top weird to me, weirder still is how much it all makes sense to me down here. Now all of that could have made me all kinds of psyched out and panicked and unable to cope. Not a soul would be able to blame me. But there you are, all snuggled up next to me, and it makes it all like a weird adventure we're taking together."

"Hell of a speech, tiger," she said with a grin, snuggling up to him. "Thank y'all back, I should have done all of this years ago, but I was all a skeered and stuff. But it isn't so scary when you've got to do it all too."

"Speaking of scary . . . "

"Yeesssss?" She let a bit of trepidation creep into her voice.

"Well, you know how you have family stuff we have to drive out and take care of, right?"

"Yup, thanks for coming along for that, by the way."

"I am going to have to call my dad. We've got a lot of shit we need to talk about."

Chapter 15

"They have in me struck down but the trunk of the tree; the roots are many and deep—they will shoot up again!"

—Toussaint Louverture

———◆———

THEY TABLED GOING out to Madison's family graveyard until the next weekend. They both had jobs, wanted time to unwind, etc. Matt avoided pointing out that it wasn't like her family was going anywhere, even though the joke was just *sitting there,* waiting to be said. He was pretty sure that was in bad taste and had the common sense to know that while she'd laugh at that if they were talking about somebody else, she might not see the humor in it here. Kaymoor had shaken them both up a bit, and his realization as to why the ghosts were like that had probably shaken Madison up even more than him.

He was back at the farm by himself tonight, he had planned it that way. Matt needed to be by himself; he had something he needed to do. But before he could be alone, he, of course, had to be subjected to his aunt and uncle's assessment of Madison. "She seemed very polite" and "That's a fine-looking girl" pretty much so covered it, though there was a side dose of "So how serious y'all planning to get?" It took longer for them to say, but that was the gist of it. So, Madison had passed the family sniff test; he'd have to text her to let her know.

Matt considered bothering Tyler, if only because it would put things off for a little bit. When he got to Tyler's room, though, he heard a very feminine sounding giggle through the door. Matt didn't consider himself a rocket scientist, but he was pretty sure that meant that avenue of procrastination was out.

Matt trudged on to his room and fired up the computer. It took a few minutes to run through his inboxes, twitter, and Facebook, but nothing of much interest seemed to be happening—because people can be inconsiderately boring when you need distractions. There were some cute "love you, miss you" messages from Madison, but nothing else that he really needed to respond to. He knew what he was doing. He was struggling to put something off long enough that it would eventually be too late to bother and then he could tell himself later that he had just forgotten. Matt was doing it so poorly that even he couldn't convince himself that it wasn't what he was up to or that any of his activities to do it with were in any way vital.

With hearty "Screw it," he took out his phone and auto-dialed.

"Hello?" his mom answered almost immediately.

"Hi, Mom, it's me, Matt."

"Oh . . . Matt . . . oh, dear. Is everything all right?"

"What? No, I'm fine, Mom, I just haven't really called much and all . . . "

"Oh . . . all right . . . umm, sorry, you caught me by surprise is all. Are you all right down there? How have you been settling in? Do you have a job or anything?"

Matt had texted this stuff to his dad ages ago; nice to see the lines of communication were in such good working order up there. "Yeah, Mom, I'm fine, got a job, got a girlfriend—"

"Oh, my, a girlfriend?" His mom cut him off.

"Yeah, her name's Madison. She's really pretty and all . . . "

"Well, that is good to hear," Mom enthused.

"Umm, Mom, could you put Dad on?" he asked, sounding as nonchalant as he could manage. "I really need to ask him something about down here, and he grew up here and all."

"What? Oh sure, let me get him," his mother replied, still sounding flustered. A moment later, she yelled, "Bobby pick up the other line!"

Matt heard his father's voice in the background; he couldn't make out the words, but Matt figured he really didn't need to. He figured it would be some variant on the theme of "Who the hell is it?"

Sure enough, a second later, his mother yelled, "It's Matt! Calling from West Virginia!"

A few moments after that, the other phone made a violent clacking noise. "All right, honey, I got it. You can hang up now!"

"Okay! Matt, if you want to talk after you're done with Dad, tell him to put me back on."

"All right, I will, Mom, love you."

"Love you too, sweetie."

The landlines were a total mystery to Matt. He'd even asked why they bothered, only to be told they were for "power outages." That made sense, he supposed, but it didn't explain having multiple lines in the house. Or, for that matter, why if he had called either one of their cells tonight, he would have gotten voicemail. Old habits die hard, he guessed. One day, kids will be thinking messages at each other, and Matt would probably be holding on to his Samsung for dear life, buying parts online to keep it functional and being made fun of by his own kids for it, assuming, of course, he ever even had a stable enough life to consider breeding.

"Hey, Matt," his father said flatly after they'd both heard the other line click off.

"Hey, Dad."

"So, what can I do for you tonight?" Still no emotion in his voice, like he was waiting for something.

Matt sighed, it appeared they both knew where it was going, might as well get it over with. "Dad, we need to talk."

"Yeah, I figured we did. So, you going to yell at me?"

"I don't know, Dad, should I?" Matt sighed again. "I just want to know why you didn't tell me; more than anything, that's what I'd like to know."

Matt's Dad let out an answering sigh and then continued, his voice containing only the slightest hint of the accent he had been raised with. "I don't know, Christ. Which version do you want, the selfish version or the non-self-version?"

"I could do with the truth, Dad."

"Problem is, they're both true. It's just a matter of how much you want to resent me later."

Matt considered it for a moment. Truth tended to be truth in his eyes, but if you ever listened to people talk about a relationship . . . he himself always said, "There's his side and her side and the truth." Maybe both versions could be equally true. "Try giving me both, and I'll try to decide which one I liked better, and we'll go with that."

Another breath made the phone muffle. "All right, I'm going to have to give you some background. You know how I always told you about your MeeMaw running off when she was young, right?"

"Yeah."

"Well, she'd never believe it, but I was proud of her. She'd gone somewhere, done things. I used to tell my friends about her adventures out in the world. They never believed me, didn't think it was even possible to just leave like that. The thing I could never figure out was why she'd come back at all. There we were, getting satellite signals from all over the place, and I'd watch them every day, there was a whole world out there. I never wanted to dig coal and I never wanted to farm, I just wanted to get the hell out.

Go somewhere, the place my mom had talked about where there were no witches and no magic and things just made common sense. And dear god, where people could talk so you'd understand them."

"You're talking about Mungo, aren't you?"

Matt's dad actually chuckled at that. "Especially, double underline on Mungo, but I was being general."

"So why didn't you ever tell me?"

"I kept meaning to, to find a way to show it to you so you could make up your own mind what you wanted. But first, you were too young, couldn't have you blabbing to everybody at school up here that your MeeMaw was a witch, that's when they call child services on you. Then, I don't know . . . it just got harder and harder. Everything was nice and normal the way I always wanted it, and I didn't want to screw it up."

"So, why'd you send me down here now?"

"You mean other than not wanting to give up my den?"

"Yeah, I figure the den was bonus material." Matt felt a smile cross his lips.

"Well, things weren't good for you here . . . your mother suggested it one night when we were in bed, and, well you did have a right to know, as weird as it was. Hell, for all I knew, it wasn't even going to be you who had it, could have been Tyler or Edwin who got it."

"Well, it wasn't them, but you already know that."

"I already do, it was mentioning Mungo that did it," his dad agreed.

The line was quiet for a moment before his dad asked, "So, what are you going to do next?"

"Mom'll tell you. Right now, things are working out pretty good down here so far. Job, girlfriend, scion of a family of mountain witches, you know, the things everybody wants out of life. Think I'm gonna let it ride a bit," Matt replied.

"Well, I love you, son. No, really, I do, even if I was a

jerk about my den; but damn it, I did spend money redecorating. If you don't decide to run back sooner, we were planning to come down for Christmas this year. We'll see you soon."

"Love you too, Dad." Dad was never very good at sarcasm, so Matt figured he missed the family of witches crack.

$$)O($$

They were driving the Xterra out to what everyone here referred to as "county". McDowell County, to be exact. If you said the word "county" in southern West Virginia, most people knew exactly where you meant. It was what was left when a full boom goes full bust. Generations of politicians had mouthed platitudes about fixing what was essentially a third world impoverished country right here in the states, but that was about all they did. Despite all the talk, for whatever reason, all these years later, the only real changes had been in the number of abandoned buildings, which had gone up. People fled, whether or not they fled far or stayed in state when the jobs left, the people left. The coal companies had taken the wealth and left "county" to fend for itself. A few mines still operated, but once the rot set in, the people with the jobs mainly didn't live here anymore either. Oddly, despair wasn't the only feeling Matt had as they drove through these small struggling towns. He had this overwhelming feeling that all this nature that surrounded these towns was just waiting for people to come through and wipe clean what had been done here and to start fresh. Like the rotting, abandoned buildings were just specks of food needing to be cleaned off to allow the plate to be used as the family's best china all over again. He couldn't help but respect those that stayed; they showed a strength to stick it out that, clearly, he perceived himself as lacking.

Matt was driving; it wasn't that Madison didn't have a car, you needed one to survive here really, she just rarely drove if she could avoid it. He'd pressed her on it once, and she'd replied, "Play to your strengths, kid." What she meant by that could be summed up by the trip they took to Dismal Falls in her car that had left him checking for gray hairs later. He wasn't sure that it was her driving so much as it was her ancient little Subaru, a vehicle that would need a major overhaul just to appear derelict. Madison liked to talk when she drove, distracting her from a car that liked to wander around the road aimlessly when it was driven, a match made in heart attack heaven. He suspected that she'd be a perfectly capable driver if the car she was driving wasn't prone to getting distracted from the road all on its own.

"Watch the ATVs through here," Madison remarked as they drove through one of the small towns along their way.

"Why in the hell are they on the road?"

"Desperation. There's an ATV trail near here; people so desperate for tourist dollars, they let them do whatever they want." She shrugged.

"Do they have insurance?"

"Who knows, thus, be careful. Unless you want to be paying for repairs on this thing yourself."

Not every house in these small towns was forlorn and tumble-down. Every fourth or so would look very nice, like someone proudly railing against the encroaching darkness. An anti-pioneer holding their own in their own spot despite the odds, despite watching it turn into wasteland before their eyes. Having the wilderness come in their own front door and yet holding back against it. The cloudy day wasn't helping appearances or first impressions, obviously.

"So, this is where I'm from," Madison said. The way she said it, Matt could see the challenge standing proudly in that little sentence.

"So, what are the hills like up in the mountains?"

"Woods, wild, wonderful West Virginia. If it wasn't for the mines still running, it would probably be a hunting and fishing paradise. Who knows, maybe the ATVers, as much of a pain in the ass as they are, maybe they're the first step in people seeing that. Lord knows the mines are on their last legs."

Matt felt like he'd passed a test here. He wasn't blind, he could see the poverty, he could see the abandonment, but he refused to act or think like the people here were pitiful. Like they were so far gone they could only receive pity now. If anything, the fact that they'd face these odds just to hold on to home and heritage was admirable. "Lot of history here," he remarked instead.

"Yeah, probably a raft of stories. All fully fleshed out with evil villains and struggles against the odds. Shame all people see, if they see it at all, is the lack of money. Somebody should write those stories before nobody remembers them," Madison agreed.

They had lunch at a Greek place, which came as a surprise being all the way out here; better still, it was good. He mentioned it, and Madison replied, "Lot of immigrants came here. Big stone building we passed is dedicated to World War One African-American soldiers, first in the nation. Whatever color you go into a mine, y'all come out black."

"I think you got a better education about life growing up here," Matt replied.

Madison looked at him like he'd lost his mind. "And how do you figure that?"

"What are you gonna learn where I grew up? How many middle-class people from identical backgrounds you can fit into identical houses per square mile? How we all pretend the world works even though it doesn't outside of our subdivision?"

Madison smiled sincerely. "You know, I never thought of it like that before, thanks for the positive spin!"

They clipped the edge of the main town in the area, Welch, before turning off onto another highway. Welch didn't look bustling either, but it was larger. So, it wasn't all ghost towns left to mother nature to wipe the slate clean again after all. For some reason, that also comforted Matt. Like how they must have felt the first time on *The Walking Dead* when they reached a settlement. Like it isn't JUST a few straggling survivors, the world still moved out here.

The sun had finally begun to come out, and now . . . it all started to look just rustic. Fields and forests began to dominate the landscape. Coal had been here, the remains could be seen here or there, the train tracks, there was a large tipple they passed still in operation, but it no longer dominated the view wherever you looked. This felt like the beginnings of what the whole county would get to be one day. Farms might even sprout up once the toxins leached away; streams would start to be fishing havens. This whole part of the county felt like it was drawing in breath in anticipation of breathing freely again.

Matt couldn't help but cheer up; well, he could have stayed dour, they were going to a graveyard after all, and near a town called War, which didn't sound promising at all (also a real town, look, the book didn't *name* them, we just report 'em as they come up), but he didn't want to. He was just as ready to breathe as mother nature here. Matt hadn't even realized until he saw the change in scenery how solemn what they had passed through had made the mood in the vehicle. He looked over and saw that Madison was smiling.

"Looking forward to seeing your relatives again?"

She made a face. "Do y'all look forward to talking to yours?"

"Well no, but I have Mungo. Wait, you don't have anybody like that in your family tree, do you?" Matt looked concerned.

"Well, we've been here almost as long as the Hawleys, so I guess we'll find out."

"God, I hope they don't yell as much. It's bad enough not understanding what in the hell he's saying, but he insists on yelling it at you on top of it." Matt shuddered.

Madison giggled a bit. "Well, they're my relatives, they probably won't be nearly so interested in y'all, so I think you're probably safe." They drove on a little further before she added, "I think I am looking forward to talking to my mamma again."

"Good thing you have that gift."

"Gift, huh? Yeah, a gift, I think I like that too. It's so much better than worrying about what's wrong with me. Turn up here and then look for a dirt road." Madison pointed.

After Matt turned, he had to stop immediately. It wasn't just that the dirt road was only a "road in theory," more like a deer trail that had gotten ideas above its station, it was that there was two of them. "Umm . . . "

"Left. After the fire, we finally sold some of the property to a mining concern. That goes up to their sidewall mine. I didn't want to, but with the taxes, it's all we can do to keep the rest of the property," Madison explained before adding, "Definitely never go to the right; they think anyone who heads up there is either a copper thief or some environmental pinko looking to do a report on MTR damage. Either way, you won't be welcome."

"Well, I didn't even *want* to go the wrong way before you said that!"

"Let's talk to some ghosts first and then we'll see, rebel boy." Madison laughed.

The road that they used to head up the hill looked almost like a dry riverbed. Rocks jutted out from under the brown dirt like axle-seeking land mines. Matt winced as he put the SUV into four-wheel drive low gear and began the trudge up the hill.

"You know, I really don't have that much experience using this thing the way it was intended," he grumbled.

"Well, look at it as making up for lost time."

"We'll have more lost time if I break it."

Madison snorted. "Like y'all said, it was intended for this. Local guy comes up here twice a year to mow, and I know damned well he's driving an old Ford that's more holes than truck; stop bein' such a weenie!"

"I am not a weenie!" Matt protested.

"Well, you're a cute weenie."

Matt paused for a moment before saying, "Well, as long as I'm cute in my weenieness, I suppose I can learn to live with it."

As promised, despite the unlikeliness, there was a graveyard up there. The stones were all small things, even by the standard of a small mountain family plot, but there were plenty of them, enough to indicate generations of this family. The grass must have been cut recently, they were all clearly visible, even with the cloud of dust from Matt braking when the plot appeared suddenly as they rounded a corner. It was a shaded area, the trees had clearly been planted for this reason only, fields and rock could be seen further up the hill from the wooded area surrounding the graveyard.

"Wish me luck," Madison said quietly.

"Hey, I'll be right here with you if you need me."

Madison got out and walked up to the elderly metal fence; it was made more like the fence around a yard than some spooky heavy-duty graveyard fencing. The original wrought-iron had been sold off years ago rather than let it be stolen by scrappers, so now it was just something cheap, something of little resale value.

Matt hung back and waited outside the gate. She could ask him in if she wanted, but it really wasn't his moment. He didn't want to intrude on hers by just barreling in after her.

Madison stepped through the gate, letting it creak all the way open. She took a few steps in and closed her eyes.

She was terrified of this, but that would only get worse the longer she let it go on. She forced herself to take a deep, steadying breath. Madison was about to open her eyes and say something when her train of thought was interrupted by a voice she knew all too well.

"Don't know what in heck y'all are so scared 'bout. Not from the woman who used to love y'all enough to change yer diapers when y'all wuz a baby."

"Mamma?"

Madison opened her eyes to see her mother standing in front of her smiling.

The tall, slender woman Matt could see from where he stood wore a pair of jeans and a flannel shirt over a t-shirt, and her hair was a deep auburn falling down her back. He had guessed before that how you appeared in death was how you remembered yourself most in life. Madison, on the other hand, almost burst out laughing because it reminded her inappropriately of the movie *The Frighteners*.

The ghostly form just kept smiling and said, "Well, y'all came to my grave, didn't ya? Who in the hell else would you expect? Sid Hatfield and Arch Moore jumping up and down on pogo sticks? Now mind, I wouldn't mind seein' that my own self, and no mistake."

Madison couldn't help herself, she laughed again, a light, airy laugh without any worry or trepidation. She had her hand to her mouth to quell the outburst when she replied, "I missed you, Mamma."

"I missed you too, sweetie."

Matt was sure he could see a tear in Madison's eye as she looked on her mother's form and had to chide himself for even this much eavesdropping and watching.

"I'd ask how you've been, but . . . "

"Well, for all that, I've been well anyway. At least I have company to talk to."

A light went off for Madison. "Oh, where are the others?"

Her mother grinned a little; Matt thought that he could see some of Madison's mischief in those eyes. "I told the old bunch of spooks they'd scare ya off iff'n they all come out rushing to see y'all at once. Seeing as how y'all only recently really found your gift and all."

"Weel that's jist abit lang enaw," said a voice from behind the pair of them.

Matt was stunned by it. It was the same brogue he could never understand and was frankly terrified of coming from Mungo, but now it sounded sweet and even lilting, and decidedly feminine.

The figure that appeared behind Madison's mother was clothed in a fine dress; her red hair was piled up in swirls on her head; even ghostly, her green eyes drew your vision to her. Matt was surprised to find that, even this many generations removed, he could see the resemblance immediately.

"Couldn't wait, could you, Grandmother?" Madison's mother said with a grimace. To Madison, she said, "Well not really my grandmother either, but the *greats* get tiresome to rattle off. This beautiful young lady would be the founder of the family here, Elspeth Cruden"

"Ummm . . . charmed?" Madison stammered.

"Hen, laird, swatch at aw 'at decoration on 'er." the woman said matter of factually.

"Grandmother, I told y'all before, it's the style now," Madison's mother chided the spirit next to her.

"Weel, Glenna, at leest th' loon looks normal. Fae, is he?" the ancient ghost sniffed.

"Ummm, Mamma? That fine-looking young man standing out there, respectfully, I might add, is my boyfriend Matt, who I think she's talking about, but I'm just guessin', and, ummmm . . . he can hear all of this." Madison's face looked worried, but Matt could see her eyes wanted to burst out laughing.

She almost did lose it when she saw a similar gleam in

her mother's eye. Her mother just smiled and called over to Matt, "Well, y'all might as well come over here, boyfriend, so y'all can have your teeth and hooves examined by us dead folk. What's your name?"

It took Matt a moment to get over the shock of being brought into this, which was something he'd been hoping to avoid. "Matt Hawley, ma'am?"

"Hawley, is it? Well-known name in these parts. And y'all can hear us? I don't suppose you're kin to Lou May and Curtis, are you?" Madison's mother asked.

"That would be my MeeMaw and Pa Pa, yes."

"My word, dear," Madison's mother said, turning back to Madison. "Look at y'all dating a Hawley boy. And from the available evidence, *the* Hawley boy. Y'all come up in the world since that Jordan boy from over Bradshaw y'all dated in High School, and no mistake."

Madison blushed a bit. "Mamma, it's nothing like that. He was working at the record store I liked, and he was new here and looked lonely. Y'all are right about Jordan, I think he's doing time now."

Matt was not particularly thrilled to hear that the initial contact had been a pity thing, even if he couldn't deny the logic of it. Of course, she wasn't going to say to her mom that she thought he was cute, so maybe he was overthinking this. Somehow, he suspected he wasn't, but look where that pity had gotten him in the long run!

"Well he looks like a lovely boy, and a nice local family, no matter how he got y'all interested in him," her mother said

"Aye, Mungo was nae a bad cheil, jist a bit lood. Hopefully, they've bred th' lood it ay them by noo," the matriarch of the family agreed.

Madison's mother turned back to her. "So are y'all ready to meet your family, dear? Your MeeMaw's been asking for ya, but she let me come out first. Your young man can wait here if he likes, or the goin' over with a fine-tooth comb option is still available if he's pining to be treated like a farm animal."

"I'd like that."

"Me too," said Matt. When he saw that all eyes had turned towards him, he quickly added, "The waiting at the car thing . . . umm . . . this should probably be for family only . . . umm . . . have fun, Madison."

"Come along, Maddie."

Matt went back to the SUV and tried not to watch. It felt rude; it was their family having a reunion, not his, and it always feels awkward to be standing to the side when some big family moment happens. Everyone is gushing with emotion, which you clearly can't share, you don't know half of the people, and you weren't there for what they were. Yet you feel obligated to participate with a hearty "Yay" or "I'm so sorry" that you clearly weren't feeling. You're a spectator, and you should have enough respect to not treat people's important moments as entertainment. Happily back in the SUV, once he saw the ghostly figures appearing all around Madison, he took out his phone and was pleased to see he had exactly enough signal to get on the internet.

About an hour later, Matt was deep into an argument in a Facebook group over whether or not the earth was flat (he was con, the book just feels the need to stress that the main character of this book believes the earth is round, and who knew you'd have to point that out one day?) when the door suddenly opened. It startled him enough that he dropped his phone, sending it under the seat. (That is the place where phones instinctively go, knowing full well how difficult it is to get them back out without opening the door.)

He recovered quickly and asked brightly, "So, how you feeling?"

Madison smiled. "Better than I have been in years, I think. Y'all have any idea how hard it is to hide who y'all really are, even from yourself?"

Matt shook his head. "No, not really. Before I got here, I don't think I had a real me to hide. That's what people like I was do, they go with the flow and never develop a real self. The real them is whatever they get told it is this week. Unless you want to say the real me was too lazy to find out who the real him was, that might work. But I would think being yourself would come as a relief if you hadn't been being yourself before. You know, one less thing to keep track of."

"You want to see the old farmstead while we're here?"

"Is it spooky?"

"Oh very, used to give me nightmares when I was a girl." Madison grinned.

"Can we not?"

"Yeah, I think we've done enough magic stuff today. Still, it's nice to have a place to belong to, something other than being in the audience for a band," she said with a smile. "Now roll, cowboy. I feel like going to the mall."

"Really?!"

"Really. After all this backwoods country mysticism, I feel the need to re-affirm that part of the real me is also someone who saw some bitchin' new boots at Hot Topic and is sure she has enough money in her account to get them!"

Chapter 16

"There are risks and costs to action. But they are far less than the long-range risks of comfortable inaction."
— John F. Kennedy, boat captain

———◆———

MATT HAD NOT bothered to go to the mall in the entire time he had been here. In reality, he hadn't really bothered with the mall much back home either. Online shopping and specialty stores were more his niches. His parents used to drag him along when he was a kid, but as soon as he could refuse, he did exactly that. In reality, Matt figured that was probably what malls even still existed for, Gen X or older adults who still remember malls fondly, like the way really old people think about flea markets. Matt also noticed that flea markets had oddly become retro-cool and back in style, showing that irony was still very much alive and well in America. It was only a matter of time before kids started flocking back to the malls to buy soft pretzels and Sbarro again under the pretext of being sarcastic. It wouldn't matter to the mall owners, as long as the money came in.

The point being, and there was one, near his house. Matt went in with a bit of trepidation, having no idea on earth what to expect from a mall in the mountains of West Virginia. It was a bit of a come down to find out that a mall in the mountains of West Virginia was almost indistinguishable from a mall anywhere else in this great land of ours. The same stores, the same products, the same people, as if they had been pushed out of a mold somewhere where they were grown to fill malls with. It had a food court, it had a record/DVD/quirky stuff store, a vitamin store, cell phone stores, a video game store (full disclosure, Matt did buy a copy of *Dead Hospital IV Colostomy Of Doom*, but he didn't feel good about himself doing it), and a Hot Topic, where they did indeed still have the boots that Madison wanted. Boots which laced up tightly to past her knees; boots that Matt did have to admit looked hot as hell on her. Though, when the girl working the cash register in the *Nightmare on Elm Street* t-shirt told them to "Have Blessed Day," Matt had almost busted a gut. It was all he could do to get out of sight of the store before he started laughing. Madison, being *from* West Virginia and being used to cashiers saying that, had to concede that it was funny in this context, just not as funny as he was making it, and he could stop laughing any time he wanted now. No really, shut the hell up, Yankee carpetbagging scum.

Purchases in hand, they left the tribute to American capitalism and made their way home to the farm. Matt made them stop at a bookstore on the way so he could buy a book by Neil Gaiman just to make himself feel slightly less like a tool of the lowest form of capitalism. Even with the need to partially assuage his guilty feelings by making a literary purchase, deep down he had to admit he was looking forward to playing the game with Tyler when they had some free time and to Madison keeping the boots on the next time they played Doctor.

)O(

Bill Baldwin was not having a good day. He was down three goons, counting today. Bill didn't know what happened, but not knowing didn't change anything, Maw Maw would not see his ignorance as a lack of culpability. First, there was the one Maw Maw had sent out to rough up the Hawley loser, because she "wanted to see something," that had somehow or other become his fault, and since it was her idea, he couldn't puzzle that one out at all. Now the two he had sent out to lean on the farmer were gone as well. It was hard to ask her to supply more for him because she got mad. Replacing them usually only ever had to happen when one of them got themselves killed in a mine, and even then, he'd get barked at for not paying more attention. Two just vanishing like this, now that was especially hard to explain to her.

He swore they committed suicide in the mines out of mischief, but she swore even louder and with a better selection of curses that they weren't capable of it. Maw Maw had tried to explain it to him once, but he had the damndest time following her logic. She'd said slaving was what they knew; they were slaves where they come from, they'd be slaves here with no problems. Maw Maw always had an explanation for everything, especially when it came to telling him why things were his fault. Well, what she said may be, but the ones that had died, had died in some of the dumbest manners possible. Mindless slave or not, it takes a special kind of idiot to step on a live wire that you had to go out of your way to find, as a for instance.

Worse still, he'd been summoned by the old bat. She'd called him twenty minutes ago demanding he get out there now. He had no idea why—at least not anything that she knew about—she couldn't know about the goons yet, just wasn't possible. Though, come to think of it, she had known about the first one before he had been able to say a word. He couldn't remember many occasions going all the way back to when he was a boy that she'd ever summoned him for a good thing. No, when she wanted him, she wanted him to do something and damned well do it now and do it right, or she wanted to yell about what she thought he hadn't done right. He'd have to tell her about the two goons he'd lost while he was there. She'd yell at him, he was sure of it; the only reason she wouldn't do something unpleasant to him was that he was family. Bill not only was family, deep down inside, he suspected that she needed him almost as much as he needed her. If only he could figure out how to articulate exactly why she needed him, maybe he wouldn't be dragging his feet every step of the way up to her porch by the time he got there.

"Boy! Get yer fat ass in har, we gotsta talk!"

Well damn! Now he knew he was in for it. With no real choice here, he went in the door calling out, "What can I do ya for, Maw Maw?"

When he entered her parlor, she was smiling. This meant nothing, that woman could do a ton of evil with a smile on her face the entire time. Still, she patted the chair he usually sat in. "Take a seat, and I'll explain it all."

He took his seat, his hands folded on his lap like some kind of poor schlub looking to get a bank loan. "What you needin' from me, Maw Maw?"

She almost looked peaceful and beatific as she sat there. Frankly, since he'd never seen that look on her face, that scared him more than anything.

"Y'all know how I said I just needed a few more territories and I could do somethin' real big? Somethin' major that would make it that we wouldn't have to take no lip from nobody evah again?"

"Yeah, it's been working out for the both of us. I get the mineral rights, and y'all been getting the power." He nodded.

"Well, I figured out a way I can jump-start the whole thing. Do it all in one night. But we got to be smart about it now! Can't afford no mistakes here! Which mean y'all got to do EXACTLY what I say. Can't be no way but how I say or it'll go wrong, and we're too close now." She smiled wickedly and leaned forward, making Bill even more afraid. "So, this is what y'all are gonna do . . . "

)O(

They were taking a day off today. Well, not really a day off, that sounded like they were sick of each other, which wasn't the case. More that Madison had some things she wanted to do today, and Matt kind of felt what with watching her reunite with her departed loved ones, maybe he should spend some more time with his own. It probably got lonely out there in the graveyard. By now, they would have told each other all the jokes they knew, so he couldn't imagine what they got up to. It might be nice to have him around, if for nothing else, he still could watch Colbert every night and come up with new material.

MeeMaw would want him some today, he was sure of that. She'd been a bit more demanding with Matt since the incident at the company store. That didn't quite seem fair; none of them got hurt, the portal got slammed shut, what in the hell was the problem? But ever since then, whenever they so much as touched magic, she'd wanted everything done exactly so. Everything she showed him since then had to be done her way or no way at all. MeeMaw used to be all milk and cookies and a fiver when his mom wasn't looking, now it was like going back to elementary school with Mean Old Mrs. Trumbaur, who would send you to the corner if you so much as looked at her funny. Mean Old deserved to be capitalized there since that was her official full name as soon as everybody in fourth grade was sure she was out of earshot. Except that one time Hunter Clemons should have looked around more before saying it. If he had, Hunter would have seen her standing right behind him and not spent a month of recess inside doing math.

Maybe he could get advice from Pa Pa on how to deal with it. His grandfather had lived with the woman most of his adult life; if anybody had the slightest clue what would placate her nitpicking, he certainly would. Matt knew he was getting desperate here, he was risking seeing Mungo by going out to the graveyard. Still, he needed someone to talk to, to say what he was thinking to; dear god, he needed advice from an actual grown-up. Not a grown-up like him, technically, a grown-up in a legal sense. Matt only counted in the minimum prerequisite as adult supervision. Nobody should actually be foolish enough to take that designation seriously enough to, say, leave a child in his care or trust him with explosives. In Matt's mind, he should still have his parents called in if the police stopped him on the street because he looked lost.

He sat down in the grass outside of the graveyard itself, still debating whether or not he should go in. He ended up deciding to pretend he was practicing a trick and not just putting off going inside the wall. Matt practiced a new, for lack of a better word, spell he'd figured out on his own. Carefully, he would grab one of the weaker strands of magic in the air and give it a command. A moment later, a butterfly or an explosion of light would float in front of him for just a moment before fading away. Matt knew that sometime soon, Madison would probably learn enough from MeeMaw to do the same thing; but for now, he was hoping to impress her with her own private fireworks display.

He was just about to release another one when a familiar voice said next to him, "Somethin' on yer mind, Matt, or are ya just lookin' ta' set the fields on fire?"

Matt jumped. He'd have jumped further, but he had been expecting Pa Pa would join him.

"Jesus! We have to put ghostly bells on you so I can hear you coming!"

His Pa Pa chuckled. "Sorry to spook ya, boy. Y'all will have to forgive the dead our little amusements."

"It's all right, I guess. I was hoping to talk to you anyway," Matt said, settling back down.

"Well, I kinda figured. So, what's on yer mind?"

"MeeMaw."

"She being a bit rough on y'all? I mean, I can guess why, but tell you what, why don't y'all tell me what happened out at that building."

"You think that's why too, huh?" Matt asked.

His Pa Pa's spirit nodded. "Eeyup. She told me all about it, and when she goes on about something at that kind of length, there's almost always a reason."

This was exactly what he'd hoped Pa Pa would say. Matt wanted to talk it all out to somebody older and wiser than him. Matt went through how he saw the events of that day; he could only imagine his version differed quite a bit from his MeeMaw's, but all he had was his version. She was a seasoned Granny Witch with a lifetime of experience, and he was a kid who last year at this time didn't believe magic was real, let alone that he could do it like some Hillbilly Merlin (there was another name there in the earlier versions of this book, but again, we don't want to be sued). It took a while to say it all, it had been a busy, confusing day, so there was a lot to unpack there, but, slowly, he reached his conclusion, more fading to a whimper than finishing it. Matt felt happier for it, though, just to tell it all to someone who wasn't there, someone who, despite being a ghost, had the reassuring nature his Pa Pa exuded.

"Well, that explains a lot." His grandfather nodded again slowly, as if taking it all in.

"Like what?"

Pa Pa looked thoughtful for a moment before finally saying, "Let me see if I can explain it. See, son, when y'all blasted that gateway shut, you were using some powerful magic. Bit higher than simple hill witch stuff, y'all tapped into the real nitty-gritty stuff the English used to get so excited about and wrote all kinds of spells that don't work trying to harness it. Now personally, I think that it should have been expected; a witch marrying a witch, well, the product of that is gonna have some strong roots even a generation removed. Who even knows what your Pa could have done if he'd embraced it? Both our families were pretty powerful to begin with, so the combination . . . Guess your MeeMaw figured with your mama not being from round har, it wouldn't come up. I think y'all done scared her a bit is all, and now she's fussin' at y'all like a mother hen 'cause she wants you to be safe. Power like that just flying around willy-nilly, Lord knows what y'all might get yerself up to."

"Standing next to the smoking crater saying 'Oops?', that sort of thing?"

Pa Pa chuckled softly. "Yep, I would say exactly that sort of thing is what she's worried about. Maybe she worries too much and can be a little too harsh about sharing her worrying with innocent bystanders. People get like that when they're spooked, they don't mean nothing by it, but it does come natural."

"Yeah, I suppose that's true." Matt shrugged.

"Iff'n it'll make y'all's life easier, I'll say something to her."

Matt smiled a little wanly. "Thanks, Pa Pa, I appreciate that."

"Well, what's a Pa Pa fer? Now in the meantime, ya' might as well keep practicing since y'all are out here. Some of them things y'all were makin' was looking mighty good."

$$\text{)O(}$$

It had been a long time since Madison and Chloe had really had time to hang out just the two of them. Between both of their new boyfriends, embracing her witch roots, which had meant adventures, and just, you know, work and stuff, there really hadn't been time. Thankfully, Matt had been cool with letting the day go so she could go pal around with her bestest pal. She figured Tyler and Matt would take the day and do something masculine. Madison assumed beer would be involved somehow, probably belching as well, definitely urination, possibly explosives, most likely somewhere inappropriate. Guy stuff! She only hoped they wouldn't have to post bail later.

Problem was, her and her bestie weren't really palling at all.

They were together, sure, they had done a few things Madison had wanted to do, absolutely, but they hadn't been palling around. Chloe had been next to her, but not really herself all day, not really much of anyone, for that matter, she was just there. At this point, Madison was wondering if there was a problem with Tyler and how she was going to tactfully ask what was on her mind and if it *was* something with Tyler, as opposed to bluntly asking. It would be out of character for it to be; Chloe had a long history of dating losers; and while Tyler's ambitions were not stellar in life, he did have a job and was generally a nice guy. Madison had dated him herself and knew that even deep into his cups and feeling sorry for himself, he'd never been abusive or mean to much of anyone. Tyler was five steps up for Chloe's normal misunderstood artist/musician asshole boyfriend of the week.

Weirder still, they were driving out past Mullens; there was almost nothing out past Mullens. Chloe had said she had to drop something off at a friend's house. That was weird too; they'd been friends for years, and as far as she knew, Chloe had never even been to Wyoming County before, not even to visit Twin Falls. When pressed about it, she said it was to drop something off for someone she'd been talking to online. Maybe it *was* something to do with Tyler after all. Chloe had barely talked all day, and when she had, it had been practically in monotone and directly to the point with none of her normal bubbly chatter added on. And now their stated destination was further out than even Madison had gone before into the coal badlands. This was all getting weird.

"Are you feeling all right?"

"Yes, of course. I'm fine," Chloe replied flatly, eyes on the road.

"How long is this going to take?" Madison asked, eyeing her friend with suspicions she didn't even have a name for but trying to keep her talking until she could figure them out.

"Oh, it won't take long at all, just need to drop something off, like I said," Chloe replied, still not looking at her at all.

Okay, that tore it. Her best friend wasn't even *looking* at her? What the hell? Normally, she had to politely remind Chloe to keep her eyes on the road! Madison reached out and tugged lightly on Chloe's shoulder. Her hand slipped away off her friend, but it didn't come away empty! A familiar ghostly shape came along with it!

"What the hell?" Chloe gasped, blinking.

A moment later, the disoriented girl put her hands to her face in shock. Which was when her very late model Ford Taurus swung to the right out of control, owing to the fact that the thing hadn't had an alignment since the Bush administration! Neither of them remembered much more about what happened next except for the loud noises.

A large black Suburban pulled up to the crash a few moments later. Two enormous men, men with their own zip codes and gravitational pulls who somehow had been wedged into suits, got out. They walked slowly and purposefully to the smoking mid-sized sedan.

"What should we do?"

The other looked in the window. "They aren't hurt badly, just dazed. We were only told to make sure the one got there. Remove her before she regains consciousness, please, and place her in our vehicle. Remember to restrain her."

The first man-mountain opened the door to the Taurus with a screech of twisted metal and reached in for Madison.

When he got the call, Tyler flew for his truck. He had to go!
As he was running, he was forced to pause when an
imperious voice called out, "Boy! Where in the hell y'all
flying off to?"

"I gotta go to the hospital, MeeMaw!"

"What in the hell fer?"

"Chloe's been in an accident!"

The old woman's eyes widened. "Hold yer horses just
a moment! I'll go with y'all, you know better than anyone
if y'all get sick, y'all come to MeeMaw!"

It should have been impossible to get in to see Chloe so
soon after she'd been brought in. It would have been in
most parts of the country and in most hospitals, but not
here. There was more than one person on staff at that
hospital who knew exactly who MeeMaw was and what she
could do. They carefully labeled her as a "consulting
physician" on the visitor's log when she felt the need to be
here.

MeeMaw did not come out to the hospital often. As
much as it pained some of the doctors to admit it,
MeeMaw's patients usually got well long before theirs did,
so they didn't need to come to the hospital to begin with.
They could only be thankful that MeeMaw was nice enough
that she didn't want to muscle into their racket too often.
Anybody who knew about the Granny Witch usually called
for her long before they called for an ambulance. Chloe's
mom hadn't even found out yet, it was Chloe's little sister,
Emma, who had called Tyler to tell him. Their mother
wasn't allowed private calls at work, even on her cell
phone, even for emergencies.

Tyler gasped when they entered her room, and rushed to the bed. Chloe was still unconscious, with bruising on her face from the wreck. One arm was in a cast, and she was hooked up to a monitor that beeped away in an irritating but reassuring monotone. Tyler's girlfriend had definitely had better days than this, and seeing her so obviously hurt broke his heart. Tyler had tears in his eyes when he turned back to the door. "MeeMaw!"

MeeMaw looked at the girl carefully for a moment. "She'll be all right, boy, never you fear. Looks worse than it is. I'll do a few things to speed things along a bit, but don't you worry none, she'll be walking out of here with you this time tomorrow. First things first, I want to know how she got here. There's most like to be something important in that story, and I want to see what it is."

"What, like a tumor?" Tyler's face was a mask of worry.

"No, nothing like that, Tyler. Why y'all got to look for the worst in everything? But y'all said she was in a one-car wreck, now that sounds strange to me. I done seen her car, ain't glorious, but it shouldn't do that. Now you be a good boy and wait outside for a little while. MeeMaw has to concentrate a bit so she can work. When I call you back in, iff'n we have time, I'll let y'all talk to her a bit, how 'bout that?" she said with a warm and reassuring smile.

"You sure?"

She might not admit it, but it warmed her heart a bit. For all the tattoos and his god-awful taste in music, her grandson was still the kind and caring boy he always had been. She nodded with a smile. "I'm positive she's gonna be fine. Now y'all run along and get yerself something from one them machines while I work, all right, sweetie?"

As soon as her grandson was gone, she looked at the girl again. There was something else there, something lingering. One of those things had been inside the girl! It left a residue so thick she could practically smell it! It was a good thing she knew something Beatrice Baldwin didn't, otherwise, as banged up as this girl was, if Baldwin had known, she'd be a lot worse than this. The girl wouldn't be here at all, Beatrice would have just made the girl vanish when Chloe had been at her mercy. What Beatrice didn't know was that just because the conscious mind can never recall what happened when it was possessed, it didn't mean the subconscious didn't sit back and watch. It didn't mean the girl's suppressed mind didn't record every word and action. If you just came out and asked, that person would have no idea. So, what you had to do was to know how to ask differently.

A few minutes later, MeeMaw shot out the door into the hall. "Boy, get out yer phone!"

"What? Why?"

"Y'all got them Googly maps or what have you on that, right?" she demanded impatiently.

"Y'all mean Google maps?" Tyler asked, wide-eyed and confused at what this had to do with Chloe.

"Yep, that's the thing," she replied tersely. "I want y'all to look up Whitman, West Virginia."

Tyler scrabbled to get his phone out and to the right page. He had no idea what all this was about, but he knew when MeeMaw was like this, he'd best do as she said. He showed the phone to her. "Okay, now what?"

"That ain't what we need, but it's close enough," she replied, looking over his shoulder at his phone. "How do y'all move that pointer thingy around to put a mark on the map?"

"Y'all just touch it with yer finger," Tyler explained, hoping this could be over with so he could see Chloe.

She took the phone impatiently and fiddled with it for a moment. Finding what she was looking for, she stabbed her finger at the phone triumphantly. "It's right there! Y'all know how to get directions to that spot from the farm?"

Tyler squinted at the phone. Son of a bitch! He could barely make it out, but he could see a dirt track there on the map, leading up to something obscured by trees. "Let me see what I can do." He operated the map feature for a minute before saying, "Yeah, I'll be damned, it recognized the road somehow."

"Then this is what y'all are gonna do. Y'all are gonna email them directions to yer parents and to your cousin Matthew, his phone, his computer, every damned email he got so to be sure he gets it."

"All right, this is gonna take a minute," he replied, bewildered and getting frustrated by not being told what was happening.

"Good. I know y'all still got that shotgun in the vehicle, and that's a damned good thing 'cause we might need it 'fore the day is out. But as soon as y'all are done with the emailing and such, we got to get driving."

"What about Chloe?"

"Figuring nobody gets hurt today, she'll be here healthy and happy to see when we get done. Y'all can write her a note or something, but if we don't get our asses in gear, yer cousin ain't gonna never see his girlfriend again."

Tyler looked at her open-mouthed for a second, stunned by what he'd just heard. Finally, he replied, "All right, let me just get to this then."

$$\text{)O(}$$

Madison's eyes slowly opened. She took a moment to assess her situation and said the only thing she could think of that encompassed the entire pastiche presented to her, "What . . . the . . . actual . . . fuck."

It was a pretty good summation, all things considered. How else do you really expect to react to finding yourself tied to an enormous boulder, staring across a ring of other monoliths at a swirling mass of neon color? It's not like you have a lot of other responses cataloged and ready for something like that in case it comes up. Even if Madison had had one ready (which, as already noted, was unlikely) she was still a bit groggy from the car accident to boot, so good for her for that pithy response.

The swirling circle of mesmerizing colors—blues and greens and oranges—between two stones across from her put the rest of the world outside of the circle deeply into shadows.

A cracked voice called out from them, "Good! 'Bout time y'all woke up!"

Madison felt she should know the woman who stepped into the circle of light. She was sure she had seen the woman before, she just couldn't place where.

A Granny Witch older than Matt's MeeMaw walked towards her, the elderly woman's face twinkling with malicious glee. In other words, tied up, mysterious light show, and a cackling witch (well not actually cackling, but it looked like an option) could only mean one thing: she was fucked! She only hoped that she'd get some explanation as to the nature of the fucking soon; nobody ties you to a stone for a good reason, witches, even less so. Still, it would be nice to know what she was up against here—other than the boulder, that was.

"So . . . ummm . . . yeah . . . I seem to be tied to a big rock and all. Any particular reason, or is this what people in this county do to treat a car accident victim?" Madison figured she was screwed either way, she might as well be bitchy about it. It made her feel ever so slightly better.

The woman laughed. "Y'all know something? Not too far back at all, I was regrettin' not killing y'all with yer mamma. But, good thing I didn't."

"I knew that fire wasn't an accident! You bitch!" Madison barked as it dawned on her exactly *who* this was. She was unable to stop herself from straining against her bonds, trying to get to the woman. At last, her brain registered the pointlessness of it, and she sank back against the stone.

"Bitch I may be, but I ain't tied to a rock, now am I? No, it was not an accident. Not easy magic to pull off against someone who works it herself. Power, girl. It's all around us, just comes down to what a body is able to use before it breaks. Y'all can get knowin' and use more, y'all can tap into the earth under yer feet to use more still . . . But I need even more than what I got. Won't need any magic at all once I open the way for 'em; they'll bring all I need and then some. But I need enough power to open the gate up the rest of the way from this side. Y'all know how I'm gonna do that?"

"Not that any of that made a lot of sense, but I'd guess from what y'all said, get more land."

"I'm gonna suck y'all dry, girl, and use your power!" The old woman cackled (Madison was right, cackling had been an option all along). "See? Iff'n I'd a killed ya', who knows how much more land I'd have to get control over before I could do this? The land'll fight ya' tooth and nail iff'n ye ain't born to it. It don't want to do this and only gives up the power I need by sheer force of my willpower. Y'all ain't gonna have a clue how to fight me. It's gonna be easy. Just need to take some time to get everything just right. There's a time and a place for these things, so y'all just get yerself as comfy as ya can in the meantime. I mean, considering the situation. And when it's all done, I'm gonna look a hell of a lot better than y'all will, young miss, I kin promise y'all that! I most definitely kin promise that."

Chapter 17

"I live my life, breathless . . . A life of constant motion and excitement. A life that many will envy, and most would avoid!"
—Eric Burdon, the Eggman

---◆---

"**C**AN'T Y'ALL go any damned faster!?"

"MeeMaw! These roads ain't exactly designed for high speeds. More fer payin' close attention so y'all don't fall off a mountain speeds!" Tyler protested.

MeeMaw sniffed at that, almost as if she didn't believe him, even though she knew for a fact that he was telling the truth of it. It impressed upon Tyler the need for urgency, something he was pretty sure he didn't need impressed upon him any more than it had been; he got it. When someone asks you if you have your gun, tells you to email someone else as if they might need cavalry, and makes you leave your comatose girlfriend to go somewhere right now, you usually have the point by then. Sniffing about how long it was taking really felt like piling on.

"Here! Turn here!" she squawked suddenly, pointing to what barely looked to be a track coming up on their right.

Tyler slowed down, practically standing on the brakes to make the turn before coming to a halt.

"What are y'all stopping for?"

Tyler sighed. "MeeMaw. If I don't put 'er in four-wheel

drive, we won't make it a hundred yards. Look at the damned thing!"

She looked at him and smiled just a little. "Sorry 'bout that, guess I'm just a little tense is all."

"Well that makes two of us," he replied, changing gears over.

The road could barely be called a road, it could barely be called a driveway, even when being generous about it; hell, calling it a path would have been being generous. Tyler winced constantly as they worked their way up it. He couldn't see where this was leading yet; it twisted and switchbacked its way up the mountainside, and with the trees and the turns, it seemed to have no destination at all but up. All Tyler could do at this point was pour almost all of his concentration into avoiding the largest of the exposed rocks sticking out of the soil as they went and hope there would be somewhere to turn around at some point. So intent was his concentration that he almost drove directly into the black Suburban when they rounded a corner! He had just put it in park and opened the door when a rifle retort exploded and echoed down the mountainside, followed instantly by the shattering of the front windshield!

"Now y'all know why I asked about the gun," MeeMaw muttered from where she had tucked herself down by the floorboards.

"What in the hell are we gonna do?" demanded Tyler, his voice on the edge of panic as he huddled nearby.

"Just fire a couple of shots up that way to keep 'em occupied and pinned down. What I got to do is gonna be round back anyway. If they're busy with y'all, they won't even notice me," she replied.

Tyler closed his eyes and took a deep breath. This was not how he envisioned his normal day of artful slacking going at all when he'd woke up this morning. "Are you fucking kidding me?" he demanded, but he found that he was saying it to the passenger door as it banged shut.

)O(

Matt was wandering back to the house on his own time, no real rush today. Without actually intending to, he was wondering what Madison was up to. He wondered if she was missing him too. This was supposed to be a day off to do non-boyfriend/girlfriend things, but he increasingly wasn't into it. Frankly, he got bored easily without her. He was friendly with a couple of Tyler's friends, and Madison had introduced him to some of her friends; it wasn't like he couldn't find something to do without her, he wasn't that pathetic. It was just that more and more, he found that he didn't want to. It wasn't as fun without her there to crack jokes for, jokes that were just theirs and that only they laughed at.

Nobody seemed to be around the house. Matt figured his aunt was off in town, Uncle Donnie would still be down at the barn doing whatever mystical barn things that didn't involve cow piss that needed doing. Tyler wasn't around, which was kind of weird. When Matt had talked to him this morning, he had acted like he didn't have anything on his plate for the day since it was Chloe that Madison was with. Screwing around with Tyler had been Matt's fallback plan here. Matt considered going out to talk to MeeMaw and trying out this newfound understanding as to why she demanded such perfection out of him, but finally decided he wasn't quite ready to be that understanding and open. Instead, he opted for firing up the computer to see if he had any messages that didn't involve boner pills or hot women in his area hoping to meet him, refusing to admit the entire time it was booting up that what he was really hoping for was one from Madison saying she was bored and to come get her.

While waiting for the computer to get past the walk and chew gum phase that it always stumbled through after turning on, he grabbed his phone to see if he had any messages waiting there. There was a text from Tyler, along with an actual message with an attachment. That had to be serious to double up like that; Tyler barely even singled up to tell you if something was up, instead relying on you figuring it out yourself. He opened up the message and read, "Madison in trbl, dircshons in mssg, haul ass-Tyler"

Ho-lee-fuck-a-rooni! Once he did a bit of translating of text to English, what he found when he opened the actual message was a set of directions and maps. He had no idea what in the hell this could be about, but it sounded serious! Serious enough that he fired up his printer and printed out the maps. He also sent it to his phone as a Google page for directions. Just to make sure, he also grabbed a solid copy of the Gazetteer map book he saw on the living room shelf before booking for the door!

"Steppin' out, honey?" Aunt Debbie called from somewhere in the house, which made him jump since Matt had thought she wasn't home.

"Yes, ma'am. Tyler wants me for something, he didn't say what," Matt replied, rushing for the front door.

"Must be somethin' important, he tore out of here with MeeMaw a while ago like the devil was on his tail."

Uh-to-the-major-league-oh, full rut-ro Raggy!

"Well, I gotta go, he wants me to hurry," Matt replied, straining his patience.

"Tell him to call me, will y'all?"

"Sure thing," he said as the door was closing.

Just as he was rushing to his SUV, his grandfather appeared before him. "Hold on boyo!" the ghost said, putting his hand up in front of him like a traffic guard.

"Pa Pa, I'm kind of in a hurry," Matt replied, coming to a stop. He had no idea what happened if you walked through a ghost, but he wasn't really ready to try an experiment right now with anything that might involve him getting coated in ectoplasm. That might not even be real, but there's a time and a place to analyze and measure things, and this wasn't it.

"Oh, I know, and I know why, maybe better than you. Pick up one of the stones from the drive to take us with y'all," the ghost told him calmly.

"What?"

"Look, I'm bettin' yer MeeMaw is about to finally have it out with that Baldwin woman; she could use all the help she can get. All the rules I know say that we're bound to the soil and stones we haunt, nobody said nuthin' about maybe moving any of them stones. We were able to go to the Goins farm 'cause it's still part of the traditional family land, but we can go further than that with a little help. MeeMaw sometimes takes me shopping with her 'cause I'm better with math. To be honest, I can probably explain it better on the way."

"Does this mean Mungo is coming?"

"'Fraid so, we'll probably need him. He's top-notch in a brawl, from what I hear."

Despite serious misgivings and worry as to his ability to drive with Mungo in an enclosed space, Matt picked up the stone anyway and got going. The SUV threw rocks as he spun down the lane, rocks with no ghosts anywhere nearby to haunt them.

𝇇

Pa Pa was elected spokesman for the group already, if only because Matt had the easiest time understanding him and vice versa. "Let me see if I can explain this . . . "

"Please," Matt replied, trying to keep his eyes on the road.

"Y'all get that there are other worlds apart from this one, a hairsbreadth away, right? Yer MeeMaw explained?"

"For the purposes of this discussion, I think I'll concede it. MeeMaw has said as much."

"Good, speeds things up. That Baldwin woman has been consorting with things on the other side, that's why their slaves show up here all the time lately. The powers that be over there been giving her their slaves to use as she wants, simply because they're trying to buy her off, and it's been working damned fine for them," Pa Pa explained patiently.

"Kinda get that. I take it she helped them get that spot at that company store?"

"You assume correctly. At least that's what yer MeeMaw suspects. Anyway, what she also suspects is that's why she's been forcing off other Granny Witches, so she can get access to the land. All those little lives buried in the rock, not to mention dominion of the ones in the graveyards, 'lest they're tended to by loved ones, letting her steal their power to boost her own. There's kinds of power a witch has to reach for normally, like those bands you see in the air, the strength to use them he or she gets from being on their own ground. A witch is most dangerous on his or her own patch. Don't mean a witch is powerless off her land, but it's rare they can handle the real big bands of power when they aren't at home. Everything that lives on that land will lend the witch the power they need to grasp bigger and more powerful bands out of the ether. That woman's been building herself an empire, as it were. What we think is she's doing it so she can blow a hole between these worlds and let the masters of those slaves into this world completely. Not this one at a time thing they been doin', but an open doorway between the worlds. Who knows what they promised her if she'd let them in, but it must have been damned fine for her to risk consorting with them!"

"That does not sound good," Matt conceded quietly and flatly. "But what does that have to do with Madison?"

"I wouldn't have thought to do it, most sane witches would have thought the idea was too horrible, but . . . think about how much power she could steal in the right situation from a full-blown living witch! Surprised she didn't figure that out sooner, only a blessing she didn't, but Beatrice Baldwin always was stubborn. Her way is always the right way, she figures, and her way until now was the old way, stealing power from the land she lords over and gettin' more land," Pa Pa said slowly.

"So, she's got Madison to—"

"Suck th' bludy life reit it ay yer burd," Mungo interjected; he'd been asked to be quiet, but he'd gotten caught up in the moment.

"He said—"

"No, I think I got that," Matt said quickly. His face was completely clouded with worry. "I've got to call Tyler." He dug out his phone and punched the auto-dial.

A few moments later, Tyler picked up. "Hey! Would you look at that! We both got signal, will wonders never cease!"

"Tyler, what in the hell is going on?"

"Well, I'm kind of in a bit of a firefight right now with a very angry person with a rifle," Tyler replied, his voice sounding remarkably calm.

A second later, an explosion of some kind could be heard through the phone.

"What in the hell was that?" Matt demanded.

"Firefight, remember? Just a sec." He heard the phone clunk, followed by a much louder explosion coming through the phone. The phone clunked again, and Tyler was back. "That ought to hold him for a minute."

"Tyler . . . now I'm going to ask you calmly, what in the holy fuck is happening there?"

"Oh, yeah. So anyway, I'm in a bit of a firefight, like I said, to keep some fat guy from interfering with MeeMaw, who I assume is going to have some kind of magical fight out back. The guy had some great big Looney Tunes hunks of meat types with him, but they went running past down the mountain a while ago, almost shot 'em 'til I saw how scared they looked. Figure all the magic in the area is kinda being sucked into whatever MeeMaw is up to. Hey, do me a favor, when y'all get here, park off to the side of the road a bit so I can get out. I figure I'll probably have to go to the hospital when this is all over."

Tyler's voice didn't sound perturbed at all, which, if anything, perturbed Matt even more. It forced him to consider that either this happened all the time or Tyler was in some kind of weird shock over it happening now. Neither answer could really be considered a positive.

"Hospital?!?!"

"Oh, not for me, I mean, he scraped me with one a while back, but I'm fine. No, Chloe's in the hospital."

"So, any chance I'm ever going to find out what in the hell is going on right now in a way that makes any real logical sense whatsoever?"

"Anything could happen, I'm kinda winging it myself here. But yeah, park out of sight and work your way around the mountain to the backside there if y'all want to help. Figure MeeMaw wants y'all for that, not to help me reload. When I hear ya', I'll keep fat boy up there busy for a bit so he don't see y'all. But hurry, all right, I only got so many reloads left here."

"Right, better let you go." Matt hung up and hit the gas. He had no idea what was happening, but he knew Madison and possibly MeeMaw were in danger! What that meant he was expected to do about it was beyond him, but clearly, something was being demanded of him here, so he better concentrate on the road he was driving way too fast down lest he stop driving on anything but open air because he missed a critical curve.

When Matt turned on to the track leading up to the house, he was positive that no matter what the GPS and the directions were saying, he had to be lost. There was just no possible way someone lived up here, or even went up here, even on a dare, by mule. If this led to a field, the field was probably fallow because they couldn't get the tractor up here anymore. Rather than gaping in disbelief longer than he already had, he texted Tyler.

"I think I'm lost"

A moment later his phone buzzed. "Wr R U?"

"A goat track"

Buzz back, "Snds rght, lk 4 my trk"

That wasn't inspiring, even after he translated, but he had to guess his cousin knew what he was talking about, so he put it in four-wheel drive and began making his way uphill. Matt winced every time he felt a rock ping off the Xterra, but he tried to keep telling himself this was what he bought the thing for. Well maybe not this exactly, he couldn't possibly see where he would have had the foresight to have considered interfering in a battle between two witches to save his girlfriend in the mountains of Appalachia in his purchasing decisions. If he'd asked about it, the salesman would have looked at him funny.

Matt had just caught a glimpse of Tyler's vehicle up ahead when his phone buzzed. Looking down, he saw "Prk thre" followed a second later by "Go rnd hill to rght." Well there it was; he had no idea what he'd gotten himself in to, but it was about to begin for real. Matt took a deep breath, reminded himself MeeMaw and Madison were counting on him, and got out. He almost dived back into the vehicle when he heard a gunshot up ahead. It took his brain a moment for it to register that it had come from Tyler and not the crazy person he was in the gunfight with. His cousin was creating a distraction for him, which was nice of him. Would have been nicer if he had warned him better in that last text, Matt had almost peed himself—something he was not going to mention later if they all got out of this alive.

Matt hadn't expected to be bushwhacking anywhere today, so he was wearing sneakers, which were absolutely perfect for a mountainside, perfectly awful. He reminded himself glumly after he slipped on the steep terrain the first time that his *Grandmother* had come this way and she hadn't been wearing Timberlines to do it with either, so he should probably shut up. He also tried to ignore the other voice that reminded him that she was born here and he had been born in a place where a cracked sidewalk was considered "rugged." The whole thing seemed to be taking forever, a forever he didn't think he had, time-wise. Matt thought he had gotten himself trained to do a little of this, going out with Madison, but he thought wrong. They had been taking trails, this was anything but. He kept slipping and sliding and having to grab tree limbs to keep from falling down the slope. Since two of the stones he'd stepped on had rolled out from under him to clack their way down towards a ravine to his right, he'd sworn off using rocks and was now trying to dig every step into the leaf mold.

Sweating and cursing, he finally saw why he was here. The tableau presented to him was something he could have never expected to see in his life outside of a movie theater! Inside a circle of ancient and thoroughly disreputable looking stones were his MeeMaw and a woman he could only guess to be the Baldwin woman MeeMaw kept complaining about. They were locked to each other by bands of magic, and from there, both of them were tied by additional strands to a thing that made him think of the portal in that old *Stargate* show. MeeMaw looked like she was not having a good time of it; sweat stood on her brow and she looked almost frail at the moment. Probably because of the ghost things that kept diving at her and then swirling away! Worse than that, he could see in the distance, through and over the trees, even more coming!

The Baldwin witch must be pulling all of the entities she'd hid in various bodies out there in the countryside to help her now! He could maybe help MeeMaw with the Baldwin woman, but he had no idea what he could do about the onrushing slaves!

Matt had completely forgotten the cargo he had riding along with him. At least he had until Mungo suddenly bellowed, "Tae war, mah fowk! Finally! We gie tae dae somethin' useful an' kick some crease!"

At his ancestor's battle cry, which everyone seemed to understand except Matt, the ghosts that had been riding along with him flooded down the hill to engage the entities from the other dimension! Almost all of them, that was, Matt could feel his Pa Pa floating right next to him patiently as Matt continued sliding and stumbling towards the fray. A few slipping steps more, he was able to finally see Madison! Just as importantly, he could see one of those shapes floating behind her, strapped to her unconscious form; she had been neutralized to keep her out of this!

He needed to do something about that first and foremost! On a hunch, he grabbed a loose strand of his own and let it fly to wrap around the strands holding the ghostly figure in place behind her and pulled as hard as he could! Whatever had been welded to her seemed lost for a moment but began to float away. It almost looked like it was shuffling off and hoping to go unnoticed by the witch Matt's MeeMaw was fighting. Matt could only figure that since it hadn't been called to do battle and had been released from its last command, it was hoping to make a break for it.

Matt let out a breath of relief to see Madison begin to stir almost immediately. He wasn't sure what he could do next, though. Matt had never really used magic to do something seriously physical like untie knots, and with the firestorm between MeeMaw and the other old woman, he was almost afraid to get any closer than this! Matt suddenly felt like he had been neutralized by his own lack of knowledge here!

"I think yer gonna need the girl," Pa Pa said as if reading his thoughts. "Those two seem busy enough, don't think they'd notice none if y'all went and got her."

Since he couldn't think of anything else useful to do right then and there, he began to make his way down the hill. Beatrice Baldwin must have suspected his presence, what with her monsters from beyond suddenly being engaged by vengeful ancestors (especially Mungo, Mungo was doing vengeful ancestor like nobody's business). Matt was so intent on stealth, he almost didn't see the stray strand of power as it suddenly lashed out at him until it was too late! It left no physical mark on the ground it struck when he dodged, but he personally could hear it sizzle like it was on fire. The old woman paid for her distraction; MeeMaw, given a brief respite, renewed her own attack! The lines of power between them now began to twist towards the Baldwin witch and away from his grandmother some. Matt decided to use the distraction to sprint the distance to where Madison was tied up!

"Hey, hon, I'm right behind you," Matt gasped, out of breath, from behind the rock.

"Matt! Thank God! Hey, sweetie, I know we've never discussed anything kinky, like bondage or anything. But I'd like to pick my safe word right now," Madison replied in a worryingly calm voice.

Matt paused as he tried to figure out how to untie the ropes. "Oh?"

"Yes, I chose 'twatwaffle'."

"Twatwaffle?"

"Yes, twatwaffle."

"Really?"

"Yes, as in GET THESE TWATWAFFLE ROPES THE TWATWAFFLE OFF OF ME!" she barked.

"Right on it, dear heart," he replied, thankful for the

outburst. She was feeling normal at least—for what the situation called for, that was.

When the knots finally came undone, he felt Madison sag on the other side of the stone. Matt rushed around the rock to find her slumped in front of it.

"Are you okay?" he asked.

"I will be in a minute. Sorry, being strapped up there for that long, my legs went numb." She smiled a little sheepishly.

Matt reached over and helped her to her feet and got her back up the hill a bit and away from the battle royal that was happening in front of the swirling lights. He could see that whatever advantage MeeMaw had was already dissipating. MeeMaw might be the better witch overall, she might have studied harder and learned more, but this was happening on the Baldwin woman's home ground. MeeMaw really only had what magic was in her or that she could bring to work with from the sky itself; Beatrice Baldwin could just keep pulling more from the very ground they stood on to replenish herself! No matter how much these hills might resent Beatrice and her treatment of them, they still belonged to Beatrice Baldwin until someone else took them.

"What should we do?" Madison asked as they stumbled a little further back up the hill.

"I . . . I have no idea," Matt admitted, defeat sounding in his voice.

"I think I do," Pa Pa said, suddenly appearing next to them.

Matt noted he looked a little disheveled for just a moment before he reverted back to his normal tidy appearance. Who knew ghosts could get their clothing screwed up in a street fight too?

"What?" Matt and Madison demanded in almost full "I owe you a beer" unison.

"Y'all remember what y'all did at that building? Y'all

know, what closed off their way in? Do that, just do it a bunch bigger."

"But Pa Pa, that was the biggest bit of magic I could get a hold of!" Matt protested.

"Well, there's two of y'all, ain't there? Work together."

"How?"

Pa Pa paused and smiled just a bit. "Me and your MeeMaw, we used to hold hands. Sounds silly since all y'all really need to do is focus on the same thing, but we thought it helped some. Or, maybe we just liked holdin' hands is all. Let the power flow between y'all a bit, wouldn't be surprised if you've already done that a bit by accident when y'all were being . . . ummmmm . . . intimate together."

The two living faces in attendance turned beet red.

Despite the crackling magical battle happening all around him, even despite the occasional bellow from Mungo of "Ah am gonnae kick yer gantin crease, ye dobber!", despite the occasional crack of gunfire from up the hill as Tyler and Bill Baldwin kept each other busy playing Hatfields and McCoys, and despite his own flaming red embarrassment over his grandfather mentioning sex, he still managed to think he saw what the ghost meant by that. He was just reaching for Madison's hand when he thought of something.

"Wait," he said, "MeeMaw and that Baldwin woman, they're hooked into that portal! If I send a bolt of magic into it, what's going to happen to them?"

Pa Pa was silent for a long moment. Even though he didn't need to, he took a long breath and let it out in a gusting sigh. "I honestly don't know. Could do anything to 'em, maybe even kill 'em both."

"But—"

Pa Pa cut him off. "Look, son, I know this is asking a lot of y'all. I know that. But look, the things on the other side of that hole thar' that woman wants to let in, they ain't just the creatures y'all seen already. What you seen is the slaves! What she wants to bring through, they'd be bringing hell on earth here, it's thems what are holding the chains on those slaves! Them what think they could always use do to make everyone a slave! I don't know what they promised her, but she is gonna hand over our world for them to put those chains on all of everyone here!"

"Yeah, but—" Matt tried again.

"Your MeeMaw is trying, son, but she can't beat her on her own ground. Y'all can't touch your MeeMaw and give her power, they're all locked into each other. Y'all can't even touch that Baldwin woman, it'd bounce right off. Lou May is gonna lose sooner or later. And if with all MeeMaw knows, she can't beat the woman . . . The only weak link in that chain they got tying them together is that portal; y'all have to do that!"

"But . . . "

"What?!"

"Should we do this now? Or should we warn MeeMaw?" Matt finally got out.

"Who do y'all think told me to tell ya to do it?"

"What the hell is coming out of that circle?" Madison let out in a squeak of fear, interrupting their back and forth.

Matt whirled to look where Madison pointed. There was no mistaking what that was. It was a tentacle. He'd had calamari before, and damn it, he knew a tentacle when he saw or ate one, which he never intended to do again. Matt was not really all that up on his horror mythology, but he was pretty sure that otherworldly tentacles were really, really bad!

As if reading his mind, Madison added emphatically, "No way around it, alien tentacles are absolutely bad for everyone! I have read a shit ton of Lovecraft, and tentacles equal total fuckage!"

Matt mentally prepared himself, well, as prepared as he could be. This was a pretty big deal, bigger than anything he'd ever attempted before, so it was more psyching himself into doing it than actually doing anything. Finally, he straightened his shoulders and put on his most Clint Eastwood looking tough guy face and said quietly, "Let's do this."

It should be noted that he still wasn't doing anything, more of a formal prelude to doing something, a precursor, if you will, to doing . . . look, we'll just shut up now, shall we, so we can all see if he actually does something?

He grasped Madison's hand.

"What am I doing here? Like, what do y'all need?" she asked.

"I'm going to find the biggest strand of magic out there. Which, frankly, I probably won't be strong enough to control. When I tell you, I don't know, think about controlling it too and pouring energy into me. Just visualize me having enough power to control it, like, visualize it obeying my order. If it doesn't work, nothing should happen, except maybe me getting some kind of backlash. If it does, when I let it go of it, let's try to get behind the rock!"

"Visualize it . . . "

"Or whatever."

"What kind of backlash?"

"I have no idea, but I do know we have to do it now!"

"*Whatever* it is, Gandalf!" she replied with her voice taking on a manic edge.

Matt scanned all around the area; he wasn't just looking for a big cord of power like last time he'd done something like this, what he wanted would be massive! He'd got sight of things like that before wafting past at a distance. He knew they existed, but Matt had never once considered trying to ride that pony. If the fate of the entire world wasn't riding on it, he sure as hell wouldn't be considering it now! To make matters worse, as he scanned about, he could see that Beatrice's strands of power had gotten to within mere feet of MeeMaw! Whatever she was asking that magic to do to MeeMaw was going to happen soon! If he didn't get his ass in gear, this would be all over but for the mopping up, and he and Madison would be the mopping up!

As if to put an exclamation point on that, Beatrice Baldwin's voice, tinged with what could only be called shrill insanity, cackled, "Well, girl! You done gave me a good fight, and it does y'all credit. But a witch is dying here today, and I don't intend for it to be me! So, I'll be taking my leave of y'all, Louise May Hawley, and taking leave of this hag body as well once this is all over!"

Matt fought with himself to remain calm and keep looking, but he was beginning to panic. Panic did nothing for keeping his second sight clear at all!

Madison broke his concentration slightly when she pointed her finger, calling out, "How about that one?"

Matt looked where she had said and realized the thing was so big that he hadn't noticed it before because his mind had decided that it was part of the sky! But there it sat, floating gently in the air, glowing white in early evening light. The biggest coil of power he'd ever seen before! Matt got together all of his courage and said the manliest thing he could think of in this situation, "Um . . . Okay . . . I guess." (But, like, way more macho than it reads.)

Using other cords of power, Matt herded the massive thing towards himself, all the while noting to give himself some credit for thinking of that. When it was close enough that it practically obliterated everything else from his view, he reached out to touch it. Instantly, he jerked his hand away from the sizzle of power the thing gave off! Reminding himself that he had to do this, and do it now, he reached out again. It was like touching an electric fence but only the tingle up your spine and through your limbs without the pain associated with it. Matt strongly suspected that if he held on too long, the pain would be along shortly.

"Now, Madison, give me anything you have," he hissed through clenched teeth.

He tried to command the thing, but in its vastness, it ignored him! He also began to feel power and, most importantly, will flow into him from Madison. He had to get this done! He tried to remember everything he'd willed when he destroyed the other portal and conjure up an image in his mind that he could only describe to the strand he was trying to command as "that, but bigger." Slowly, ponderously, he could feel the order being implanted onto the massive strand of power. Still not sure if anything would happen, he released it to hopefully do as he had asked.

"Run like hell!" he barked the moment he remembered that something might actually happen, dragging Madison after him to the dubious shelter of the stone she'd been tied to just a little earlier. As they fell gasping in the shade, all they could hear was the hiss and sizzle of the fight between the witches and his ancestors beating up the beings from beyond the gate. Matt began to panic. What if it was just too big and there was no way, even with Madison's help, that he could get it to take an order from him!? What should he do now? He had to do something or else they were all doomed, god, why was he such a fuc—

The world went white!

CHAPTER 18

"If any of you cry at my funeral, I'll never speak to you again!"

—Stan Laurel

———◆———

AND THEN IT wasn't anymore. There was no more magic sizzling in the air, there was no battle being raged all around them. All that remained in its place was an immediate deathly quiet and the peace of a normal dusk.

At least it was quiet for a moment, until Matt heard Mungo gasp out, "Whaur did th' cowards gang?"

Matt slowly got to his feet, helping Madison up as well. They made their way around the stone to see what had happened. The other stones stood upright, but the swirling portal had gone, taking whatever creatures had come to Beatrice Baldwin's beck and call with it. He could see the elderly witch of these hills lying where she had fallen. Looking across the clearing, he saw another crumpled shape. It took him a moment to register what it was.

"MEEMAW!" he cried, sprinting to his grandmother's side.

He turned her on her back and saw her eyes were shut. Matt looked for breath and saw not the slightest movement from her chest. In a panic, he tried to remember how to do CPR, yelling, "Come on, MeeMaw, stay with me!"

Matt felt something soft on his shoulder. He whirled to ask Madison if she knew CPR. Instead of his girlfriend, standing there was MeeMaw, smiling sadly at him. She looked far younger than the body lying next to him, but he had no problem recognizing her for who she was. Standing next to her was his Pa Pa; somehow, he looked younger too, like he had been waiting for her to help him shed the weight of the years.

"MeeMaw?" he choked through the tears flowing down his face.

"It's all right, baby. It's ALL all right. Y'all done real good here today. I'm proud of you," she said softly.

Matt turned to her body and looked back. "But . . . "

"That's okay too, my sweet child. Really, it is. We all got to go some time, ain't none of us forever and ever. I had a heart attack saving the world, and that ain't so bad for the local hippy witch, and don't think I don't know what they said behind ma' back. I could have had that same heart attack lying in bed a week from now dreaming about something silly and petty. I think I done pretty damned well myself." The ghostly figure knelt down and took his chin in her insubstantial hands, yet he could feel them as if they were as real as anything. His grandmother tried to wipe his tears away, and a look of consternation flicked across her face to see that it was beyond her powers. She added, "It's all done, and y'all done better than anyone could have possibly imagined. But now it is done, and what I want y'all to do for me is to take me back to the farm where I belong. Y'all can do that for me like my special little boy, right?"

Matt nodded and put his arms under the frail elderly body that was now so suddenly and violently vacant and picked her up. It was time to go home.

☽◯☾

Bill Baldwin watched the vehicle he'd been engaged in a gunfight with for the last several hours suddenly start backing rapidly down the road. That was a damned good thing and no mistake, he was just about out of cartridges. Bill figured it must have been the same for the asshole down there. He figured the guy must have come for the girl, thought he'd gun his way home to getting her and didn't reckon on Bill being up here and armed. *Good riddance to bad rubbish* was what Bill figured.

With all the hubbub, he hadn't thought to check on Maw Maw for a while now. To be honest, even without a hubbub, he was afraid to go down there. He didn't want to get too close; what she was doing down there was no business of his. But, what with her spooks jumping out of his bodyguards and all, something must have happened mighty important. He figured he should at least get a look-see as to what it was and ask if he could get some more of them goons to make up for the ones he'd lost recently while he was at it. When this all started today, that's what he'd been meaning to ask in the first place, might as well get on with it.

Bill had to push and shove a bit to get the back door to open. There was always an accumulation of detritus against the thing from being in the woods like this, and Maw Maw just didn't get out much even using the front door, let alone the back. When she had taken herself down the hill following the goons with the girl, she'd already been out front waiting for them. It was getting dark out here, so he went back inside real quick and got himself one of the cheap little flashlights he insisted the old woman have around in case her power went out. No sense in breaking his neck just because he wanted to be nosy about Maw Maw's business, after all.

It wasn't until he was outside that it dawned on him that something was wrong. It was dead quiet out back, like, not just the woods in the evening quiet, quiet as the grave quiet, the kind of quiet that gave you chills up your spine! He couldn't see whatever magic Maw Maw was about, true enough, but whatever she'd been doing involved a kidnapped girl, for one thing. There ought to be some noise down there by the old stone circle, shouldn't there have been? Even if it was only Maw Maw wandering around scuffing about on her own now, and then there was a body that would need getting rid of.

"Maw Maw?" he called out.

Good lord, what if the old biddy hurt herself? he thought. Bill picked up his pace, skidding down the hill, sending leaves and rocks flying as he went. The beam of his flashlight bounced off one of the big rocks up ahead, so he called out a little louder, "Maw Maw? Y'all down here?"

When he stepped around the first big stone, Bill immediately could see why it had been so quiet. The girl was gone, and judging from the way the old woman's body was just lying there, so was Maw Maw! Bill rushed over to her, knelt down, and checked for a pulse. He didn't expect to find one, nor did he, but he knew from the mines you had to do that. He'd been taught that when he was young, even if they'd been crushed by a slide, check for a pulse. Bill had thought it was pretty stupid then, but old habits die hard and all.

Bill started to cry a little. He probably wasn't really all that sad about her dying, he'd prayed for it often enough, but it was his childlike reaction. You cried when a relative died, that's what you did, so that's what he was going to do. After a moment or two, he got furious. It had to be that girl! There may not be a mark on Maw Maw, maybe the doctor would say it was a heart attack or just old age or something, but still. The girl was here when she died, and she had every reason to want his Maw Maw dead! It had to be that damned girl! Well, he had an idea who she was, and damned well knew who her friend was, he'd get his boys to . . .

Finally, something else got through to him. His goons had run off. Whatever had been keeping them slaves to Bill had left them. The thought crept over him like an animal stalking its prey before it pounced on him and dug its claws in! He suddenly realized he might have bigger problems than trying to foist the blame for an old woman dying on some girl. Bill had no earthly idea who would be showing up for work at his mines tomorrow! For that matter, he had no idea who was working at his mine right now!

Bill scrambled to his feet and began running for his Suburban out front. He could call this in later. Right now, he needed to see if he still had working mines! No mines, no President's office at the company. No President's office at the company, no Senate campaign. No, suddenly Bill Baldwin had far bigger problems than some daft old woman finally biting off more than she could chew!

$$\text{☽O☾}$$

Matt was glad to be back inside after the funeral. Overall, it had been a somber occasion, and he was glad enough to be done with it. Matt couldn't help wondering who funerals were really for. He thought maybe it was for the living to be told how much everyone loved and felt sorry for them rather than the dead person, a great big "buck up little soldier" for the grieving family where everybody offered to help out in this time of strife by making potato salad. He might have found it more comforting if he had known half the people there. It would also have been more comforting still if the recently deceased hadn't been there, occasionally sniffing with distaste and saying things like, "I can't believe she had the audacity to wear *that* to a funeral, but I suppose it's no business a mine, I'm only the one in the box!"

He was finally back in MeeMaw's living room. Matt supposed it was his now. Nobody had said much, nobody seemed to have to. MeeMaw had passed away, and as the person in residence with the power, the house passed on to him, it was somehow understood. It seemed that happened whether he wanted it to or not. Thing was, he knew he wasn't going back up north, but a fella likes to think he has a choice in these matters instead of suddenly having his uncle bring home boxes to "help him move out to the house." It was just weird to have his parents staying in his old room while he had his grandmother's house more or less given to him. His dad had made the situation even clearer that he was glad Matt was happy, and so was he, up north, and Matt should redecorate the old place, down here.

"Hun? People brought a lot of food, what in the hell do y'all want me to do with it all?" Madison called from the kitchen.

Oh yeah, that was the real reason he wasn't leaving, if he was being honest with himself and everyone else. He'd have to learn to like being the local source of healing and magic here, but he already knew he loved Madison and was willing to do all that because she was here. Which was a good thing since she had just gotten her security deposit back when they'd moved her out of her apartment.

"Do we have the room?"

"For now, but no way we're eating all this!"

"We can feed Tyler, he needs to eat something other than pepperoni rolls and fast food anyway," he called back.

"Well, I think Chloe might be changing that," she said, coming out of the kitchen to join him on the couch, or more on his lap, which was on the couch, so close enough.

"Fine, we'll have them over for dinner a few times."

She touched his nose with her finger. "How 'bout you? Y'all all right?"

Matt shrugged. "Hard to say, really. I mean about MeeMaw, well our, by which I mean you and me, our loved ones never really leave, do they? About having to learn to help all these people locally . . . "

"Daunted?"

"Major daunts."

"I'll be helping."

He kissed her lightly. "And you have no idea how much I love you for it."

"I can be like that little girl in the Shake and Bake commercials, 'An' I hepped!' It'll be fun."

"You have a strange idea of fun."

"Love me?"

"Oh, like you don't know," he said with a grin.

"Still, it's nice to hear."

"I think I'd like to take a walk alone for a bit, though," he said, his face turning serious.

"Good, y'all need to think, and I have a surprise for you."

☽○☾

He needed to take a walk, more importantly, he needed to talk to someone. Okay, there was a specific someone. Matt wanted to talk to MeeMaw some. He slumped against the wall in the same spot he had occupied when he'd come out here to talk to Pa Pa last.

"MeeMaw! You about?"

MeeMaw appeared right next to him. She appeared to be wearing a party hat.

"Am . . . I interrupting something?" he asked, surprised by the hat.

"Oh, the rest of the family just likes to throw a bit of a shindig for new people on our 'big day.' It can wait, we've got all the time in the world now anyway. What can I do for y'all?" MeeMaw said, smiling.

"What am I gonna do?" Matt practically wailed.

"Do? What all of us have done. Learn the people, learn the land as you go. It's not normally like this, y'all know, right? If it was, I'd have had a heart attack years ago. Nope, it's mainly fixing boo-boos and trying to tell 'em to take care of themselves, really." She shrugged.

"But it's not like I'm very good at this; hell, half the time I can barely take care of myself," he replied with his head drooping.

"Matthew Hawley, you look at me right now, young man!" she snapped. What could he do? He looked. "Now you listen to me, and y'all listen good. Pa Pa has told me that maybe I've been a bit hard on y'all. He's right about that, I have. You want to know why I was?"

"I don't have a choice, do I?"

"Perceptive. I was hard on y'all because you are the product of two families of witches. Y'all got more oomph in your finger than I got all over. Y'all scared me, Matt, not like I thought you'd do something mean or bad with the gifts the good Lord gave you, I worried y'all would do something bad by accident. I love you, boy, and I didn't want something like that on your conscience or mine," she explained, a sudden smile flashing when she was done. Her face softened further. "Y'all are my lil sweet grandson, and I wanted to protect y'all from yourself. Maybe I should have told you more often, but I'm proud as punch of you, boy. Always have been. I love y'all with all my heart, Matthew Hawley, and I'm proud as all get out with you."

"Really?"

"Really. Don't worry so, I'm here for the calling if y'all need me. Now, if'n y'all don't need me . . . "

"One more thing."

"Yes?"

"Send Mungo out for a moment."

"Really?"

"Really."

A moment later, Mungo's deep voice bellowed, "Wa in th' heel ur ye interruptin' me when Ah was havin' fin?"

"Mungo?"

"Whit?!"

"I won't tell anyone if you don't want, but could you please just talk without the outrageous accent? I know damned well you can, and I know you like to visit, and I could do without the Mad Scot routine," Matt said flatly.

"Bloody hell!" Mungo slumped down the wall next to him. His head turned and he stared hard at Matt. "So, may I ask, how did you figure it out?"

"I listened to your story. You were a guest in a nobleman's house, wooed his daughter, and made your way to, and in, the new world like a gentleman. So, knowing that, do you really think I'd believe you'd talk like a hard drinker in a Glasgow pub?" Matt said with a grin.

"Oh, that is good! Maybe your grandparents are right, boy! Maybe there is a lot more to you than meets the eye. Makes me glad you came from me! I don't let any of the others know until they've been dead a good fifty years, it's a good way to talk around people if I want to, especially to the Missus. Worked when we got to the new world too; people would think we were dumb savages and wouldn't even notice we'd fleeced them on a trade. Would you believe you're the first warm one to deduce it in all this time?" Mungo was actually laughing. "Wait until I tell Wynda!"

The two of them sat in silence for a moment, enjoying their secret and the evening air before Mungo said, "So, if you don't need me for anything else . . . "

Matt got to his feet. "No, but thank you for this. I'll be sure not to tell anyone."

"Now that I do appreciate, young Matthew."

Matt started walking back to the house, feeling better than he had for quite some time now.

)O(

When he opened the door to the house, he found the surprise Madison had mentioned. A display of magical lights right inside the door flashed gleefully in a way that only he could see. They were carefully arranged to make a drawing of a witch, right down to the hat, floating in the air in front of him. But this was no ordinary old cartoon Halloween hag, this witch was done like one of those nineteen forties pin-up girl paintings, in garters and nylons, a bullet bra, the hat, and a smile. Next to her, there was an arrow pointing upstairs. So, Matt went up—there was an arrow and everything, after all.

When he found her upstairs, he discovered that Madison was wearing the exact same outfit, only better because it was Madison.

On that note, we should probably end this book right . . . about . . . there.

About the Author

Paul has lived all over the country before settling in Appalachia over fifteen years ago with his wife Leslie and their son. He also has two adult children living in his native Pennsylvania. He is the author of two previous horror-comedy novels. Paul is a member of the Horror Writers Association, appearing on the panel for horror-comedy at the 2021 Stoker Con. While he has put out quite a bit of fully serious horror in his career, he has also never answered the question, "Is everything a joke with you?" correctly once in his entire life.

MORE FROM
MADNESS HEART PRESS

Exotic Meats and Inedible Objects by Rachel
Rodman
978-1656681171

The Reattachment by Doug Ford
978-1393464846

Encyclopedia Sharksploitanica by Susan Snyder
978-1-955745-99-4

Trench Mouth by Christine Morgan
978-1-7348937-9-3

All Men Are Trash by Gina Ranalli
978-1-7348937-3-1